A PROBLEMATIC PARADOX

A PROBLEMATIC PARADOX

ELIOT SAPPINGFIELD

G. P. PUTNAM'S SONS

G. P. Putnam's Sons
an imprint of Penguin Random House LLC
375 Hudson Street
New York, NY 10014

Library of Congress Cataloging-in-Publication Data
Names: Sappingfield, Eliot, author.
Title: A problematic paradox / Eliot Sappingfield.
Description: New York, NY : G. P. Putnam's Sons, [2018]
Summary: Thirteen-year-old Nikola Kross's world is turned upside down when her father is abducted by aliens and she is suddenly transported to a special boarding school for geniuses, but things get even stranger when she realizes she has certain abilities that put her entire school in grave danger.
Identifiers: LCCN 2017010099 | ISBN 9781524738457
Subjects: | CYAC: Genius—Fiction. | Extraterrestrial beings—Fiction. | Boarding schools—Fiction. | Schools—Fiction. | Science fiction.
Classification: LCC PZ7.1.S2643 Pr 2018 | DDC [Fic]—dc23
LC record available at https://lccn.loc.gov/2017010099

Trans-species universal language and sensory vocabulary version may be viewed, touched, smelled, heard, and communed with at the Parahuman Mediocre Literature Repository, Bolivar, Missouri 65613.

Printed in the United States of America.
ISBN 9781524738457
10 9 8 7 6 5 4 3 2 1

Design by Eileen Savage. Text set in Leitura News.

For my wife, Stephanie, for deciding to
tolerate many things over and over.

*"More than all the trees in
the world . . . I forget the rest."*

1

MISS HICCUP AND THE BEEF MAILBOX

As I sat beneath a cat poster in her tiny, sparse office, I wondered if Miss Hiccup's real smile resembled the painted grimace she wore around students. No adult human can be that chipper all the time. Maybe it was the poster. She had one of those motivational posters, with a cat hanging from a branch and the caption HANG IN THERE! below it. I've always wondered if anyone was actually inspired by that kind of thing. Maybe Miss Hiccup was one of the fortunate few who gazed at that cat and thought, *You know, if that cat can hang in there, so can I!* It would explain a lot about why she and I didn't exactly get along.

Miss Hiccup was pretty, in an institutional kind of way. She was a thin woman who wore pencil skirts and had long golden hair that was only a little dry and frazzled. I could relate—my hair always looked like I dried it with a high-voltage power line. Her face was not unkind. I could even imagine that she had a sense of humor hidden behind her big, fashionably nerdy glasses. Despite that, there were moments when I could swear there was an absolute, searing hatred of the entire world in those eyes.

It was my favorite thing about her.

My second-favorite thing about Miss Hiccup was the hiccuping. That was where I'd gotten my personal name for her. She had an actual legal name, but "Miss Hiccup" was more fitting and more fun because she seemed to have a permanent case of the hiccups that got worse when she was stressed, which was all the time, in my observation.

When Miss Hiccup cornered me on my way to the bus, she ruined the best part of my day. Instead of boarding the bus to freedom, I had to trudge back to the counseling office for a few minutes and then kill time till the late bus arrived to collect the stragglers, detention inmates, and band kids.

Miss Hiccup spent some time just sitting there, smiling and making eye contact. It's the oldest trick in the book when you want someone to open up. Most people hate uncomfortable silences, so they tend to talk in order to fill them. I'm not most people.

A minute later, Miss Hiccup hiccuped, twitched, and said, "Is your backpack okay?"

Of course she wanted to talk about backpack-in-the-toilet incident #74. It was a new thing as far as she was concerned. The only reason she knew about it *this time* was because whoever had stolen it had really stomped it in good, and I wasn't able to get it out on my own. The counseling office is directly across from the bathrooms, so I figured they could help, since I was a taxpayer and all.

I made a mental note to ask the gym teacher next time. He was good at overlooking that kind of thing.

"My backpack is fine," I said. "I switched to a waterproof one a while ago, so it doesn't even smell. It's antimicrobial."

"Smart thinking," she said with a warm smile that was almost, but not quite, sympathetic. "I thought we could talk about *fitting in* . . ."

"Why don't I start?" I offered.

"Do you have something you—*hic!*—you'd like to talk about, Nikola?" she said, sounding like she was in desperate need of a drink of water.

"No," I said. "But you said you wanted to talk about fitting in. I feel like I should address that. I *do* have trouble fitting in, but I'm in a good place with it at the moment. Not a lot of angst going on here. Nothing to concern yourself with."

This was mostly true. I'd been looking forward to attending West Blankford Middle School about as much as I was counting the days until my next trip to the dentist, and the fact that my classmates were as horrible as they had been the previous year wasn't exactly a shock. I wasn't having a blast, but I wasn't disillusioned. Kids are usually mean to people who are different, and people don't come any more different than me.

My name is Nikola Kross, and I'm a weirdo. A freak, if you prefer. I'm a peanut butter and sardine sandwich in a vending machine full of candy. I'm a twitching platypus curled up in the corner of a cardboard box of puppies. I'm off track. You should probably get used to that. Let's back up a bit.

I'm a thirteen-year-old girl attending middle school in North Dakota. It's not my looks that make me odd. Well, that's not the main thing. I'm no taller or shorter, bigger or smaller than the median range for those characteristics. I have a nose that is a bit above the normal width and length, but not to the point where it becomes remarkable. I have a few freckles here and there, and my eyes are brown. I wear glasses with shatter-proof lenses and an embedded digital display that I designed myself and is currently broken. My hair is very curly, long, brown, and a bit mane-like. It's always a mess, but I don't care enough to spend the time to tame it when that time could be better used sleeping in. That's what I look like. Do me a favor and remember it, because I hate describing myself.

What makes me weird is that I'm a genius. Most people who say that are bragging and are about to pull out their Mensa card in an effort to impress you. I'm not bragging. I really am a certified genius, and it shouldn't impress anyone. Talking about how smart you are is like boasting about how big the engine is in your car: you still have to obey the speed limit, and what really matters is *where* you drive to, not how much noise you can make on the way.

High intelligence runs in my family like a genetically transmitted disease. My dad is an amateur scientist (he prefers the term *research hobbyist*). He spends his days running our home particle accelerator, experimenting with exotic meta-materials, or just trying to remember where he left his shoes. Mom was an experimental poet, but she disappeared when I was a toddler. Dad says she's dead now, or might as well be dead, since we've certainly seen the last of her. Sensitive guy, my dad.

In case I haven't lost you completely, we're also fabulously wealthy. Back in the midnineties, Dad patented some interesting semiconductor designs as well as those plastic hooks that stick to your wall without tearing up the paint. Those inventions, along with a few dozen more, fill the bank account monthly. If it helps, that doesn't mean I ride in limousines drinking sparkling cider. As soon as the deposits clear, Dad blows all the money on home improvements. That might be nice, but our home is a big lab, so for us, a "home improvement" doesn't mean a new hot tub; it means a new supercooled cloud chamber or a few upgrades on our personal supercomputer cluster.

To a degree, I blame my parents for my outcast status, and not just on a genetic level. Dad is distant and terminally distracted. Instead of toys, I got circuit boards and soldering irons for Christmas so I could make my own. When I was little and asked for a bedtime story, he'd narrate the schematics for a microwave oven before giving me a firm yet loving bedtime handshake. When I had trouble sleeping, he'd describe how people die from sleep deprivation. I like to imagine my mom might have been a bit more . . . parental, but if she and my dad fell for each other at some point, then I have to assume that she was every bit as eccentric. Some people just stink at being parents. It happens.

It's not all their fault, though. I've made some bad decisions. If you want to make friends in school, it's not a good idea to bring an untrained robotic panther to class without permission, or to program a drone helicopter to follow you around and shoot chocolate candy into your mouth, particularly if its aim stinks. You should also avoid testing experimental artificial food products on your classmates. Silicon polymer foam birthday cupcakes might be calorie-free and nontoxic, and taste wonderful, but if you give someone explosive diarrhea *even one time*, they tend to hold it against you.

I don't entirely regret my bad decisions, but things weren't easy for me at school. If someone sat down next to me at lunch, I first had to find out whether they'd lost a bet, or if they were planning some prank at my expense. This sometimes backfired: one time, I yelled at a girl because I was sure she was up to no good, but it turned out that the other seats were all taken, and she had to eat standing up. Still, she was rude to me the next week, so I don't think I missed out on anything.

You need to know all that because that's why Miss Hiccup was talking to me. I'm not *fitting in*. Big surprise.

"You see, honey . . . ," Miss Hiccup said, dragging the last word out like she was talking to an injured poodle, "I know you put on a brave face, but I've heard from—*hic!*—from a lot of your teachers that some of the other children have taken to . . . um . . ."

"To being awful to me?" I suggested. "Salting my chocolate milk? Insulting my parentage? Addressing me with the most derivative and unimaginative—"

"Well," she interrupted, "as a matter—*hic!*—as a matter of fact, yes." She de-tented her fingers, reconsidered the decision, and re-tented them. "I thought it might be helpful for you and I to discuss some st—*hic!*—some strategies to help you *mesh* a little better with your peers. I think with a little effort on your part . . ."

She went on talking, but I knew where she was going, so there was no point in waiting through the hiccuping. "Why aren't you talking to *them?*" I said. "They're the ones being mean! Do you have any *strategies* you can discuss with my peers to help them stop behaving like the worst parts of *Lord of the Flies?*"

"Pardon?"

"It's a book. I have a slightly waterlogged copy you could borrow, if you're interested. It's about some nice children who get stuck on an island and start behaving like American middle schoolers? I just mean that you might consider focusing your energies on the people who pick on kids who are different."

"Welllll," Miss Hiccup said, in a very noncommittal, guidance counselor-y kind of way. "That's just about everyone in the school, and—*hic!*—we're going to have better luck working on how *you* interact, rather than changing the tone of the entire school. There's a seminar going on at the community college this week for kids who—*hic!*—who just need a little help learning how to show people what a great, interesting, fun person they can be! I thought we could—"

"That's nice of you to say," I said, "but I don't understand: if everyone in the school is prejudiced against great, interesting, and fun people like me, and there's nothing actually wrong with me, why is it easier if I do my best to be as wrong as the rest of them?"

"Well—*hic!*—I wouldn't put it th—*hic!*—that way."

I know I'm supposed to be respectful of adults, but I couldn't help myself. "I would hope not. When you tell a person who is being bullied that it's their own fault for being themselves, it's important to say so in the nicest way possible. Right?"

"How many times have—*hic!*—you been in my office this year? Ten? Fif—*hic!*—teen? There are some—*hic!*—some simple changes you can make that will—*hic!*—make a real difference."

I forced myself to smile pleasantly, as if she'd said something helpful. "If you don't want me in here all the time, I suggest you stop dragging me in here all the time."

She made a sad face and looked like she was about to interrupt, but I sensed an opportunity to power through and get out of there. "I really appreciate your advice. Thank you so much for taking the time to talk to me. I'm going to go outside and wait for the late bus now. You can say that you tried your best but just couldn't reach me. Have a nice year!" I got up and got out before she could stop hiccuping and call me back.

I wondered why she felt the need to talk to me about *fitting in* at all. I was actually starting to like a little salt and pepper in my chocolate milk. They'd been doing it my whole life. Did it bother me? Sure. But I wasn't going to let it get me down, and I *sure* wasn't going to turn myself into one of them. I like being me more than I dislike being an outcast.

I made a mental note to speak with my dad that evening about possibly skipping middle and high school altogether and going straight to college. I wouldn't even need to apply. The first time our class took standardized tests, we got letters from the state asking why I wasn't on an accelerated track. But Dad had nixed the idea on a dozen occasions already— something about developing my social skills in an appropriate environment. As if no one can develop social skills in college. He even told the school to stop letting me take the tests, I guess to keep me from getting any more bright ideas about it.

The middle school had a swing set on the edge of the playground, which was the best place to wait for the bus. It had a view of where the bus arrived, and was far enough from the stop that I would not need to talk with anyone.

But there was already a group of kids hanging around the swings when I arrived, with one big guy occupying my personal favorite seat. He was large, unusually so. Sometimes the guys from the football team hang around after practice with their pads still on. Maybe this one wanted a quick swing before putting on his street clothes.

I turned to leave but ran right into one of the loitering kids. He was solid—but soft somehow, like the walls of a padded room. I mumbled "Sorry" and went to move around him, but the rest of the apes had crowded around me. It was then that I noticed the gang hogging my swing set was, in fact, girls.

I use the term *girls* in the loosest sense of the word. Their leader, the one who had been sitting on the swing, had long, highlighter-yellow hair braided into pigtails and was wearing makeup like she'd broken into her mom's stash for the first time. She looked at least as tall as my dad—about six feet—although it was hard to tell because she was close, and I was having problems understanding what was going on with her limbs. Her arms were much longer than they needed to be. They were so long I wondered if she could stop herself on the swings with her hands instead of her feet. Her legs were weirdly short, though. I don't really remember what her face looked like. She was ugly—I remember that. Not ugly like the opposite of pretty, but ugly like . . . well, it's hard to say. She was ugly in the same way that plane crashes and cancer are ugly, if that makes sense. I don't remember any of their faces, actually. I just knew I'd never seen her or any of them at school before. Why had I even assumed they were students?

I said "*Excuse me,*" but they didn't react. The three before me were decked out in long flowery skirts, chunky costume jewelry, and brightly colored hoodies, which they kept pulled over their heads, kind of like monks with tragically bad fashion sense. Being encircled by them was like standing at the bottom of a very unfriendly well.

Miss Giant Longarms, who wore a too-tight sequined guitar T-shirt above a denim miniskirt, finally broke the silence. "Hi, Nikola," she said. Her excessively high and girlish voice didn't match. It was like a tiny junior cheerleader talking to me from inside a mailbox made of beef. Rotten beef. The smell of bad meat hit me the moment she spoke, and it was all I could do to keep from retching. She was smiling broadly, I think. I distinctly remember teeth.

"Can I help you?" I said, cursing the lack of adult supervision on the playground that afternoon. Where was everyone?

"Yes!" she said cheerfully. "I'm sooooooo glad you asked! We love it when people want to help us, don't we, girls?" Her friends nodded. The girl reached out to shake my hand. Her hand looked moist.

I recoiled, which is rude, but I *really* did not want to touch her. "Who are you? How do you know my name?"

"My name is Tabbabitha. And we, my dear," she said as she spread her arms to include her friends, "are going to get you out of this place! You're going to join our team. Isn't that great, girls?"

"Yup," said the first thing.

"Uh-huh," said the second thing.

"Yah," said the third thing.

"Yeeeeah," I said, marking a narrow opening between the first and second thing I might be able to duck through. "Look, I think your team is great. Big fan, seriously. Whatever you guys are into, I think you're the best in the world at it."

I googled *dealing with bullies* once. It said to empathize with them, defuse situations with humor or distraction, and, if those fail, get help. Something told me none of those options was going to work. I got the instant impression Tabbabitha wasn't the kind of girl who even understood jokes that didn't involve someone getting hurt. I was pretty sure I would have problems summoning empathy for her, anyway. I decided for the immediate yet polite exit plan.

"Well, hey!" I said, looking at where my watch would be if I wore a watch. "It was great meeting you, Tabitha, but I should be getting—"

She smiled again, baring teeth that seemed better suited to taking down an antelope than making friends. "It's Tabbabitha. You're a lot like your daddy, you know. Very smart, and rather stupid at the same time. It's irritating, trying to reason with people like you. You don't *listen*. Most of you people are smart enough to take directions."

I didn't like the way she'd said "you people." I didn't like the rest of what she'd said, either. My fear was fading and I was starting to get mad again. "Look, I don't know what your problem is," I said, raising my voice in hopes it might bring an adult, or at least another student, "but I think you should leave me alone."

"My friends and I have come to extend an offer," she said. "We think you're a bright girl. We'd like you to join us, help us work out a few simple . . . projects, and we promise to leave you and your father alone afterward. That's all! Don't you want to get out of this . . . town? Your dad must have oatmeal in his head living in a dustbin like this. It took us forever to find you, in fact." She leaned unnervingly close. Things were getting creepy. A breeze whirled around us. A dry leaf shook in the air as it fell. "You'll have fun. Trust me, you *want* to come with us. Let's go."

As she talked, I was hit with a wave of unease—kind of like the way you feel the day after you've gotten over the flu. Normally, the big, ugly moose of a girl could have shut my mouth with a glare, never mind the creepy way she was talking to me, and I actually agreed with her about West Blankford, but nobody insults my dad. That was over the line.

I leaned in through the eye-watering stench until we were only about an inch apart, and looked her straight in the . . . face? "Listen, Tabbabitha. I don't know why you want my help. But you're acting like a real creep, and I can't help noticing that you smell like microwaved roadkill. I want nothing to do with you, and I'd like to leave now."

Tabbabitha stepped back. "I won't pretend I'm not disappointed, but I *am* impressed. You're quite the little firecracker. Normally I take what I want, but it's better if you offer your assistance willingly. Long story. I'm sure you'll have a different perspective later. Talk soon!" She shouldered me aside as she shuffle-waddled off the playground.

Was she using her hands *and* feet to walk?

No. That would be weird.

2

MR. HAPPYBEAR'S
EMERGENCY BACKUP PLAN

I spent most of the ride home being struck again and again by just how creepy all the things Tabbabitha had said were, especially that last comment—*Talk soon*. I'd have called my dad, but he never had a phone on him for more than a couple minutes before it was good and lost. I found myself wishing, for the first time ever, that I knew where my Happybear Bracelet was.

My Happybear Bracelet was some kind of tracking system that was connected to a wireless implant in his ear. It would transmit a message if I pushed a button on the bear's nose or if I went outside the geographic area I was supposed to be in on any given day. It would also tell him where I was in real time and play audio of what was going on in the room if he wanted to turn it on. You know how every young girl wants to have her parents essentially listening in on everything she says and does and watching her every move? Yeah, me neither. Plus the bracelet was ugly. It was made from thick electrical cable with fabric insulation, attached to a cartoonish bear's head pendant that was supposed to look happy but looked more like what an evil clown would think a happy bear was supposed to look like. The thing had always struck me as paranoid and overprotective, considering crime in West Blankford was almost nonexistent. Long story short, as soon as my dad had forgotten he wanted me to wear it at all times, I stopped wearing it.

Besides, what would I tell him? *Hey, Dad, I ran into some bullies at school, so keep an eye out for teenage girls asking for favors?* What favor had Tabbabitha wanted anyway? She wanted *something* from me, but she hadn't said what it was. Maybe she was running some kind of study. Or selling Ghoul Scout cookies. Whatever she'd wanted, it was something she could *take*, but wanted me to *give* instead. A kiss? I shuddered at the thought.

I got the idea that Tabbabitha was probably used to failure in endeavors that didn't involve intimidation. Maybe boxing was her calling. Or some other activity where long arms and a personality as charming as a garbage disposal would be an asset.

In the end, I decided life is too short to worry about every little thing strange bullies say. Instead, I worried about what to do when I got home. Maybe I'd try to get the software for version two of my fake UFO up and running. The last one had caused a bit of a problem with the air force, so I was using radar-dispersing materials on the new version, which made it a lot heavier and more difficult to pilot. After that, I thought I might play some video games. Maybe the new *Scientific American* had come. I had every expectation that the afternoon would be a pleasant one.

I'll go ahead and tell you: I'd just completed my last day at West Blankford Middle School. I'm telling you because nobody told me, and I kind of wish someone had. I would have enjoyed riding the bus a lot more if I'd known I'd never do it again.

The bus let me off in the vast parking lot of an abandoned SuperMart. Did I mention that my home was an old discount warehouse store? No? Well, it was. Dad loved the place—it already had a dedicated data line, so we got great Internet service, the power system was able to support the unreasonable demands we placed on the grid, and the store had enough room for Dad's equipment and supplies.

Our living quarters were a pair of mobile homes set up in the back corner of the building where the electronics section had once been. They had been redone, so the accommodations were pretty swanky, if you ask me. One of the homes was for me and held my bedroom, a small living room, and our dining room. The other was for Dad and contained his bedroom, our computers, and a library. It might sound miserable, living alone inside an abandoned warehouse store, but it was pretty great. I almost never had to clean, my front yard was tiled, and I could crank my music as loud as I wanted.

The bus groaned and drove away the moment my feet

touched the concrete. I noticed that Dad had left the front doors wide open, which was not entirely unusual. Dad might be a scientific genius, but if he wore all clean clothes and remembered to make sure his shoes were tied and his socks matched, he was doing pretty good. I made sure to lock up the moment I was inside. You think *your* dad complains about the heating bill? Imagine heating a building that could hold a couple medium-sized airplanes.

Our entryway still had a claw game left over from its previous life. I pulled off my shoes and coat and tossed them into the bin, then kicked back onto the sofa, nestled where shopping carts had once been stored. As I'd programmed it to do, the claw grabbed my coat and shoes from the bin, pulled them inside the glass box, and hung them on hooks. It then retrieved the steel-toed boots I liked to wear around the house. I'm particularly proud of that machine, but a lot of good shoes and coats lost their lives to it before I got it right.

Once my boots were laced, I picked up the megaphone we keep by the sofa.

"I'm home," I called.

The lights were still on, which was typical during the day, and Dad's golf cart was still where he had parked it to drop me off that morning. We had golf carts because the front doors are a fifteen-minute walk from the trailers due to the labyrinth-like arrangement of equipment and materials inside the building. It was weird that the cart was unattended, but not unheard of. One time, Dad decided to take a walk in the field behind the building because he thought he had seen some rare butterfly. By the time he discovered it had actually been a cheeseburger wrapper and a rather cunning breeze, he was deep into some farmer's soybean field and needed to hitch a ride home. In his defense, it was a very pretty cheeseburger wrapper. He kept it pinned to a board in the dining room.

I pointed the megaphone into the middle of the store. "Dad!" I called. "Can I borrow this fuel rod?" I listened to my request echo through the building and die. Me playing with a fuel rod is just the sort of thing that should have freaked him out, but . . . nothing. Peering out the doors, I could see our minivan still parked in the EMPLOYEE OF THE MONTH spot. The forklift, delivery truck, and bicycles were still where they belonged, too. He was probably home. Wherever he was, he had wandered off without his trusty golf cart. This situation could mean only one thing: *I had an excuse to drive the cart.*

Golf carts are faster than they look, and harder to control, too. I got to the trailers without doing any damage apart from a tiny dent in a copper cylinder marked DANGER CORROSIVE HAZARD. Nothing was leaking or on fire, so I marked the trip a success. My silvery mobile home was just as I'd left it, as shabby and familiar as a pair of old jeans.

I was feeling a bit peckish, but all I had for food was a dozen leftover Pizzatillos from breakfast. The breakfast dishes were still out, and a pitcher of milk had started curdling on the counter from either the night before or the night before that. I made a mental note to rinse it out in the next few days.

When a person leaves home and strikes off into the

unknown to have adventures, face mortal peril, and perform remarkable feats of daring, I feel they are entitled to a good meal beforehand. At least something warm. Or a granola bar. Really, *anything* but a dozen cold Pizzatillos would be okay. They're little tortilla chips wrapped around spaghetti sauce, cheese, and a meat-like substance. The product is microwaved until it's good and soggy, resulting in something the ads call *The Tasty Snack Your Kids Crave!* This is mostly true, except for the part that is a lie, which is all of it. Pizzatillos are not tasty, and kids don't crave them. I think Pizzatillos are referred to as a "snack" in the ads because to call them "food" would count as false advertising.

I ate all twelve.

When I checked Dad's trailer, I found his clothes for the day laid out on his bed. This meant he was still in his pajamas, wherever he was. He was never *that* forgetful. I wondered if something might actually be wrong.

One of his cheap cell phones was still on the table (he kept losing them and buying new ones, so we had dozens lying around). I grabbed it, got back in the golf cart, and drove to the security office at the front of the building, dialing every number I had for him, just in case. I heard phones ringing here and there in the building. None picked up.

My dad is a bit of a nut about security. When you keep several million dollars' worth of equipment, dangerous chemicals, radioactive isotopes, and proprietary designs inside your house, a dead bolt on the front doors doesn't cut it. I took the stairs two at a time and found myself in the dim gray office that had once been used to catch shoplifters and now housed the most advanced security system this side of the White House. A bank of green lights on the wall confirmed the video logs from the day were still recording. I'd last seen Dad when I left for school, so I pulled up the video from that morning and watched myself leave on the bus while Dad waved by the front doors.

The bus passed out of the camera's sight, and my dad went back inside. Not long after, a single black SUV pulled into the lot and parked in a far corner, as far from the doors as possible. Someone parking in our lot wasn't unheard of—sometimes people pulled over to mess with their phones, eat lunch, or have a nap, if they had been on the road for a while. Dad hated it and was always strangely worried about anyone on the property. When he saw someone out there, he'd wander out and kindly ask them to get lost after a minute or two. He didn't make an appearance, but that was probably because he didn't know they were out there yet.

I ran the tape forward, zooming through a lot of nothing until I saw something move. I resumed playback and saw Dad walking across the parking lot toward the SUV. How long had it been there at that point? I checked the time on the play-back: 3:51 PM. That would have been about ten minutes after my conversation with Tabbabitha. The vehicle had been sit-ting there for about eight hours at that point. I was trying to see if the SUV was even occupied when the other cars arrived.

Four black SUVs pulled into the lot and circled past the

stopped vehicle, which started and joined the back of the line. The SUVs made a wide, lazy turn and came to a stop by the front doors. This left my dad in the middle of the lot, with five black vehicles blocking his path back inside. Seeming more annoyed than worried, Dad approached the first vehicle, trying to peer through its window. A second later, the window rolled down, and he appeared to be engaging in conversation.

Four seconds later, Dad stepped back from the door of the SUV and looked around nervously. It wasn't hard to recognize the universal gesture of checking for witnesses. He was scared or in trouble. My heart began to pound slightly, and I leaned in close. Then I had to lean away because I was fogging up the monitor. Dad was still talking, but at the same time he was edging around the front of the SUV and furtively pulling a phone from his pocket. The passenger door on the front car swung open. A bulky woman flopped gracelessly out into the parking lot, like someone had decided to dump a pile of dead squids on our property. When she straightened, the woman was impressively sized—she looked about a foot taller than Dad. She had long light-colored hair braided into pigtails and unnaturally long arms. The camera resolution was poor, but I knew exactly who it was.

I called her some names then, but I can't put them down here, because I'm not allowed to use those words except in special circumstances. Instead, I'm going to tell you the exact *opposite* of what I said: I called her a little friendly ray of sunshine. I said she was a real peach, and that I hoped she would live a long and happy life, and would end up in heaven someday.

Seeing Tabbabitha seemed to change Dad's perspective, too. He stared goggle-eyed at her while she spoke to him. Then she extended her arms like she wanted to give him a hug, which took a minute, because extending those arms was a considerable task. And then Dad ran straight into her embrace like they were old friends! She wrapped her arms all the way around him twice. Well, it looked like twice, but I figured that was impossible.

"What are you doing?" I shouted at the screen, which did not respond.

Dad stepped back and gestured toward the building. It looked like he was inviting her inside. She nodded, and the two of them walked toward the front doors, his arm over her shoulder. A terrible thought occurred to me. What if I was about to see them walk inside and not come out? Was she still in the building?

Just in case, I grabbed a stapler from the desk, opened it wide, and held it like a weapon while I watched the video. In retrospect, this wouldn't have been all that useful, unless she came at me with a sheaf of papers she wanted to keep separated, but it was something. If I had been a little more clever, I would have remembered that I met her in person shortly after the video had been recorded, so she couldn't have hung around long.

"STOP!" I shrieked at my father. "Don't let her in! Where's your brain?"

As if he heard me, Dad halted and took a second look at Tabbabitha, carefully withdrawing his arm from her shoulder. He smiled quizzically at her; then his expression changed into one of absolute horror. He ran for it, bolting across the parking lot like an Olympic runner, albeit an Olympic runner in fuzzy slippers.

"Go! Go!" I shouted at the monitor. "Don't let her get you! Run! *Move, Dad!*" I was gripping the stapler so hard that it ejected a single staple, which bounced harmlessly off the screen.

Frightened scientists can move quickly, but unfortunately, so can SUVs. A moment later, the cars had cut him off, and several burly figures "helped" him into the back of one. He didn't fight them, but there wouldn't have been much point if he had. Tabbabitha strolled to the cars, looking quite put out, either at being rejected or having to walk that far, and the vehicles left in single file again, as unceremoniously as they had arrived. I fast-forwarded. The tape was nothing but empty parking lot video after that until the bus pulled up to drop me off.

I sat there for a couple minutes in a dead panic. I was sweating like I'd run a mile, and a dozen questions popped into my head. Was my dad dead? Where would they take him? Where would I go? Who should I call? Should I hide somewhere? Was that morning's absentminded *See ya later* the last thing I'd ever get to say to him? At times, the room went a bit blurry and swimmy. I stood up purposefully and then sat back down again, realizing I hadn't the first idea of what to do. My dad had been kidnapped, and I'd just watched it on TV.

I tried to recall everything he'd said in the past few days. He hadn't mentioned being in trouble with anyone or owing anyone money, apart from one of our neighbors to the south who was claiming our automatic lawn mower had traumatized their cats. Our talk at dinner the night before had been about the work he was doing with anti-hydrogen, which is a kind of antimatter, but that was all theory and speculation. He had also been tinkering with an instant translator device, but for some reason it only worked when you wanted to translate Esperanto into Farsi, and even then it translated all food-related words into *chicken*. It would be darn useful for Esperanto speakers visiting Iran with a hankering for a dinner of chicken chicken with chicken sauce and a tall glass of iced chicken to drink. For everyone else, it needed work.

He had also mentioned working out the details of how to construct an intelligent computer system that thought like the human brain, and how I could go about importing some-one's brain into a computer, if I ever needed to. He'd wanted to know if I had any friends looking to make some money as research subjects.

I logged into the security mainframe with Dad's user ID and password, which I had managed to hack ages ago because the man had some pretty ridiculous notions about how many hours of video gaming per day is appropriate. There were no logged entrances or exits other than when we left in the morning, and there were no unauthorized computer activities or other security issues, apart from what I was doing at that particular moment. Then I checked his calendar to see if he had any appointments or if he was expecting anyone. The date had nothing on it except one entry, a reminder for our standing Tuesday dinner: *5:00 pm call tacopocalypse—taco fiesta special.*

I remembered my Happybear Bracelet again and cursed my stupid desire for privacy. Sure it looked like something designed for a toddler, but I could at least have gotten in touch with Dad. Instead, I'd gotten rid of it. But where? I could have sworn I'd stashed it somewhere in the security office. I looked around the room and imagined I had something I needed to hide. That led me straight to a cupboard located inconveniently in the corner behind a heavy filing cabinet.

A couple hard shoves later, I found Mr. Happybear staring creepily at me from under a book called *Aunokw Xuogwea*, which was about how to decode basic ciphers. I snatched up Mr. Happybear, pressed his nose, and waited.

Nothing happened. The battery was dead, of course. The bracelet had been in that cupboard for a couple years, at least. I stuffed it into my pocket and went back to the security footage as I tried to figure out what to do next.

I searched the other security feeds, rewinding and fast-forwarding through hours of recordings from six different cameras. Nothing else of note had happened. I didn't know what else to look *for*. Then I rewatched Tabbabitha and Dad talking and the thugs tossing him into their car, and looked for license plate numbers. But the plates looked blurred, like there was some kind of plastic film over them.

I fast-forwarded again until I saw the bus dropping me off after school. I was about to go back to my trailer when I noticed something else on one of the screens. The five black SUVs. They pulled into the parking lot like they did in the other footage, but something was different. What was different?

I paused and checked the time on the recording.

4:53 PM.

I looked at the clock: 4:53.

The video was live. I switched all the other cameras back to live mode. It didn't look like anyone was moving around outside the store, and the doors on the SUVs were still closed.

Maybe they had come back for something in the lab. No, they could have gotten whatever they wanted when they had taken Dad—he'd left the doors wide open. There was only one thing in the lab that hadn't been there before. Me.

It was time to set aside abject terror and consider my options. I could probably hide in the SuperMart for a month or more. The place was a mind-boggling maze, and I knew every inch. I doubted a newcomer could even locate the bathrooms without GPS. That would work for a while, but they were sure to find me eventually. They'd only need to wait me out. I could call the police, but if I called the cops, would the kidnappers just leave and come back later? Would the cops put me in foster care until Dad was returned? Would I be any safer in foster care at some stranger's house than I was in my dad's fortress of a laboratory? I grabbed Mr. Happybear from my pocket and pushed his nose again. Nothing.

Dad had probably known people were looking for us and wanted me to have a way to find him, and I'd thrown it away because I wanted to be trusted like an adult. It turns out *I* wasn't the one he mistrusted. I shouted at the cartoonish plastic bear head and, in frustration, threw it on the floor. It hit with a sharp *crack* and split neatly in two. A single watch battery bounced free and rolled away.

Something important to remember in moments of crisis: your brain stops working at 100 percent if you aren't careful. For instance, I'd forgotten that it's possible to change batteries in gadgets.

I snatched up the bracelet, retrieved the battery cover, and threw open a filing cabinet door, revealing a pile of thousands of batteries of all sizes, styles, and shapes, all brand-new.

A minute later, I was holding a reassembled Mr. Happybear, whose eyes were glowing a rather threatening shade of red, which meant it was on. I went to push the emergency nose button but was suddenly hit with a wave of doubt.

Dad had drilled into my head that I should *never* push the button, except in a major emergency. In hindsight, I probably should have asked him what constituted a major emergency. Had he meant hazardous waste spills? Creepy girls with unsettling propositions? Unexplained absences?

Maybe I was being paranoid. What if the vans had come to drop Dad back off? Maybe he'd fainted, and they'd taken him to a hospital. Tabbabitha *had* let me go without a fight that afternoon.

I went back to the security monitor and saw the doors on the front SUV swing open. Four people emerged from the darkened interior. Three were tall and burly-looking, and while I could not make out a face, there was no mistaking the mailbox-shaped figure that hopped out and started waddling toward my front doors. She was carrying something—was that a sledgehammer?

I pressed the bear's nose as hard as I could. The eyes blinked for a moment and then . . . kept blinking. Nothing was happening.

I pushed the button a second time. Nothing again. I pushed it about three hundred times in the next four seconds—still nothing. Then I remembered I was supposed to *wear* it. Just as I slipped it over my wrist, a startling crash rang through the store, followed by a second crash. I didn't need to see the monitor to know the sound of a sledgehammer meeting the bullet-resistant glass on our front doors.

Mr. Happybear's eyes quit blinking. A tinny computerized voice spoke from the bear. "Say! It seems like you're kinda freaking out a little bit! Is everything okay?"

God, I hate voice response systems.

"No," I said as clearly as I could. "Contact Melvin Kross."

"Out of range. Cannot contact. Sorry, Nikola. What seems to be the problem? Tell your friend, Mr. Happybear!"

"Out of *range*?" I roared at the bracelet. "How far could he have gone in the last hour? What's your range?"

Mr. Happybear's eyes blinked sarcastically. "Gosh, I'm just not able to answer that question. I'm sure sorry, Nikola! What seems to be the problem? Tell your friend, Mr. Happybear!"

I had a few things I wanted to tell Mr. Happybear, all right, but kept them to myself. "People are breaking into the house and my dad has been kidnapped," I said instead.

Mr. Happybear thought about this. "It sounds like you're having a problem with ABDUCTION and maybe a little bit of HOME INVASION. Is that correct?"

"*Yes!*" I screamed at the bracelet, realizing the crashing noise I was hearing over and over wasn't just my heart but the steady noise of someone about to break through the front doors.

"Awww," Mr. Happybear said with infuriating slowness. "Sounds like you're having a pretty tough day on account of the *ABDUCTION AND HOME INVASION*. I'm sure sorry about that, Nikola. I'll tell the security system. Have a great day!"

I was about to ask what that meant when a completely different voice spoke. It seemed to come from everywhere in the building all at once, as if the building itself was speaking.

"Securing facility," said a reassuring woman's voice. This was followed a tenth of a moment later by an entirely un-reassuring sound. A huge booming crash ripped through the lab, sounding like ten eighteen-wheelers had hit the building from all directions at once. A glance at the security monitors told me what had happened: a giant metal door had slammed shut over the entrance and presumably over every other route in or out as well. Had they always been there, hidden in the floor or over the ceiling? I reminded myself to ask Dad how he'd done it when I saw him again.

On the security camera, Tabbabitha was sitting in front of the door, holding the splintered handle of her sledge-hammer, regarding it like she'd never seen anything like it before. The woman's voice spoke over the intercom again: "Passive resistance mode activated. Please proceed to Mobile Housing Unit B."

Mobile Housing Unit B was Dad's affectionate nickname for my trailer. I didn't know what good it would do to go there, but it was a plan that didn't involve talking to Mr. Happybear, flapping my hands in panic, or curling into a fetal position on the floor. Two seconds later, I jumped onto the golf cart and put the pedal to the metal. Dad's golf cart rocketed forward at the alarming speed of twelve miles per hour, which didn't seem as fast as it had earlier that afternoon.

The lab suddenly looked frightening and inhospitable. More so than usual, anyway. All the main lights had gone off, and there were alarms and strobe lights flashing all over the place. This must have been by design, because while I could navigate the lab with my eyes closed, a stranger would have a hard time with the canyons of crates, equipment, chemicals, and other random objects. At least, I hoped this was the case, because as I drove, I could hear a massive roaring and crash-ing sound coming from the front doors. Someone was ram-ming an SUV into the security doors. They would be inside before long.

By the time I rounded the second corner of our mini-golf

course, past the Christmas decorations and plutonium storage unit, which marked the halfway point, I could tell they were inside the building. By the sound of it, at least one of the SUVs was taking care to crash into everything it could on its way to find me. The racket was deafening, and a distinct odor of chemistry told me that some compounds that weren't supposed to be combined were mingling somewhere. The lab was about to become a difficult place to breathe.

There was another skidding and crashing sound—had they just hit the piano? My golf cart crept along, slowing as the battery power depleted. It hadn't been charged all day, after all. I passed a couple dead ends, rounded the third corner, and was now technically driving farther away from the trailers, which was the only way to get there. It was nerve-racking, but if the path to the trailers had just been straight, they would have run me over already. I was almost to the last turn when I was greeted by a shadow on the far wall of the building: it was an outline of the cart and myself. The SUV's headlights were pointed right at my back.

I pushed the accelerator as hard as I could, but it made no difference. The SUV revved its engine and squealed forward, less than fifty yards away from me. I screamed at the cart, "Go, go, go! Come on!"

Maybe it was my screaming, or maybe the SUV crossed the wrong sensor, but at that moment, the reassuring woman spoke from the intercom once again. "Active resistance engaged. Plug your ears, please."

Because I was swinging the cart around the final corner, I

needed my hands and couldn't reach my ears at that moment. A second later, I wished I had. From somewhere high above the rafters, a tongue of blinding blue light reached down and met with the roof of the SUV. *Lightning.* Indoor freaking lightning struck the SUV. The sound was incredible. I've never heard anything like it, and neither have you. Trust me. It was so loud I felt it—like getting slapped on the entire right side of my body all at once. The shock spun my cart around and actually pointed it in the right direction. Down the aisle of crates and newly flaming junk, I could finally make out the trailers. There was a welcoming golden light shining on the closest one, and I drove straight toward it. My ears were ringing like crazy, but I could just make out the engine of the SUV trying to start again. The lightning must have blown out its electrical system.

After what seemed like ages, I made it—jumped off the cart, dashed into the trailer, and turned to push the door closed.

The security system must have known where I was, because the moment I closed the door, every light in the building went dark, and I could feel a deep vibration thrumming beneath my feet.

It felt like an earthquake. Breakfast dishes vibrated off the table, and cups slid off shelves in the kitchen. The pitcher of milk problem solved itself. Over the ringing in my ears and the clatter of falling dishes, the reassuring woman's voice spoke one last time: "Please fasten your safety harness. Departure in ten, nine, eight . . ."

Safety harness? The room was black, I was more scared than I had ever been in my life, and I was being asked to fasten a *safety harness?* In the kitchen? I had trouble finding the butter, let alone a harness I had never seen. I figured the closest thing was my recliner in the living room.

"Five, four, three . . ." Another loud crash outside. One of the vans had just smashed into Dad's trailer next door. I dashed into the living room, jumped into the recliner, and, for whatever reason, pulled the lever to stick the footrest out so I was basically lying down.

"Two, one, departing . . . Thank you for engaging the security system. We hope you are very satisfied with your security enhancement experience. If there have been any problems, please call . . ." The woman continued talking, but I stopped paying attention about the same time that everything in the trailer went rocketing past me, like the whole unit had been stood on its end. Either that or the trailer was moving very quickly, very suddenly. If you could sit inside a bullet and get shot out of a gun, I think the sensation would be pretty similar.

No matter what was actually happening out in the darkness, I think it's safe to say that I was not very satisfied with my security enhancement experience. I closed my eyes, held on, and, as I always do in difficult situations, recited the ABCs over and over in my head, both forward and in reverse. Before long, I would either be safe or dead.

Either way, my problems were over.

3

GOING TO IOWA. ON PURPOSE.

The next few minutes were kind of a blur. There was a lot of movement, an incomprehensible amount of noise, and a smidgen of mindless terror. I felt as if I were riding in a poorly designed bullet train, or maybe a roller coaster, but without the comforting shoulder harnesses or being able to see where I was going. Tables, chairs, books, dishes, and every other item in the unit bounced around violently. A framed cheeseburger wrapper fell from the wall, cracking the glass. Occasionally, everything in the unit, myself included, would slam against one wall or another, indicating either a turn or that the entire place had gone on its side. There were sharp bumps that lifted the recliner and me completely off the floor, and swooping dips that reunited myself, the recliner, and the floor with bone-rattling suddenness. I was able to muster one positive, conscious thought: unless those SUVs had rockets in the back, they weren't going to catch me any-time soon.

Eventually, the ride slowed and stopped with a thud. Everything slid forward with a final, exhausted lurch, and faint light streamed in through the curtains. The sudden motionlessness and silence were startling in contrast.

I couldn't tell, but I thought the light was sunlight. It *looked* like natural evening light—my trailer had always lived under the glow of a bank of fluorescent lights, so the warmer, uneven illumination was difficult to identify. First thought: I *really* needed to dust.

After weighing my options and considering several courses of action, I decided to grip the armrests of my chair and whimper for a minute or twelve. After I'd done that, nothing had changed, so I got up and went to the door. I drew in a deep, fortifying breath, opened it, and found myself face-to-face with a small gray goat.

The goat made eye contact for a moment before sidling roughly past me with a grunt. It strolled into what had recently been my living room and pooped on the floor. It was like he'd been waiting all day for me to open the door so he'd have a warm place to poop. He looked up at me, said "NA-a-a-a-a!" and started eating a portion of the living room rug he had not defecated upon. Apparently, the goat considered himself a homeowner and wasn't worried about my opinion on his redecorating.

I took a last look around my trailer. I wanted to crawl into my bed, put on a movie, and wait for everything to blow over.

But you can't escape from someone and then wait for them to find you. You have to keep moving. I grabbed a bag and a change of clothes, and threw open the door a second time.

A wide meadow now surrounded the trailer. Cool, fresh air greeted my face, and soft-looking patches of grass spotted the browning landscape. There wasn't a building in sight. I was not alone, though. A handful of goats were trotting over to check out the new arrival.

I left the door open and stepped outside. "Help yourselves, guys. Eat, poop, and be merry."

"NA-a-a-a-a-a-a-a!" said the goats, and they proceeded to do just that. Behind the trailer was a foreboding concrete tube with rails like train tracks. I would have thought it a drainage pipe or the entrance to an underground garage had I not just emerged from it with all my worldly possessions. The tracks extended past where the trailer had stopped, and I could see how they were so buried and overgrown with grass that someone might not notice them, unless they happened to step right on one. Squinting a bit, I could make out a huge paw print stenciled on the side of a distant water tower—the logo of the West Blankford High School Wild Boars. I must have been a couple of miles outside city limits.

I could also see a pillar of black smoke rising from about where I reckoned our home was located, but decided not to think about that yet.

Mobile Housing Unit B looked like it had been through a war or two. Deep scrapes and gashes adorned every surface, and at least one metal panel had been ripped off altogether. On the opposite side of the trailer was a rusty barbed-wire fence and a gravel road that appeared to lead directly from nowhere to nowhere. This was convenient because I had nowhere to go.

I said goodbye to the goats, hopped the fence, and started walking.

It was growing dark, and the thought occurred to me that a flashlight would help me see where I was going. But that would only help if I'd had some idea *where* I was going. I was just *going*. I would have called family, but apart from Dad, I didn't have any. I would have stayed with friends, but you know the flaw in that plan.

I tried pushing the button on my Happybear Bracelet again. Just as before, the eyes blinked a second, and the bracelet spoke to me in a tinny electronic voice.

"Say! It seems like you're experiencing a stressful situation! Is everything okay?"

"Contact Melvin Kross."

"Out of range. Cannot contact. Sorry, Nikola. What seems to be the problem? Tell your friend, Mr. Happybear!" said the bracelet, just as before.

"Can you call me a cab?" I asked.

"Gosh, I'm sorry, Nikola! No taxi services are available in this location. Transportation has been requested," Mr. Happybear said. "Would you like to hear a joke?"

"No," I said, wondering what kind of transportation came after rocket-propelled trailer.

"Okay!" the bracelet said. "What's the difference between *A SLICE OF PIE* . . . and *A PUPPY*?"

I closed my eyes and sighed. Every instinct in my entire body told me to ignore the question and keep walking. I figured the odds of Mr. Happybear knowing a good joke was about one in a billion, especially since it had been programmed by my dad.

I couldn't stop myself. "I don't know. What's the difference between a slice of pie and a puppy?"

Mr. Happybear's eyes blinked once. "Perhaps you should find out before you eat your next slice of pie!"

Let me tell you, if that bracelet hadn't been my only link to Dad, it would not have survived the evening.

I hadn't walked five minutes when a pair of headlights appeared over the crest of the hill I was descending. A moment of panic turned to relief: the lights were not the high, square lights of the SUVs. The approaching vehicle rode low to the ground and with a distinct rattle.

I needed a ride, but for a girl my age, hitchhiking is typically considered about as reckless as Russian roulette. At the same time, I was tired, and there were certainly people after me. People I couldn't hope to escape on foot. As the car drew nearer, I decided to risk it and stuck out a thumb. Like magic, the car's brake lights lit up, and it rolled to a stop alongside me, the brakes squealing. A purple-tinted passenger window cranked down haltingly, and a voice spoke from within: "Er, ah, Niko—*hic!*—Nikola?"

My worst fears were confirmed as the window lowered

enough to make out the face of Miss Hiccup. "No," was all I said.

"No? No what?—*Hic!*—"

"No, today is bad enough already, and I refuse to believe that you're here, miles from heaven knows where, offering me a ride. Please stop existing. You are making me doubt that the universe still makes sense."

Miss Hiccup's trademark kindly smile was nowhere to be seen. Instead, she angled her head down to glare at me over the top of her spectacles. "Look, Nicky. When you first came to our school, your dad brought me a pager and gave me a pretty generous—*hic!*—er, payment. The deal was that if the pager ever went off, I was supposed to come here, pick you up, and drive you somewhere. So get in and we can get—*hic!*—get this over with."

I wanted to keep walking, but this Tabbabitha person had resources, transportation, and friends who didn't mind breaking the law to get at me. I had my feet, a pair of boots, some clothes, and a ride, which was apparently a part of Mr. Happybear's nefarious plan. I held my breath and opened Miss Hiccup's car door.

"The name is Nikola," I said, climbing in. "I see you didn't spend the money my dad paid you on a car."

Miss Hiccup's eyes flared. "There is absolutely nothing wrong with my ca—*hic!*—car, young lady."

You know how something can be so ugly it becomes cute? Like those wrinkly dogs? That doesn't work for cars. Miss Hiccup's car was a brown, green, orange, and brown

El Camino. If you've never seen one, it's a car in the front, a truck in the back, and a crime against automotive design from bumper to bumper. Miss Hiccup's El Camino appeared to be pieced together from the ugliest parts of all the ugliest El Caminos ever created.

"Okay," I said. "Spill it. What's going on? Who were those people?"

She shrugged and stared ahead. "No idea. I told you what I know. The pager beeped, I put down my ramen noodles and got in the car. Is your dad a fugitive or a spy or something? I bet he makes drugs, doesn't he?"

I didn't think so. "He's a scientist," I said.

"Yeah, because scientists occasionally skip town without their kids from time to time. Your pop sounds like a real stand-up guy."

"He didn't *skip town*. He's been . . . abducted," I said, finding it strangely hard to admit the situation to another person. I know this will sound weird, but it felt a bit . . . *embarrassing*. Like it might feel if you fell down stairs in front of everyone.

She turned to look at me. "My own pop was a real schmuck, too. We had a saying in my house growing up: Things were bad, but they were always going to get better next week. Of course, next week never happened, you know? You can't keep waiting for a thing that isn't coming. I hope you aren't."

She was studying me in a quizzical way that made it clear she expected an answer.

I shook my head. Part of me wanted to correct her, but something told me I shouldn't. I was a little bit floored by the change in her demeanor. She was always so kind and sweet. How much of that had been an act? Grouchy, brutally honest Miss Hiccup was starting to grow on me.

"So where are we going?" I asked instead.

She sighed. "Iowa."

"We're going to Iowa? On purpose?"

She laughed heartily. "And that ain't the half of it."

"What do you mean?" I asked.

Miss Hiccup repressed a snicker and almost repressed a smile. She was enjoying herself.

"I don't know anyone in Iowa," I said.

She turned on the radio, filling the car with loud static. She turned it off again. "Sounds like that's about to change."

I would have felt better if she didn't look as happy as she did. She'd stopped hiccuping, too. "What's so funny?"

She took on a contemplative look. "You know, Nicky, the rotten thing about being a guidance counselor is that you have to be so damn *nice* to everyone. You have to be nice to the crappy, sassy little kids, no matter how awful they are. You have to be nice to the other teachers, even the ones who make you call them *doctor* because they have a PhD in physical education or home economics or something. And when you're done with all that, you have to be nice to the *parents*: 'Oh, hey, I haven't even glanced at my kid's homework in three months, but would you mind kissing my butt while I yell at you because he has a C in English?' It gets old. It isn't natural—being that nice all the time."

"Okayyy," I said, "but where are we—"

"Last week," Miss Hiccup went on, "a kid stole a cigar from that gas station down the street from the school and smoked it in the boys' room. You know what happened? He got busted. They hauled him into *my* office and told *me* to deal with it. The moment he hit the chair, he puked. He puked *in my purse*. And he'd been eating corn! My *keys* were in there, Nicky. I have to touch those *every day*! But I had to be *nice* to the little vomit fountain. I had to say, 'Oh, that's okay, let's get you cleaned up.' I would have cleaned the little cigar-stealing barf bomb with a fire hose if I could have gotten away with it."

"You don't own any guns, do you?"

She pointed a shaking finger at me, a warning look in her eyes. "Can it, sister. I'm never going to see you again, so I'm going to give you a gift: I'm going to tell you what your problem is."

She brushed an errant lock of hair out of her eyes and continued. "I know you're smarter than everyone at school. That's great, but it's been pretty inconvenient for me. Do you know how big a pain it is to find teachers who aren't scared of teaching you? It sucks, trying to teach a classroom of kids about photosynthesis and having one kid point out that you're mispronouncing some word none of them will ever remember anyway. Do you honestly expect a public school teacher to know what wavelengths of light produce the most nutritive output in switchgrass? We don't pay them enough to even look up switchgrass online."

She turned on the radio and tried tuning it, but all she found was the voice of a man shouting about something in the Bible. She turned it off again and continued her monologue. "And you know what? Those other kids *are* wrong, and you *are* right. Those other kids are horrible people. They're going to grow up and become horrible adults, and you'll have to deal with them without anyone to take your side. There's no changing that. All I can do is send letters home to all the parents, but the parents don't read them. You know why?"

I started to answer, but she was going strong and didn't want to be interrupted by something as insignificant as me answering her question.

"Because the parents are horrible people, too. So yeah, it's more convenient to tell you to quit being weird and to blend in."

"Well, I just think that—"

She turned on the radio a third time, tuned it, and smacked it with the flat of her hand. This time it produced a sound that was about 80 percent static and 20 percent music, which was apparently good enough, because she left it on. "Here's the worst part: I kind of like you. I see myself in you."

I cringed involuntarily.

"Teachers say that all the time, great way of bonding with a kid, and it's usually a lot of bull, but I actually mean it. You're a lot like a younger me. When I look at you, I see some of the stuff I like, a *bunch* of the stuff I hate, and some of the stuff I'd change if I could. So here's what I'd change: You need to learn how to meet people halfway. Allow people to be imperfect. Get out there and make friends with jerks and idiots and terrible people, because when you stop looking for the worst in people, *that's when you see the good stuff.*" At this point, she turned up the radio and made it clear we were done with our little heart-to-heart. "Why don't you take a nap? The trip will go faster. You could sleep till we got there and not miss a thing."

- - - - - ✳ - - - - -

The sun hung low on the horizon. For a moment I thought it was the sunset, but the chill in the air and the ache in my neck told me it was morning. I sat up and looked around. Miss Hiccup was still asleep, so it must have been pretty early. She looked so peaceful that it almost made me want to like her. The landscape was flat and empty in all directions, making it seem almost as if we were standing still. Fading clutches of early snow clung to the earth here and there, harbingers of the coming winter. The El Camino, which had not broken down or burst into flames during the night, was moving along at a good clip. I drew a deep breath and stretched. Off in the distance, a lone stag leaped a wire fence and continued on his way to wherever stags go. The hum of the road, faint static-music, the vibration of the engine, and the wind noise were so soothing that I found myself being lulled back to sleep.

I bunched my backpack up against the window and started getting comfortable again when something occurred to me. I didn't have a driver's license, but from what I understood, it was very bad for a person driving a car seventy-five miles an hour down the interstate to be sound asleep, no matter how peaceful she looked.

"WAKE UP, MISS HICCUP!" I screamed in a panic.

Miss Hiccup was so startled that she jerked upright in her seat, wrenching the wheel hard to the left. The El Camino lurched obediently and started spinning out of control. For a few terrifying seconds, the shrieking of burning tires and the shrieking of Miss Hiccup and myself broke the formerly placid morning silence. The world spun wildly around us, and I lost track of which way was forward and which was back. In a move of desperation, Miss Hiccup slammed on the brake, spun the wheel in the opposite direction, and engaged the left-hand turn signal (for good measure, I suppose). Just as suddenly as the spin had begun, the car jerked to a halt, ending with us parked in the center of the road, pointing straight forward with a whirling tornado of tire smoke fading away around us.

The world seemed utterly silent, save for the gentle grumble of the engine and the placid *tic-tic-tic* of the turn signal, which Miss Hiccup disengaged without comment. The stag had stopped and was viewing us with what looked like disdain.

My traveling partner drew a deep, shuddering breath and spent about a minute staring straight out the front window. After pondering her mortality, Miss Hiccup put the car back into gear and started driving again.

Not long after, she turned to me. "Miss *Hiccup?*"

Did I say that out loud? "Pardon? Say, do you know where we are?"

"You called me Miss Hiccup," she said.

Crap. "No. No, I didn't. You probably dreamed that," I said.

She cocked her head to the side. "Do you know what my name is?"

I sighed. There was no getting around it. "Not . . . exactly? It's nothing personal. I just never managed to remember it."

"Nothing *personal*? There is nothing more personal than a person's name. What made you settle on Miss Hic—*hic!*—Hiccup? Why not"—she straightened in her seat and took on a stoic expression—"Miss Pretty Blond Woman Who Should Have a Boyfriend but All the Men in Town Are Intimidated by a Woman Who Doesn't Feel the Need to Constantly Re-Inflate Their Egos at Every Opportunity?"

"Oh, yeah," I said. "It's funny you should mention that, because that's my other nickname for you, Miss Pretty Blond—er, you know, what you said just then."

"Hm," she said, unconvinced by my masterwork of a fib.

"People forget things. I'm sor—"

She twitched. "For God's sake—it's printed on my door. There are certificates on each of my walls and a six-inch sign on my desk, *and* you have a photographic memory."

"You have to admit," I said lamely, "it suits you, what with the—"

"I think we've established that I have the ability to kill us both without much notice, have we not?"

"Yeah."

"So let's just drop it. 'Kay?"

4

CORNFIELDS AND ZOMBIES

Miss Hiccup produced a set of directions scribbled hastily on a yellowed scrap of paper. I recognized my dad's handwriting and overcame the urge to grab it and clutch it to me like a cherished teddy bear.

As the hours wore on, the directions took us more and more off the beaten path. We went from the interstate to highways, then to county roads, and eventually to gravel roads with names like F-21. Before long, the directions resorted to descriptions: *Take the first left turn after the rusted-out tractor with a scarecrow leaning on it* and *Turn right four miles after the speed limit sign with a bullet hole in the lower left corner.* Other landmarks, like *the large dead horse* and *the house that burned down* had long since been cleared away or decomposed, so we were left looking for blackened earth or the sort of place a horse might choose to enter into rest. These led to occasional wrong turns, and before long, we were choosing roads based on whether we thought we'd tried them yet.

While this was going on, I made a few attempts at conversation, all of which were rebuffed. Miss Hiccup was making a conscious effort to avoid getting to know me any more than she had to. I respected her decision, but it made for a rather dull trip. "So why did Dad say he was setting up this plan, anyway? You must have had questions," I tried finally.

Miss Hiccup had been focused on scanning the fields for what the directions referred to as *an enormous beehive* and didn't answer at first.

"Hello?" I said.

"What? Oh, sorry," she said. "I was pretending not to hear you. Your father did explain. But his explanation was bizarre, and I'm not sure if any of it was true."

There was a pause. After almost a minute, I couldn't take the suspense anymore. "AND?"

"What?" she said, as if she had drifted off into a daydream. "Oh, I'm not supposed to tell you. I just thought you'd like to know you're missing something really fascinating and mysterious."

I rolled my eyes. "You've made your point; I'm sorry I was rude to you. Now, can you just tell me what my dad was up to? A lot of stuff has happened, and I'm a little scared. You don't have to be hateful the whole time." My voice cracked as I said it, and I figured I should stop talking in a hurry or I'd start bawling for no reason.

Miss Hiccup looked at me with—was that sympathy? If it had been anyone else, I would have thought it was. "Listen, I really hope everything works out for you. I like you as much as a person can possibly like someone they don't particularly care for. I mean that."

"Um, thanks?" I said. "Beehive! Turn here!"

The beehive wasn't hard to miss. *Enormous* didn't even begin to cover it. I've consulted a thesaurus and have determined the best word would be *Brobdingnagian*. Roughly the size of a backyard shed, it had a perfect oval shape, like the beehives you see dropping on mischievous cats in cartoons. It was surrounded by a visible cloud of bees and was accompanied by a low drone that I wished I could not hear from three hundred feet away over the engine of the El Camino.

Miss Hiccup had to slow down to make the turn, and I kept my eyes locked on the hive the entire time. How many bees were out there? My most conservative estimate was in the neighborhood of two to three billion.

Miss Hiccup saw me staring. "They aren't going to come get you, you big chicken. They're happy guarding their hive over there."

"Oh, ha-ha," I said, but it was good to be reminded that they weren't about to swarm the El Camino.

Then the bees swarmed the El Camino. I was never less happy to have an adult proven wrong. The bees were gargantuan by bee standards. Each one at least the size of my thumb, with huge multifaceted eyes and stingers the size of sewing needles. They also appeared to take much more notice of us than insects typically would. Within a few seconds, the car was at the center of a furious black-and-yellow storm. They started landing on the windows, crawling around to get a better look. I held my breath, and my heart stopped as one made eye contact and tapped its stinger on the window. *Tap-tap-tap*, like knocking on a door.

And then, to make matters worse, Miss Hiccup started slowing down. I took a deep breath and attempted to address the situation with her. "WHAT ARE YOU DOING?" I screamed while helpfully smacking the dashboard. "GOGOGOGOGO!"

Miss Hiccup had her own take on our circumstances. "THE BEES ARE ALL OVER THE WINDOWS. I CAN'T SEE ANYTHING. DO YOU WANT TO CRASH?"

As a counterpoint, I offered forth a forecast of possible outcomes. "THEY'RE GOING TO GET IN AND EAT US. THEY'RE GOING TO STING YOU TO DEATH AND MAKE ME WATCH. THEY'LL STEAL YOUR WALLET. THEY'RE GOING TO CARRY THE CAR AND STUFF IT INTO THEIR HIVE AND TURN US INTO HONEY."

Then the bees were doing something. A perfectly circular space in the swarm had opened at the center of the windshield. In the middle was a single bee. It looked at each of us in turn, seemed to nod, and winked (can you wink a compound eye?), and the bees were gone in a blizzard of black-and-yellow fury.

I was going to live. Miss Hiccup and I sat motionless and silent for a time. Eventually, she turned to me, her voice a bit hoarse from screaming. "Ah, so, um . . . do you need to change your pants?"

"No!" I said. "God! Why? Do you?"

She seemed to consider the notion and wiggled her hips back and forth tentatively—testing the waters, so to speak. "Nope," she said. "Let's hit it."

The El Camino started right up as if nothing had happened. We drove along the dusty, gravelly road in silence, seeming to agree that we didn't need to discuss Beepocalypse One any further. At the peak of the next hill, there was a hard bump, and we found ourselves on a wide, smoothly paved street.

The change in surroundings couldn't have been more jarring. I'd been staring at cornfields and wheat fields and soybean fields for hours on end, and within a blink of an eye, we were in the middle of a town. An actual wooden street sign read, MAIN STREET.

For the first time, I laid eyes on what was to become my new home. It was a small town, like countless others we had passed at a distance on the way, with the exception that most small towns in the Midwest have given up, either allowing their downtowns to fade into decay or giving them over to identical clusters of megamarts, chain restaurants, and gas stations.

This little city was thriving. Each of the shops, offices, and other establishments was well lit, clean, and open for business. Colorful awnings and crisp flags flapped smartly in the light breeze. A large display of fresh fruit stood unguarded before a corner grocery store. The smell of apples permeated the car as we passed, and my mouth watered.

Most of Main Street's buildings were made from red brick or brightly painted wood. Intricately decorated gingerbread-style houses stood here and there along the street with more lining the side streets. Despite that, I did spot a few deviations from the theme—a sleek, modernist construction that would have done Frank Lloyd Wright proud stood at one corner. A perfectly cubical house lined on all sides with deep blue and green glass panes shifted to orange and red as we passed.

The side streets also held a smattering of charming storefronts. I spotted a rainbow-striped candy shop, a music store that looked like a giant boom box, and a few larger, more respectable-looking buildings that could have been banks or offices. The streets themselves were clearly marked with white and yellow lines that looked as fresh as if they had been painted the day before. Every street was decorated with wrought-iron streetlamps, signs carved from real wood, and extra-wide sidewalks stocked with bike racks, drinking fountains, benches, tables, gazebos, and other pleasant amenities every few feet. I had to wonder: was this a town, or had we driven into some kind of theme park?

"We have reached our destination," Miss Hiccup said in her best GPS voice. We parked opposite a large brick-and-stone courthouse at the center of town. It shared the central square with a large park, replete with benches, picnic areas, and a couple athletic fields. Not far down the street, in front of the General Relativity Store, stood a large wooden display rack that held sketchbooks, pens, markers, small musical instruments, music players, digital cameras, some Frisbees that glowed eerily in the midday sun, and a couple pairs of roller skates that appeared to be moving slightly back and forth on their own. A sign on the display read only PLEASE RETURN WHEN FINISHED.

Never had I seen a place so instantly charming and welcoming. It was the sort of place I could spend weeks exploring. I only wished they had had the foresight to put up a sign announcing the town's name. A visitor would have no idea what this place was without one.

I pored over the road atlas while Miss Hiccup fixed her hair in the vanity mirror. There wasn't supposed to be a town here at all, if I was reading it correctly. According to Miss Hiccup, we were supposed to know what we were looking for when we got here. But here we were, parked on Main Street, staring at the Pi R Circle Bakery and Coffee Shop, Professor Dave's Discount Hardware, and the Social Function Café, and the only obvious thing was that this town had some pretty bizarre ideas about what businesses should be named.

There were more odd things I was starting to pick up on that hadn't been obvious at first glance. For starters, nothing anywhere mentioned the name of the town. Even weirder, though it was almost 2:00 PM, the place looked empty. Like everyone in town had just recently decided to stop home for a morning nap and would be back in two shakes of a lamb's tail. That's corny, but I could imagine people living in such a place measuring time in lambs' tail-shakes.

Another mystery: apart from Miss Hiccup's El Camino, I didn't see a single car. Having absolutely no traffic in the middle of the day was unusual, even for the smallest of towns. On the other hand, the bike racks were stocked full with bicycles, as well as scooters and other contraptions I did not recognize. One such contraption was chained to the rack just in front of the car. It appeared to be a normal bicycle, with a small fan mounted to a tall, spindly pole above the back wheel. I wondered if it was for ventilation or if it was actually intended to provide thrust. Next to it was something that looked a bit like a metal backpack with short plastic legs. Farther up the sidewalk was a rack that held what was clearly supposed to be some kind of jet pack. Weird.

Miss Hiccup consulted her directions again, as if they would somehow give her more information than they had a moment before. I could see her searching for signs and coming up just as empty as I had. She sighed grumpily and hiccuped at the same time.

"Any ideas?" she asked.

"None. Is someone supposed to meet us?" I asked.

Miss Hiccup shrugged. "The directions just say 'park on Main Street downtown' and that's all."

Try as I might, I could not shake the feeling that something incredibly bizarre was about to happen.

I first saw it in the reflection of the Social Function's windows. A large object sprouted from the lawn of the courthouse immediately behind us. I cranked down the window and craned my neck around in time to see something moving up and out. The thing resembled one of those big radio towers you see from the highway, with the red lights on top. Something that looked like a thick fluorescent light tube ran up its center. After rising about twenty feet into the air, the tower—which appeared to be mounted on a hinged, rotating base—tilted downward until it was pointed at the sky at about a forty-five degree angle. The tube glowed bright green a moment, then vivid blue, then green again. It went from green to blue faster and faster until it somehow became orange, and a streak of blinding golden light shot from the tip. The beam struck an impressively large metal platter that hung above an office building across from the town square. The platter glowed bright orange and emitted a sound like I'd never heard. It was a single note but somehow more beautiful in its purity than anything I had ever heard in my life. It echoed everywhere at once, like every inch of the town was making the sound, not just the platter. After about three seconds, the beam was cut off. The laser cannon, or whatever it was, stood erect once more and dropped back under the lawn of the courthouse, and everything was silent again.

Then every door in town opened in unison. It was like the buildings had come down with a bad case of structure flu and were vomiting people. Things went from ghost town to bustling downtown in thirty seconds flat. Every sidewalk was clogged with people moving at various speeds. Actually, *people* was the wrong word. They were all children. The oldest was maybe seventeen, and most appeared to be about my age or younger. Some of them rolled on skates or skateboards, but most just wandered past, not looking terribly enthusiastic. One girl approached the bike rack in front of us and strapped the weird backpack thing onto her shoulders. The short legs immediately reached down, met the sidewalk, lifted her about an inch above the pavement, and strolled away. Several of the kids slowed to stare at Miss Hiccup and me. Miss Hiccup stared back, agape. I smiled and waved timidly at them, not knowing what else to do.

"They're zombies, aren't they?" Miss Hiccup whispered, her hand on the ignition.

"No," I said. "They're all kids."

"Ugh," she said, cringing lower in her seat.

Two girls strolled in front of the car. The younger one had brown hair cut into a smart bob and wore a tartan skirt and a T-shirt that read *I solved Fermat's Last Theorem and all I got was this T-shirt*. She was tiny, like she might only be six or seven years old. When she glanced up at the car, her face lit up. "Hey! Nikola! Helloooooo!" she shouted, waving like a maniacal monkey. The older girl, who was about my age, looked so similar that she must have been the older sister, except that she had deep, naturally red hair. She glanced at us and rolled her eyes for our benefit. Then she calmly wet her finger in her mouth and stuck it into her little sister's ear.

"*Eeeeeew!*" the little girl protested.

"Where's your head, Fluorine? Leave them alone. You're going to be late again."

Fluorine nodded and scampered through a door wedged

between storefronts that read ENGLISH AND COMPANY, INSUR-ANCE ADJUSTERS SINCE 1942.

The older girl approached and crouched to speak through my open window, smiling apologetically at us. She was a bit shorter than average, with pleasantly full features. She had the sort of face that lets you know the person is friendly and nice without having to know anything about them. "Sorry, she's completely out of order today—chronologically speaking. I'm Rubidia, and you're probably looking for the courthouse right behind you. They must be waiting for you in there." She turned to leave.

"How do you know—*hic!*—know they're waiting?" Miss Hiccup called.

Rubidia glanced back over her shoulder and smiled, like it was a stupid question but an entertainingly stupid one, at least. "Because the bees didn't kill you! Welcome to the School!" she called as she dashed through the door her sister had just entered.

Just then the laser-cannon thing sprouted from the courthouse lawn again, shot its strange beam against its target, made another indescribable and gorgeous noise, and was gone. The streets were once more silent and empty.

Miss Hiccup looked at me. "I don't know what the hell any of that was, but I think you're going to fit in around here perfectly." She leaned over me, yanked at the rusty door handle, and shoved the passenger door open wide.

I got out, grabbed my bag, and looked back into the car.

Miss Hiccup wore a blank expression I couldn't read. "Aren't you coming in?" I asked.

"Nope. It's not on the instructions," she said, holding up the tattered list we'd been staring at. "Send me a postcard, kid," she said, reaching to close the door.

How was I supposed to do that? "I don't have your address or your actual name."

"No kidding?" she said with a laugh, and tried pulling the door closed.

I held it open a second longer, reached in, and snatched the directions out of her hand. My dad had written them, and apart from an old photo tucked in my bag, they were all I had to remember him by.

"Take care," I said, slamming the door for her.

"Hope things go better for you," she said through the open window.

"You too," I said.

It was weird, but I kind of meant it.

Inside the building, I encountered a reception desk manned by a heavyset older man who was busy scribbling on papers with one hand and typing about eighty-five words a minute with his other. He wore one of those green accountants' visors they used to wear to make text easier to read, but it was on backward. Without stopping either of his activities, he gazed up with a welcoming smile as I approached.

"You are Nikola Kross." A statement, not a question.

"I am," I said.

The man coughed and scratched under his chin. He looked like a shaved Santa. "Welcome to the School. I'm Mr. Einstein—no relation—and you're looking for Dr. Plaskington, room 204. Upstairs, staircase on the right." He gestured to one of two identical staircases that bookended the little desk.

At the top of the stairs was a stately wooden door with a brass plaque that read DR. PATRICIA PLASKINGTON, and, below that, PRINCIPAL, PROPRIETOR, PAL. I almost missed it, but below *that*, some clever person had scratched a single additional word: POO.

I opened the door and found a rather plain and humble small office with light gray walls. The first thing that caught my eye was a poster tacked haphazardly to the wall above a metal filing cabinet depicting a familiar cat dangling from a familiar branch. The caption beneath read NATURAL SELECTION. A chess table stood under a window, and presiding over it was a rather frail-looking old lady who appeared to be in her early 300s, with a heavily lined face and a halo of wild, curly white hair. She looked like she weighed about seventy pounds, fifty pounds of which was cranium. A thick gold-and-ceramic necklace strained the structural integrity of her neck. A phone on the edge of her desk was ringing, but she made no move to answer it.

The old lady gestured at a chair. "Please stop thinking so loudly. It is rude, and I am trying to concentrate. Sit."

I sat. I was running out of whatever keeps a person going

in the face of extraordinary circumstances. If I had had one wish at the time, I would have wished for one normal person who would give me some straight answers without any nonsense. Looking back, if I could now pass a message to myself at that time, it would be this: *Get used to it.*

5

THE SANDWICH INCIDENT

Instead of greeting me, shaking my hand, asking me about my trip, or really doing anything socially acceptable, Dr. Plaskington stayed hunched over the world's most beat-up chess set. Several of the pieces were broken, chipped, charred, or otherwise damaged in some way, and bore signs of hasty and shoddy repair. She held up a hand to silence anything I might say and said, "What are you planning this time, you malevolent snipe?"

"I really haven't settled on a plan at the—"

"What?" she asked. "Oh, not *you*. I'm talking to *her*."

This was in reference to the person on the other side of the board. If there had been someone sitting there, I would have understood perfectly.

She studied the chessboard with ferocious intensity. It

was a full five minutes of silent deliberation before she made her move. I watched and waited. The phone stopped ringing.

After careful consideration, the doctor reached into a drawer beneath her chess table and produced a long-necked butane lighter with a trigger grip, the kind you'd use to light a charcoal grill. She reached out and deliberately set the white queen on fire. Then she sat back in her chair and folded her arms with an air of complete satisfaction. "HAH! Ms. Botfly will never see that coming!"

"Okay," I said. "Say, if you're not too busy, would you mind telling me where I am?"

She seemed to really notice me for the first time. "Oh, you remind me of your father. I remember him sitting right where you are, still a little scared, demanding that my assistant remove the blindfold. 'Who are you people? Where are my parents? Blah, blah, blah.' He certainly had spirit, your father." Dr. Plaskington shook her head with a wry smile. "We had more stringent security back in those days, you see. This particular campus was relatively new at the time, and we didn't have the bees and all the other autonomous security measures we have today."

"What a fascinating story," I said. "Next could you tell the one about where I am right now and why I'm here?"

"You are at a school, my dear," she said, spreading her arms in an expansive gesture. "This is my school, the Plaskington International Laboratory School of Scientific Research and Technological Advancement, but most students just call it the School, since that is a somewhat unwieldy name and many young people lack the commitment to spend the extra ten seconds it takes to pronounce it correctly. I spent decades building this school, and if a few seconds are spent in the pronunciation of its venerable moniker, then *frankly—*"

I cut her off. "Ma'am, I'd love to hear your thoughts on how people pronounce the name of your school and watch you set innocent chessmen on fire, but I think I might be able to concentrate better if I knew whether or not my father is dead."

Dr. Plaskington looked a little guilty. "I can see how that would be a distraction. Your father is an old friend of mine. One of our finest students. Allow me to put your mind at rest immediately: he has paid for everything well in advance."

"Right, but he was kidnapped, and—"

"Abducted, yes. I heard about that. Got an email yesterday. It said something about an alarm and that you were being brought here as soon as possible. I only wish he'd allowed us to arrange for the transportation. Did you ride on a car?"

"Ride on a car? Well, I was inside . . ."

Her eyes brightened with interest. "Of course! Out of the elements, very clever! You just pour some petroleum distillate into a reservoir, aerosolize and pump it into enclosed spaces, set it exploding, turn that linear force into rotary motion, and a few cogs and gears later, you're rollin' down the river!"

"Er, yeah, that's the general idea," I said. "But it's a road."

"Yes, yes. It's *boats* that travel on rivers!" she said with a wink, like that was a bit of insider knowledge she and I shared. "I can't *wait* for you all to get past this *obsession* with personal mechanized conveyances. We don't allow them here."

"Them? You mean cars?"

"And boats, but mostly cars. It's the noise, can't stand it. Plus they inspire laziness and dependence. Our campus is compact enough that a student can get anywhere on their own two feet. If you want to get around any other way, that's up to you."

"You knew I was coming? Do you know where my dad is?"

"I do not know," she said, suddenly serious. "But I can tell you with absolute certainty that your father is alive and well. Those who have taken him do not want him dead and would gain nothing from him being dead. That, however, is all we know."

The chess piece was now burning in earnest and becoming something of a distraction in itself. "I haven't even called the police," I said. "Should we contact the authorities?"

"Oh, they wouldn't have much success with the Old Ones."

"The—the Old Ones?"

"I'm sure your father filled you in. We can be reasonably certain they are behind his disappearance. He's quite valuable to them, and they've been attempting to locate him for some time. It appears they've finally been successful. The problem is that we have little way of locating *them*. We're working on it. They may be more intelligent, but he's got—"

"Hold the phone." I stood up, finally able to ignore the burning chess set in the corner. "*Nobody* is more intelligent than my dad. He's the smartest person in the world."

"I've run the numbers, and that is correct—by a margin

of about three percent, insofar as you ascribe mental abilities to the potential accomplishments of a particular mind. The problem is that even though he might be the smartest *person* in the world, he's certainly not the smartest *being* in the world. As you know, the Old Ones—"

I threw up my arms in frustration, wishing there was something inexpensive-looking nearby I could break. "Look, lady. I don't know what you *think* I know, but what I *actually* know is precisely *squat*. Well, I know some people came to see my dad, and that weirdo Tabbabitha came to my school, and she wanted me to—"

Dr. Plaskington went white. Well, whit*er*. "You were . . . approached?"

"Yeah, by a charming young lady named Tabbabitha with the arms of a gorilla and all the charisma of a rubber boot filled with refried beans. She told me I should go with her, and I told her to get bent."

The old lady cocked her head to one side, surveying me quizzically. "It is quite remarkable that you were able to resist doing what she asked of you. It took your father years to learn to see through their disguises and to resist their suggestions. Very few humans who encounter them are able to tell them no and live. You say it appeared to you as a young girl?"

"Well, kind of like a girl, kind of like a mutant, except less pleasant than your average mutant."

The principal became suddenly grave. "Remarkable. I need you to tell me everything she said to you—everything that happened—beginning to end."

I told Dr. Plaskington about my whole insane day, my visit to the counselor, Tabbabitha and her friends, her conversation with my father, and the catastrophe they unleashed inside our home.

The doctor appeared to be paying attention, a look of concern growing on her face as I finished. She nodded succinctly. "The Old Ones clearly wish to collect you, much as they did your father. It is fortunate you have finally come here. We've been asking Melvin to send you to us for ages. Your test scores are phenomenal."

"What tests? You looked at my grades?" I asked.

"Good heavens, no," she chuckled as she sprang to her feet and strode to her desk. For an old lady, she moved surprisingly quickly. "No, typical school grade structures are imprecise and primitive. We publish standardized tests and make them available to school districts at no cost. It's one way of locating students who might do well with a more challenging education. One you took a few years ago alerted us to your location—not many students can manage a perfect score, even on the trick questions. Frankly, you are a shoe," she said.

"Sorry, what?"

"A shoe! No question about it. You're more than acceptable."

"A shoo-in, you mean?"

"See, there you go, being extraordinary already," she said. "My school is terribly exclusive and can only accept a handful of humans every year. We've been saving a spot for you for some time. Was your father the reason you only took the test

66

once? I assume after our initial offer was rebuffed he didn't want anyone else discovering how remarkable you are."

"He did ask that I not participate in statewide standardized—"

"That's Melvin for you. Always a step ahead. Well, half a step ahead. If he wanted to hide you, he could have stopped you from taking even the first one, but I can't blame him for not anticipating it. Of course, that's probably how *they* found you."

"So what about my dad?" I asked, growing exasperated. "Is he going to be okay?"

"Oh, he'll be *fine*! If I'm not mistaken, they got a lot more than they bargained for when they picked up old Melvin. I wouldn't be terribly surprised if they showed up with him asking for a refund. To be honest, I'm shocked they thought he would be a good acquisition."

"They don't want him dead, then? They won't hurt him?" I asked. I was beginning to feel a little hopeful.

Dr. Plaskington shrugged. "Who knows? They'll *threaten* to murder him, of course. Probably try a little torture, mind control, solitary confinement, the odd beating, that kind of thing. But I doubt they'll kill him, at least not right away."

The woman's forecasts made me feel a little faint. How could she talk about such terrible things like they were the weekend weather forecast? The doctor shared my dad's talent for empathy, it seemed. "Can we go find him?" I asked. "We need to mount a rescue mission. I can help."

"You mean assemble a small group of teenagers with

unique abilities and personalities to go on an adventure into the unknown, seeking your lost father, but incidentally learning a little about themselves along the way? That sounds fine on paper, but the Old Ones would destroy your sanity, kill you at least once, and bury you in a bad neighborhood under an intentionally misspelled grave marker. No—best to leave this sort of thing to the professionals. I have notified the relevant authorities, and they are investigating the incident."

"Fantastic. So will they want a statement or something?"

"Yes. You're making it right now."

That didn't quite sit well with me, but Dr. Plaskington pressed on. "Our methods of tracking people are quite sophisticated. If he appeared in a crowd in Times Square without his memory, we would know. If he was dropped onto a life raft in the middle of the Pacific Ocean at this very moment, I would be notified within ten minutes. If he was abandoned with no radio and twenty minutes' worth of oxygen on the surface of the moon, we could get him home safely."

This made me a bit skeptical. "How about Narnia or the center of the sun?"

"Don't be flippant. We are capable of a great deal more than you imagine. If he wants to be found, and I'm sure he does, then we will find him . . . eventually."

"Have other people been kidnapped by the Old Ones before?" I pressed.

"Oh yes, loads. Barely a month goes by when we don't—"

"Do you get many of them back?"

She considered this. "Almost never, but this time I'm very

confident. Your father is quite resourceful. If anyone can survive the Old Ones, he can."

My head swam. Something told me Dr. Plaskington was extremely capable and *essentially* honest but not *100 percent* honest. I could tell she wasn't giving me the whole story, but I probably wasn't going to get much more out of her. She was telling me what I wanted to hear but not necessarily what I needed to know.

Dr. Plaskington fixed me with an intense gaze and took my hand in hers. "I need you to trust us. We can't find him if you aren't kept under protection. Right now your father is our top priority. If you left here, or if you allowed yourself to be captured, he would become our second priority."

Maybe Dr. Plaskington knew looking for Dad on my own was exactly what I had been thinking about, or maybe it's what she'd want to do in the same situation. In any case, I didn't have any idea where to start. For the moment, I decided it was best to trust her or to act as if I did. Without realizing what I was doing, I felt the outline of my old Mr. Happybear Bracelet in my pocket. As I touched it, the bracelet vibrated faintly, reminding me it was on. If nothing else, the bracelet was still a link to my dad. With time, perhaps I could figure out a way to make use of it.

Just then a small piece of information that had been fluttering about in my brain came to rest in my consciousness, and I let my thoughts about the bracelet go. Something the doctor had said a few minutes ago. "You only admit a handful of *humans*?" I asked.

"Yes," said the doctor, not at all derailed by the subject change. "But I don't mean that literally. An actual handful of humans would be just the one, unless you had rather absurdly large hands or were trading in miniature people." She chuckled heartily. "I think we can all agree on that!"

It seemed I needed to be more specific. "I meant to ask what other—beings?—other than humans could be accepted here."

"Well, parahumans are always welcome, but that's because they're almost always extraordinary. We have a jackdaw as well. Jeff is his name, I believe. Really, anyone exceptional is welcome at my school. We have sliding fee scales to—"

If you could have seen me just then, I probably looked like someone who was holding an invisible Rubik's Cube with both hands and was extremely angry and confused by it. The phone started ringing again. Had she just told me . . . "What? Look. If you're going to start telling me—wait—" There was so much happening that I didn't know where to start. "So who are the Old—" I suddenly wondered how the "authorities" were going to get in contact with me, when it struck me a second time that she had just told me I would be attending school with aliens, at which point the room began spinning in that rather upsetting way things spin when they're standing perfectly still, and I decided to inquire into one particular niggling issue: "WILL YOU PLEASE PUT OUT THE FIRE ON THE CHESSBOARD? IT IS DIFFICULT TO CONCENTRATE WHEN SOMETHING IN THE ROOM IS ON FIRE."

The old lady smiled in an infuriatingly kind, bemused fashion. "It is not my move, young miss. I do not cheat."

She looked ready to go on, but before she could, a tiny drone helicopter clattered into the window. Knocked off-kilter, it nearly fell, recovered, drew back, and, with a very discreet *pop*, did something that caused a single pane in the window to shatter into a shower of dust. It flew in, maneuvered over the burning queen, and dropped perhaps a spoonful of water onto it. The queen was extinguished with a faint *hiss*. The craft then reached out with a tiny saw mounted to a spindly robotic arm, sliced the head off a black bishop, and carried it out the window.

Dr. Plaskington scrunched her face appraisingly. "I guess Ms. Botfly *did* see that coming. Where were we?"

I took a calming breath. "You were about to explain what a parahuman is, who the Old Ones are, and *what on earth is going on at this school.*"

"I don't think I had intended to discuss any of that, but I certainly can, if you'd like. The prefix *para-* comes from Greek, meaning 'alongside' or 'other.' A paralegal is someone who isn't quite a lawyer; *paranormal* means something that isn't quite normal. Parahumans aren't quite human, but we're pretty darn close."

"We?"

"Why, yes, I am a parahuman, like many of the students here. You might have picked up on my superhuman charm and wit."

"How many of you are there?" I said, choosing not to address the presence or absence of charm and wit.

Dr. Plaskington nodded emphatically. "There are loads

of us! Nationwide, I'd expect we number a few thousand, depending on who you ask and whether you count those parahumans who aren't in contact with the wider community. Here at my school, on the other hand, we have parahumans coming out of our ears. Again, not *literally*. I'd say the School's enrollment is about nine percent human and ninety-one percent parahuman, and, of course, Jeff."

"So you're an almost-human? What is the rest?"

"Alien. We parahumans as well as our cousins, the Old Ones, are descended from visitors from the beyond. We came to this earth long, long ago and have endeavored through the generations to blend in as well as possible. Many of us are quite good at it."

"You're aliens? I don't . . ." I was about to say I didn't believe her, but then I realized that I kind of did. "Why did you come to Earth in the first place?" I asked.

"Why did your great-great-great-great-grandfather immigrate to the United States?"

I'd never seen a family tree that extended back farther than my grandparents, who I was told lived in Montana. "I . . . I'm not even sure who that was. Do you mean—"

"Try to understand: you're asking me the same question but with about three hundred more *greats* thrown in. The extremely short version is that we do not know, but we have no shortage of theories. You'll learn more later on in your Parahuman History and Paranthropology classes."

"Are you parahumans trying to take over the world, enslave Earth's population, or kill us all?"

Dr. Plaskington's disappointment was obvious. "Oh, don't be so prejudiced," she said. "Apart from our staggering intelligence, occasional gifts, superior physiques, and devastating artistic abilities, we parahumans are quite a lot like you. We seek nothing more than to live in harmony. Most of our kind are not welcome in 'normal' schools for the same reasons you were probably a bad fit at your last one. Our school, in contrast, will accept any student as long as they're bright, mature, and equal to the workload and intellectual rigor. Your father didn't explain any of this?"

"No," I said, wondering when my dad had started keeping secrets from me. For a guy who tells his kid every revolting detail of what a fifty-year-old man has to go through during his annual checkup, this was a pretty big omission.

Dr. Plaskington picked up her phone and set it down again to stop its ringing and began to shuffle through her desk, riffling through papers and pulling out drawers. "Did you happen to see a sandwich lying around here?"

"No. So the Old Ones, they're the same as you? You called them your cousins."

Dr. Plaskington paused, and it was clear she was a little offended by the question. "They are our cousins like chimpanzees are yours. We *were* the same but have since parted ways. They got nastier while we made ourselves more like you humans."

"So why did the Old Ones want *me*?" I asked.

The doctor leaned in close. "I believe it may have something to do with the prophecy."

73

"The . . . prophecy?"

"No, I'm just jiggling your cable. You humans do love a good prophecy. To be honest, I haven't the faintest idea. You are young and untrained. You don't have any strange abilities or supernatural talents that I can discern. My best guess is that they wanted you for leverage—a way to inspire cooperation in your father."

"So why do they need my dad?"

She shrugged again. "It can't be for anything good. Probably for his creativity. Your father is very inventive, and the Old Ones can't imagine their way out of a paper bag."

I was starting to realize Dr. Plaskington responded better to more direct questions. "What is it the Old Ones want to do? What are they attempting to accomplish that kidnapping my dad and me might help them with?"

She stood, seeming suddenly inspired, and searched through a huge handbag on a table in the corner. "We aren't completely sure, and several theories will be covered in your classes, but the upshot is that about fifty thousand years ago the Old Ones essentially ruled the world, and most agree they'd like to have it back. But listen to me, going on about ancient history when we have more pressing concerns! No sense in discussing all that for free when your classes are already paid for. What you need to know right now is that the Old Ones are still around and still trying to disassemble your civilization."

"So it's like a cold war with them? A standoff?"

"It's more of what you'd call a *hot war*, in that it's being fought every day and we are at all times under constant attack. Why do you think this school is put together like an impenetrable fortress?" She raised her hands as if indicating all the obvious stuff I should have seen, but there hadn't been so much as a fence that I remembered.

I shrugged. "It seemed kind of penetrable to me. We drove here."

Dr. Plaskington pointed sharply in my direction. "You were *allowed* in. You crossed the gap and did not cease to exist, you were cleared by the bees and were not stung, and you were not utterly destroyed by our sonic cannon or any one of at least ten other active countermeasures."

"Those *bees* were security? How did you train them?"

"Those bees aren't trained. They're robots. Robots that are designed specifically to defend against the Old Ones and other unwelcome visitors. If the Old Ones persuade gullible humans to rise up against us, the bees could drive them off or kill them. If the Old Ones attack the School personally, as they have done in the past, the bee stings deliver certain chemical and electromagnetic devices that would be excruciatingly painful to them." She returned to her seat and opened a drawer. "Read about them in here, if you like." She handed me a pamphlet with the title *How to Keep the Bees From Killing You.* Pleasant.

She was now producing other pamphlets from her desk and handing them over as she spoke. One was entitled *Real-World Camouflage and the Visibly Alien Child*; another was *They're After YOU, Dummy!* My favorite had a cartoonish picture of a huge monster with about a million tentacles that was clearly about to murder a small, terrified girl. This one was called *Why Didn't Mommy Pay for the Optional Electronic Defense Classes?*

Dr. Plaskington went into what sounded like a rehearsed speech. "The world is a dangerous place once you've been linked to the parahuman community. My school will provide you with a top-notch education, but that's only part of the deal. We'll also guarantee your safety while you're here and train you to defend yourself so you can survive on your own if you should ever choose to live outside a protected community. One hundred percent of our students leave here one hundred percent ready to protect themselves and their families against the Old Ones. *That's a guarantee.*"

It was a bold statement made a little less bold by the next pamphlet she gave me, which was entitled *Safety Guarantee Terms and Conditions* and was written in something like two-point font. I could barely make out the first line—which began, *Guarantee does not assure or imply a refund of any funds or other payment.*

I made a mental note: *If I ever get murdered by the Old Ones, good luck getting my tuition returned.* "So do I just . . . go to school, or . . . what happens next?"

"What happens next is we make every effort to locate your father, and you remain here to begin your education. I'm certain you will distinguish yourself in many ways. Plus, that tuition money has been sitting in your account for far too long—it's long past time to put that cash to work for you!"

"So," I continued, "I'm supposed to be attending school here, and I'm just going to *forget* about whatever is happening to my dad. Like, 'Oh, Dad's been kidnapped; guess I'll study for Biology.'"

"That is a rather concise summary," Dr. Plaskington said, "but still essentially true. What else would we do? Would you have us provide you with transportation and one of those ridiculous human projectile weapons . . . what do you call them? With the tubes, like a metal spitball in a straw?"

It took me a moment. "A . . . gun?"

"Yes! Thank you," she said. "Do we give you a gun so you might perform a house-by-house search? Where would you begin? Mexico? Peru? Perhaps the Mariana Trench? One of Jupiter's moons? All of these are options."

It was time to shift gears again, I decided. "Tell me more about the Old Ones," I said. "How did they rule the whole world? What kind of powers are we talking about?"

A few moments of silence followed in which she appeared lost in thought. Then she held a single finger aloft just before she leaped up, strode across the room, and pulled open the bottommost drawer of the metal filing cabinet. After rummaging behind several hanging folders, she emerged holding a truly enormous submarine sandwich. An errant leaf of lettuce slid out and filed itself under EXPULSIONS.

Dr. Plaskington's triumphant expression resembled those on fishermen photographed with their record-breaking catches.

She took a bite the size of a softball and began chewing

thoughtfully. I wondered if she was able to unhinge her jaw like a snake. It would probably be impolite to ask.

Speaking of impolite, Dr. Plaskington did not let a two-pound mouthful of sandwich deter her from speaking. "The Old Onsch are . . . intherdimenshinal creatursh . . ." She swallowed hard. "Sorry. The Old Ones are malevolent interdimensional creatures who share a single hive mind—it's covered in your pamphlets." She must have misinterpreted my surprised expression, because she held the uneaten end of the sandwich out to me. "Want some?"

Even though Miss Hiccup had so generously purchased me nearly ninety-nine cents' worth of gas station cookies just six hours before, I was pretty hungry. "What the heck," I said, and took a bite.

One time, when I was a little kid, my dad took me to a fancy restaurant. I think it was to celebrate my first publication in the journal *Nature*. In the bathroom, they had these fancy colored soaps that looked a bit like candy. I was young and a bit naive, so I took a bite out of a sweet-looking yellow one.

I bring this up because I would gladly go back in time and finish that entire bar of lemon-bleach soap if it would erase the memory of Dr. Plaskington's sandwich from my mind. I would finish every bar of soap in the restaurant and wash it down with blue toilet water. The moment the bite was in my mouth it was instantly on fire. It took every ounce of determination I could muster not to vomit on the spot.

The doctor smiled warmly. "Good, eh? My own culinary innovation—peanut butter, aged tuna, bhut jolokia ghost peppers, and a little elemental gallium to cut the spiciness. I use only *weapons-grade* peppers."

She smiled and patted my hand as I coughed and attempted not to black out. "Okay! You need to move into your housing, get a class schedule, ah, and I'm forgetting several other things. I *would* like to give you a complete tour of the campus so you feel at home here, but I'm terribly lazy. Here's a map instead." She handed me another small pamphlet from her desk. "As I mentioned, your father paid everything in advance. You have a spending allowance for meals and supplies, so go nuts."

This particular pamphlet contained a map of the entire town. Houses were labeled with the names of students living there. The rest of the buildings seemed to be the types of establishments you'd expect to see in your average small town (the Social Function Café), but many places had two names— what the signage said and the actual purpose of the building. For instance, the Mane Event Beauty Salon was actually the Marie Curie Center for the Radioactive Arts. I located the English and Company building and discovered that it was the Theoretical Literature classroom.

"The school is the whole town," I said, my voice still hoarse from the world's worst taste test.

"Yes. I got a great deal on it many years ago. There was an asbestos plant here that closed down for some silly reason—fantastic stuff, asbestos—so the place was practically abandoned already. I simply bought out the vacant buildings and set up shop. I'm sorry to rush you, but I have an urgent appointment just now, so we have to wrap things up."

I think we both knew she was talking about the sandwich.

She went on: "So if you have any further questions, you are always welcome to make an appointment or consult the Chaperone."

"What's the Chaperone?" I said.

"It's an advanced artificial intelligence program that helps monitor and manage day-to-day activities here. You'll meet her soon enough."

"Her?"

But Dr. Plaskington was no longer taking questions. She pressed a button on the desk. "Mr. Einstein! What's that girl's name?"

A voice filtered into the room. "It's Nikola. She should be in there now. Why didn't you ask her?"

"No, no, no. The other one!"

"Jane?"

"No! Sharpen up!"

"Francine? Penny? Dlphklixtia? Bingo? Hypatia? De—"

"That's the one! Hypatia! She's giving this one a tour and taking her to her house. They're roommates now, so make that happen, too."

"Yes, okay," Mr. Einstein said over the speaker. "She'll be right up."

I had one more question. "How can you be absolutely certain my dad is okay?"

"Come again?" the doctor asked.

"You said you were 'absolutely certain' that my dad was alive and well. How can you be so certain?"

"I told you, dear. I got an email."

"Yes, but from who?" I asked, wondering if the parahumans had some kind of former-student tracking system.

"From your father, of course. Who else could speak authoritatively on the subject?"

My dad had emailed her? "Why didn't you tell me?"

"I did. I said very clearly that I had gotten an email. You really should pay closer attention when people are speaking to you. Would you like to see it?"

"Yes! Why wouldn't I?"

"I was starting to wonder that myself, but some families aren't that close. Here you go." She slid a tablet across the desk to me, which I snapped up.

A message was already loaded on the screen. The sender was listed as *Unknown*, and the subject read *re: Melvin Kross Abduction*. Below that, it said:

Good afternoon, Patricia,
    I feel it is urgent to inform you that I have been abducted by the Old Ones. They took me by force from my home this afternoon and have transported me to a location I cannot identify. It is dank and the food is

poor. They have behaved with rather shocking violence and cruelty toward me. Worst of all, there is no Internet access here. Because of that, I am sending this via an emergency onetime transmitter of my own design. Just a little piece of engineering I cooked up a few months ago that uses a remote linking node . . .

He goes on here for several paragraphs about the design of his onetime transmitter, which can send a single message from any location in the solar system and guarantees the message will not be filtered as spam when it is received. You probably don't want to read about it.

I am alive and mostly unharmed, if a little irritated. From what I understand, they attempted to abduct Nikola as well, but the individual who left to do this has just returned with severe burns and a distinct attitude problem. This leads me to believe Nikola was able to evade capture. I have left instructions with a local educator named Miss Halstron that Nikola should be brought to your school in such an event.

Halstron! That was Miss Hiccup's actual name.

I would very much appreciate it if you could make preparations for their arrival and allow them entrance without attempting to disintegrate or otherwise cause them to cease living.

Please assume responsibility for Nikola's care, education, and feeding while I am indisposed. As we have discussed, she is more than equal to the challenges of the School, and I am certain she will perform remarkably.

Please be aware I still have the receipt for the payment I put down toward a full education, so you can forget about billing me a second time. I have already begun making plans for my escape and should be free within a few weeks, or several years, depending on how well everything goes. They may also kill me. You know how they are.

It is very important to me that Nikola continue her education and life with as little disruption as possible. Because I do not want to cause her unnecessary distress regarding my condition and location, please DO NOT share these details with her. Instead, tell her I have gone on vacation with a friend and that the abduction attempts were a prank. In addition, please give her a copy of the text below. She will be able to read it.

Warm regards,

Melvin

Below that was a series of garbled characters that I instantly recognized as our personal encryption scheme. I had learned it at the same time I learned how to read, so it was second nature to me, even though it was indecipherable to anyone else.

This part said:

Nikola,

I hope this message finds you well. I have decided to go on vacation with my old friend Carter Reagan, who you have never heard of but is a very nice person who likes to pull practical jokes involving violent abduction attempts. LOL. We are having a great time at our destination, although I can't remember where that is at the moment, so don't try to join me, even though that would be nice. The School is an excellent learning institution, and I think you may enjoy it almost as much as your school back home. Please try to get along with your peers and learn as much as you can. I hope to return soon because I have become accustomed to your company and hold you in high regard.

With significant affection,

Melvin

PS: Do not, under any circumstances, taste the sandwich.

6

HYPATIA THEODOLPHUS

It was around that moment when there was a knock at the door and I was introduced to my new roommate.

Hypatia Theodolphus had long, curly blond hair that was so shiny and perfect I had to wonder if it had been transplanted directly from a Barbie doll's head. Her face, highlighted with improbably blue eyes, was plump and cheerful, and her cheeks bore the rosy hue of someone who had recently been caught out in a blizzard. Have you ever seen those paintings of cherubs by Raphael? Hypatia would fit right in with that crowd, if the cherubs didn't think she was too obnoxiously cute. Her figure was curvy in all the ways mine is angular, flat, and straight. She wore a cute little skirt, cute white frilly socks, cute shiny black patent leather shoes with cute little buckles on them, a hair ribbon with a matching buckle, and just generally looked more put together and stylish on a random Wednesday than I've looked at any point in my entire life.

Instantly, I knew I was in for trouble. The girl in front of me was an essay in junior high female perfection, down to the last detail. Without saying a word, she made me completely self-conscious, which was very rude of her, in my opinion. Here I was, thinking that even though my dad was missing, at least I would be exempt from the popularity and beauty contests that were traditional American middle schools, and the winning entry was standing in front of me.

I smiled, or to be honest, I was trying to smile, so it was more of a grimace.

She smiled back. "Sorry I'm such a mess. I have a break on Wednesdays, and I was taking a nap when Mr. Einstein called."

"Yeah," I said. "I'm a mess, too, but with me it's more of a genetic thing."

Hypatia smiled. "Nonsense! You look fine! The disheveled look is all the rage right now."

Normally, at this point in the conversation, I would say something that Miss Hiccup might have called *inflammatory*. I decided that if we were going to be roommates, I could hold my tongue for the moment.

If she noticed my teeth were clenched almost tightly enough to crush them, she said nothing. Instead, she launched into a commentary on our schedule. "We have class together at the Main Street Deli/Quantum Mechanics Lab at 3:21 PM. They're doing a quantum suicide experiment today,

so we can't be late or we'll have to go first. That gives us"—
she checked her watch—"twenty-two minutes to show you
around, which should be sufficient. Please keep up, and
take down any questions you have on your computer so they
don't distract us from the schedule. Hold still."

She lifted her tablet, pointed it at me, and took a photo.

"Is that for security or something?" I asked.

"What? Oh—no. I'm trying to meet more people, so I have
a goal of making one new acquaintance per week. You're the
second this week, so I get next week off if I want."

"So the picture is for . . ."

She shook her head, sending her hair bouncing all around.
"For the spreadsheet! Now, grab your computer and we can
get going."

"I don't have a computer on me," I said.

Hypatia sighed, like I'd just sat on a slice of blueberry
pie. "*She hasn't been given her supplies yet?*" she asked
Dr. Plaskington, who had gone back to staring at her chess
set and had just forced down another massive portion of her
sandwich.

"What? Oh, I'm not paying attention anymore, terribly
sorry." She flicked her hand dismissively in our general direction. "Have a nice day!"

"I have my own tablet," I said, reaching for my backpack.

Hypatia rolled her eyes and produced a smartphone.
"You'll need a new one. Regular electronics won't work here
and couldn't handle the software you'll need to run anyway.
We'll visit the bookstore, but we're going to have to cut out

my proper schedule management discussion to make up for time." Her expression made it clear I should feel very disappointed at missing out.

"Shucks," I said.

"Don't feel bad. It's not your fault. Let's go, then!"

- - - - -*- - - - -

We walked back through the lobby. "This is City Hall, as you probably noticed," Hypatia said. "It's the administration building and all the teachers' offices, and other important stuff is here. The defense department is located in the basement, so if there's ever a tornado or bad storm, or some kind of attack, this is where we assemble."

"How often are we going to be attacked?"

Hypatia thought it over. "Depends on what you mean by 'attacked.' The Old Ones are constantly probing the gap around the school, looking for a way in. That's an attack, in a way. If you mean to ask how often a bad person ends up running around trying to get people, that's never happened. Security here is very strict, and we still run drills and take defense classes to prepare for if something does happen, and to be ready for when we aren't at school anymore."

Dr. Plaskington had talked about that. "So someone who is a student here is more likely to get attacked out in the real world?"

She shrugged noncommittally and held the door open for me, nodding in a *hurry up* kind of way. "The Old Ones tend to leave normal people alone—to them, regular humans are more like cattle or potential servants, but once you're linked with the parahuman community, they consider you a threat."

Great, I thought. *Now I get to spend the rest of my life looking over my shoulder.* Maybe that was why Dad had never sent me to the School. If I had a kid, would I let them in on a secret if I knew it might be dangerous?

Hypatia took my arm and led me away. "I can tell you all about the Old Ones later. We just completed a unit on them in Xenopsychology class."

"Xenopsychology?"

Hypatia flounced down the stairs and onto the sidewalk, tossing her hair like they do in shampoo commercials. "The study of alien psychology. How other intelligent life-forms think."

"Does this town have a name?" I wondered, hoping she hadn't been too serious about holding all questions.

"Well, it used to be called Fair Plain, but after Dr. P. bought it, she renamed it after her great-great-grandfather. The official name is unpronounceable to humans and translates as a grave insult to parahumans. We usually refer to it as the School Town."

"Dr. Plaskington's great-great-grandfather's name is a grave insult to parahumans?"

"It is *now.* Can we get moving again? Time's wasting."

As we walked past City Hall's front lawn, a twelve-foot square of grass slid under the ground, and from where it had been, the gigantic laser cannon rose from the darkness and pointed itself at the target across the street. It was a little more disconcerting to see the thing operating up close, but I played it cool and only screeched a little.

After it had done its thing, Hypatia explained: "It's a sonic cannon, focused sound waves, like a laser beam but without all the heat. The light you see is molecules in the air excited by the vibrations," she said. "It was built with defense in mind, but right now it's set on its lowest possible intensity and lets everyone know when class is over. Like a bell you can hear everywhere in town." She saw my concern. "It's perfectly safe. You could stick your hand in the beam and it would only tickle or give you a headache."

I watched it lower back into the lawn. "What if it was set on medium?"

"Then it could cut a battleship in half like a hot knife through butter. It would certainly hurt your hand then, so I wouldn't recommend it."

"What would happen if it was on high?"

She appeared to ponder this. "Probably something very bad. And very loud, I'd guess. Shall we go?"

"Why not use a bell as the bell?"

Hypatia sighed. "Not all species hear the same sonic spectrum, do they? Some parahumans prefer hearing a multi-frequency chime like the cannon produces when it strikes the resonating platter. Plus, it's way cooler."

The firing of the sonic cannon had signaled the end of a class period; by the time we reached the street, scores of kids were streaming out of buildings. I recognized the girl who had introduced herself earlier. She was deep in conversation with a brown-haired teacher who must have been in her thirties. They were arguing. A boy sporting a full beard, who looked like he might have been more at home in Siberia wrestling bears for money than in a classroom, strolled down the street hand-in-hand with a girl. She was pretty enough to charm a bear so you wouldn't *need* to fight it, so I guessed they made a good couple. A particularly handsome boy, who might have been of Native American descent, was cruising down the street on something that wasn't exactly a skateboard. It wasn't a skateboard, because where a skateboard has wheels, this board was covered with legs, like a millipede times a hundred. He flashed a winning smile as he passed and, in what I assume was the deepest voice he could muster, said, "Ladies . . ."

This might have come across as suave if he had not also jauntily tossed his backpack over his shoulder. Adjusting his backpack might have gone fine except for the fact that a pen had fallen out when he did it. Losing the pen wouldn't have been a big deal if he hadn't noticed it and said, "Whoa, dropped something," in an absentminded fashion—which is, of course, a harmless sentence except when you're riding a skateboard with a thousand legs that are apparently trained to come to a dead stop when someone says "Whoa."

Long story short, the skateboard stopped and the boy kept going, which sent him tumbling painfully down the sidewalk. Personally, I find it hilarious when boys hurt themselves by being stupid, but Hypatia was deeply upset. She ran to his side and was already hard at work nursing him back to health before he had a chance to finish injuring himself. "Tom! Tom! Are you all right?" she was saying. I figured she either had a huge crush on him or a tendency to freak out over the smallest problems. (Spoiler alert: the answer is *both*.)

She knelt at his side and pulled out her phone. I wondered if she intended take pictures or call 911, but instead she started an app and pushed a few buttons. Then she reached into her book bag and produced a white pouch that said FLORENCE NIGHTINGALE'S UNIVERSAL NURSING POWDER. She tore the packet open and dumped a liberal amount of white powder onto the cut. Then she pointed her phone at it and pressed a button that said CUTS AND ABRASIONS in a list, right below BALDNESS (MALE PATTERN), CANCER, and COLLAPSED MUTA-GENIC CARTILAGE DISORDER (PARAHUMAN), and right above DETACHED RETINA.

The stuff must have done something, because Tom started making a lot of noise—it was clear that whatever was happening under the powder was a lot less pleasant than face-planting on the concrete had been—but not thirty seconds later, the rest of the powder fell off and not a single visible injury remained.

He grinned broadly. "Thanks, Hypatia!"

Hypatia was about to respond when he called, "BOARD!" and his skateboard-thing scrambled over to his side from where it had been sunning its solar panels on the grass. I noticed that some of the tiny legs were rusty and a few were broken and hung limp. This board had seen a lot of action.

"Naughty board," he admonished, shaking a finger at it.

The board made a forlorn beeping sound and drooped a bit. Tom stepped back on and was off before Hypatia could call "You're welcome!" to the empty street.

"What was that white stuff?" I asked, interrupting her wistful stare at the corner around which Tom had disappeared.

"Oh, that—just a project I made for Health class last semester. Cellular repair nanobots, microscopic robots that are supposed to fix infections and patch wounds. It got me a B-plus."

"*Only* a B-plus? But that's amazing!"

Hypatia shrugged. "It doesn't work on anything serious, and there are some, ah, side effects. Works on scrapes and bruises pretty well, though. Besides, assignment grades don't count toward anything."

I was shocked at her modesty. "Hypatia, that stuff could change the world! You could sell it for millions."

"When the world is ready, we might sell it. But it still needs work, and humans aren't ready for serious nanotechnology yet. Weaponized nanobots could kill everyone on Earth in a month or two if they self-replicated, plus they're too small to see individually, so you'd never see them coming." She shuddered.

I hadn't realized until then that she was a parahuman, too. "You know," I said. "You parahumans seem to have a pretty low estimation of us standard-model humans. We're not all murderous goons."

"Of course you aren't. Some of my best friends are human, but all it takes is one bad egg."

That didn't seem fair at all. "You *honestly believe* that if you shared that nursing powder with normal people that they would just automatically start killing people with it?"

"It's happened before. One parahuman has a few drinks and tells a few jokes about nuclear fission reactions, and five years later you all have figured out how to make a bomb out of it. We do share plenty of things. Just not the really advanced stuff. That's how we pay for all this." Hypatia gestured to the town in general.

"The money from inventions pays for the school?"

"Some funding comes from that, but most comes from tuition and donations from parents and successful former students. The School only takes a cut if you invent something as part of a class assignment. See that big kid over there?" She indicated the bear fighter I'd noticed earlier. "That's Percival. He designed the last few GPS satellites that went into orbit, but NASA thinks it was a team of researchers at Stanford University. He put the plans together for extra credit last year. I remember because I spilled tea on his computer and almost destroyed the whole project. One of our graduates, I think her name was Amanda, invented airbags—you know, like when you crash your car? It was a kindergarten arts and crafts project. They were supposed to be surprise party balloons. You could hide them around the house, and when you yelled 'Surprise,' they would pop open."

"I thought an airbag could take a kid's head off."

"That's why they're in steering wheels and not party stores."

"So this school brings in all kinds of money, and they charge people to attend. Why isn't it . . . you know . . ."

"All golden streets and butler robots and free candy on every corner?"

"I hadn't meant that exactly, but yeah," I said.

"They spend a *lot* of money on security. Not just here, either. The Old Ones could cause all kinds of havoc if not for certain programs the School pays for. You know those metal towers you see from the highway, the ones with the red blinking lights on top?"

"Yeah, radio towers?"

"Well, most of them really are radio towers, but about one in five is a dimensional anchor that prevents the Old Ones from opening a rift in space-time to suck all the air off the planet to kill everyone. They're very expensive. Then there's the scholarship program." Hypatia moved a little closer and lowered her voice. "I've also heard rumors that Dr. Plaskington has a bit of an online gambling problem. I'm sure a lot of the money goes for that, too."

We walked, and Hypatia pointed out six or seven restaurants that served as dining facilities. "My favorite is Guido's Italian Abbodanza, but you should stay away on barbecue night. I also like Forbidden Planet because they have video games and a quiet area. I usually have lunch at 11:05 and dinner at 5:15. You can go to dinner anytime between 4:00 and 7:00, but I've worked out that 5:15 is the optimum time for minimal delay in seating and maximum carryover satiation so I'm not too hungry before bedtime. If the scheduled meal is heavier fare, like steak or some other kind of red meat, I'll go a little earlier bec—"

"Let's just agree that you've given it a lot of thought," I said. "So what's that?" I pointed to a large squarish building, hoping to change the subject before she started talking about when she used the bathroom.

"Oh, that's the gym. Since we're kind of on our own here, there aren't any interschool sports, so we have our own tournaments. There are football and basketball teams and all that, but the really fun sports are the ones invented here. I'm on the black hole tennis team, for instance."

"Black hole tennis?"

Hypatia got a bit excited. "It's soooo fun—instead of a ball there's a miniature black hole, and the rackets are strung with hypermagnetic antimatter fiber, so they can move it without even touching it, depending on what the charge is."

"Well," I said, "that sounds lethal."

Hypatia dismissed this with a wave of her manicured hand. "It's not as dangerous as you think. The ball is suspended in a temporal disruption field, so the black hole doesn't swallow you up if it hits you; you usually just get kicked out in a couple minutes. Last Thursday night I got hit with a really fast serve and—*bang*—I was at home and it was time for breakfast. Good thing I had my homework done in advance."

"Yeah, it'd be terrible if you were sucked into a black hole and didn't get your Chemistry finished," I said.

"Har-har. You can joke about not taking homework seri-ously because you've been in human schools up until now. Give it a week."

I liked that she was able to process sarcasm, but didn't think it was the right time to let her know that I would almost never take homework seriously. I had a feeling that if Hypatia and I were going to cohabitate without murdering each other, I'd need to use a lot of diplomacy.

7

THE BOOKSTORE BOOKSTORE

Hypatia checked her tablet and gasped. "We have *got* to hurry. We'd barely have enough time if the bookstore visit was quick, but the Bookstore Bookstore is never quick. Still, they take care of all your supplies, so one stop takes care of everything."

"The Bookstore Bookstore? What do they sell? Camping supplies?"

Hypatia didn't get the joke. "Yeah, they have a few tents, but they also sell books. It's one of a few stores in town that actually carry some of what they claim to have—hence the name. Except that instead of trashy romance novels and woodworking magazines, they sell the latest academic and scientific literature, any kind of supplies you can imagine . . . and trashy romance novels," she said.

Something told me there was a small pile of these novels squirreled away somewhere in her room. I really wanted to needle her about it, but since we just met, it would be a little rude to accuse her of reading trashy romance novels.

"Speaking of magazines," Hypatia said, "I think I read something of yours once, in the journal *Nature*? You were running computer simulations to predict the frequency of genetic mutations in fruit flies exposed to magnetism?"

"Yeah," I said, caught completely off guard. I hadn't thought anyone other than my dad had read it at the time. I was flattered, to be honest.

"I remember it because your results seemed cooked to me. I get far more accurate results simulating it on the school computer using my own algorithms, and your predictions are miles off what we get when we mutate them in controlled circumstances in the insect lab. I can show you sometime, if you want."

"So how many of those trashy novels have you bought?" I asked.

Hypatia's cheeks turned bright red, and she nearly dropped her tablet. "Never you mind, nosy!" she said, holding her bag a little closer to her side.

I knew pushing her on the subject might not be a good idea. "Because I've heard the Bosoms of Fire series is really good," I said.

Her blue eyes widened and simultaneously faded into a deep brown. "It's *Blossoms* of Fire, and they're actually historically accurate character studies—*Why am I telling you this?* We're off schedule. Let's go!"

"Wait," I said. "Your eyes just changed color."

"They do that, yeah. I hate it."

"Why? They're pretty."

"Oh . . . thanks," she said a little sheepishly, her eyes going bright green in the space of a second. "I'd prefer to blend in completely. My folks worked hard at making me as human as possible. I guess they missed the mood ring eyes. Let's get your books, huh?"

The Bookstore Bookstore occupied a corner lot on the adjacent side of the town square. In the windows, a number of mannequins were sitting in beanbag chairs, reading novels, wearing PLASKINGTON INTERNATIONAL LABORATORY SCHOOL sweatshirts, and sipping imaginary beverages from school-branded mugs. Another mannequin stood over them, holding a rather frightening-looking firearm that glowed blue from its barrel and rocking a pastel blue polka-dotted backpack. A lady mannequin turned her blank face to me and waved as we approached. She held up a book in her plastic mitten-hand and gestured to it like it was the best thing she'd ever read. It was *A New Student's Guide to the School*. The sign by the mannequin's chair changed to inform me that the book was on sale for just $29.99.

Mechanical mannequins—not a bad idea. Had it known I was a new student?

"That's a terrible book," Hypatia said. "Completely outdated and overpriced."

I can't be sure, but I think the android mannequin heard her, because she tilted her faceless head back and forth in a sassy way, dropped the book into her lap, and made a *get outta here* gesture at Hypatia, who ignored all this completely.

The lady behind the counter called to us the moment we opened the door. "Stop upsetting the display! I just got them calmed down. Last weekend some jerk told them that mannequins are supposed to get minimum wage, and they've been threatening to join the artificial intelligence union all week. What's the point of employing robots if you have to treat them like people?"

Although I placed the clerk's age at about fifty, something made her seem much younger. She had three ponytails in her hair, one going straight out the top of her head, where not one, but two pairs of glasses were perched. Her shirt was white and bore a coffee stain down its center. Broad dimples framed her mouth, and her heavy-lidded eyes were at once calm and scrutinizing.

She produced a third pair of glasses from a pocket on her blouse and placed them high on her nose. "Come in, come in," she added.

Books were everywhere. Shelves were packed three books deep, blocked from view by other stacks of books and buried in fallen piles of more books. There must have been hundreds of thousands of them, new stacked atop old. I could just tell there were treasures hidden in the corners of those shelves, buried under dust and copies of automobile repair manuals for every single GM car made in 1993. I liked the store immediately.

"Wow," I said, mystified, wishing we had time for shopping.

"I know," Hypatia whispered. "It's an utter *disaster*."

Metal, plastic, electronic, and cardboard signs hung at random intervals made it clear the categorizing system was like none I'd ever encountered. Instead of fiction and non-fiction sections, there were Truth and Lies sections. Within the Truth section, signs pointed out subsections such as THERMODYNAMICS, BIOGRAPHIES, ANIMAL HUSBANDRY AND ENGINEERING, FRENCH CULTURE, MARK TWAIN AND KURT VONNEGUT, and EXPLOSIONS, among others. The Lies section advertised POPULAR QUANTUM THEORY (HUMAN/NEW AGE), SCIENCE FICTION, GENERAL HISTORY, AUTOBIOGRAPHIES, BOOKS WITH KISSING, ETIQUETTE AND GRAMMAR, BOOKS WITH SHOOTING AND PUNCHING, and ARMED ANIMALS.

Hypatia must have noticed that I had already charted a course toward ARMED ANIMALS, because she grabbed me by my backpack and pulled me to a stop.

"We have five minutes," she said. "Get your things and we can get out of here. This place gives me the willies—not even an attempt to alphabetize. I'll be in the self-help section." A moment later, she was standing in the Lies section under a sign that read BOOKS THAT VALIDATE YOUR LOW OPINION OF YOURSELF.

I was about to ask how I was supposed to find what I needed when the clerk addressed me. "Child. You are new.

Please come over here." The woman spoke in a high, proper voice, with a slight accent of some sort that I could not place. German, maybe?

"Is it that obvious that I'm new?" I asked.

"I could tell. People say that I am shockingly perceptive, and on that count, they are absolutely correct. My name is Ms. Muriel Botfly. What is your name, young man?"

"I'm Nikola," I said. "*Miss* Nikola Kross."

"*Miss* Nikola?" she said, shaking her head and making a *tsk-tsk* noise. "Such a stupid name for a boy. I can see why you go by your middle name. You must be in fourth grade?"

"Seventh. And I'm a girl."

She smiled. "No, I'm certain you're in *eighth* grade, Mr. Miss. Please do not contradict me. Additionally, we do not ascribe to the grade structure, either in periodic evaluation or in the overall progress of your education. Kindly disregard that 'eighth-grade' nonsense at your earliest convenience. I'll be your Electronic Combat instructor, so you're going to need to get on my good side. Now—Dr. Plaskington sent over your schedule, as well as an order for a small wardrobe and household items. You arrived without clothes? Is this correct?"

"Just a few things . . . I didn't have time to pack, really. There were these—"

"Nudity is not tolerated at this school," she said sternly.

There was a long silence as I considered how to convince her I did not intend to attend classes naked. I decided to change the subject instead. "So, books. I think I need some."

"You certainly do," she said, producing a large paper bag.

"I've assembled your books just over here." She indicated a large oak bookshelf behind her.

"Which ones?" I asked.

"Well, all of them! The shelf will be installed in your room this afternoon, along with enough clothing and other personal effects to get you through the school year. Do you have a weapon yet?" she asked.

"For what?" I said.

"For causing injury to people or creatures and either destroying or damaging objects, of course. What kind of weapons do they let children play with these days?" She leaned forward and stared into my eyes. "You look like the kind of boy who would enjoy a good tachyon temporal tampering beam."

Hypatia popped out from behind a huge stack of books that threatened to topple over at any moment. "You don't want that one! They blast things *before* you decide to shoot at them."

This seemed to make sense to Ms. Botfly. "Yes, your friend Hyperion has a point. They *are* rather unpredictable but guaranteed to only shoot at things you would have shot at on your own eventually. Perhaps a magnetic singularity, then?"

"Are you trying to kill her?" Hypatia asked. "Remember the new kid last year? You sold him one, and he was almost crushed when it pulled in a dump truck from the highway."

"Ah, yes. Terrible mess that was," she said. "How about a *used* magnetic singularity, then? Half off. Just a little dent. They're very durable."

"No, thanks," I said. "Just curious, though: why do I need a weapon? Am I going to be attacked?"

"Eventually," she said. "I've seen your schedule. We've also had problems with nanobot rebellions, sporting competitions gone wrong, superintelligent breeds of animals bent on world domination, psychopathic robot monsters . . . those are particularly difficult . . . my Creative Robotics students are usually to blame." I could have been mistaken, but it seemed there was a distinct note of pride in her voice.

She held up a massive black sword that seemed to stab itself in my general direction of its own free will before setting it aside. "You are required to be ready to defend yourself at all times while at this school. Self-defense is not a skill—it is a collection of good habits, and if you are to live a normal life in the outside world, you need to start internalizing those habits now. We conduct defense spot checks after students have attended a full year."

"Defense spot checks?" I asked.

Hypatia's head appeared once again. "Last month she jumped out from behind a vending machine while I was having dinner, and I hit her in the head with my plate. That kind of thing."

"That kind of thing *indeed*. You barely passed that assessment, young lady. You can't hit an Old One in the head with a dinner plate and expect them to fall over."

"But what about the bees? Aren't they supposed to take care of dangerous things?" I asked.

"They're excellent but localized. If you want to hold down

a job, you can't very well go to work in a cloud of defense insects. Besides, they're rather stupid," Ms. Botfly said. "The upshot is that you'll need a weapon for combat and self-defense classes. How about a nice AR-15?" She produced a frightening-looking machine-gun thing and set it on the counter. "A true classic, no frills, available in black, camouflage, or bubble-gum pink. Comes with five hundred rounds of nonlethal ammunition."

"What's that?" I said, pointing to a shiny, metallic purple device on the shelf behind her that looked a little bit like a remote control with a trigger.

"Ah, the new gravitational disruptor," she said, producing another from a cardboard box kept under the register and handing it over with the faintest reverence. "One of the rechargeable models. It's also a hand warmer, has a built-in alarm clock, and can store over a thousand of your favorite songs. Nowhere to attach a bayonet, however."

The disruptor had a small handle, not quite as large as a pistol's, and a trigger that looked like it might be at home on a video game controller. The top of the disruptor had several buttons and a small screen, which at the moment read:

SAFETY ON

100% CHARGE

PLEASE KILL RESPONSIBLY

I looked to Hypatia, who didn't look too concerned for once. "I'll take it."

"Very good!" Ms. Botfly said. "I'll have it delivered this . . ."

She trailed off and was paying attention to a small window open above the front door. I followed her gaze and saw the tiny drone helicopter I had seen in Dr. Plaskington's office. It flew in the window, zoomed over to us, and beeped a few times.

"A mine on that square, you say? Well . . . here." She rummaged under the counter and returned with what looked like a miniature jet pack. "Slip this onto the bishop and leave it hovering *over* that square, then take the knight and call check." The little claw on the helicopter took hold of the jet pack and zoomed back out the window.

"You're Ms. *Botfly*," I said, connecting Dr. Plaskington's chess opponent with the woman before me.

"I already told you that, young man. Pay attention. Now, with the books, clothes, gravitational disruptor, your required school computer, and other standard supplies, your total comes to . . ." She did some calculations in her head. "Nine thousand, two hundred eighty-one dollars, and ninety-four cents. No checks, please."

"I'm supposed to have an account with the school," I said.

Ms. Botfly's face lit up. "In that case, I'm throwing in the magnetic singularity for twenty dollars. Not like it's your money, right? Now, stick your hand out."

I did as she asked, and she set a little metal thimble on my thumb. A green light blinked, and I was suddenly aware that it had stabbed something through my skin.

"Ow!" I shouted, sucking on my injured thumb.

She took the thimble and set it on a corner of her keyboard. "Blood sample for authorizing your purchase. And here you are, Nikola Kross. It says here you're female. Did you know?"

"I've had my suspicions."

"Hm," she said. "You should have your records updated." She went back to the computer, typing ferociously. "And here we are! Your receipt and your class schedule, *Miss* Miss Nikola," she said with a wink. "Here are the books you need for the rest of the day and your computer with the standard-issue Kevlar computer cozy with a pink turtle design." She handed over a screen a bit like the tablet Hypatia had been using, only a little larger. I had issues with the pink turtle, but I wasn't about to question her for fear of how bad the next selection might be.

We were on our way out when her small helicopter flew back into the store. Well, I'm not sure you could call it flying. Whatever you would call limping for something that is supposed to remain airborne—that was what it was doing. It scraped through the portal over the door and flung itself wildly around the room like the death throes of a housefly, bouncing off the floor, ceiling, and stacks of books. As it buzzed frantically past, I noticed a small horse's head lodged in one of its rotors.

Ms. Botfly reached for the injured machine, calling to it like it was a sick pet. "Oh, B-129J model autonomous quadracopter, what did she do to you?"

"There's a knight in one of the rotors," I offered.

"I see it!" Hypatia said. "Why are its eyes blinking?"

Ms. Botfly must have known the answer to this question, because she immediately gave up trying to catch it. She shouted, "DOWN!" and vaulted the counter and tackled Hypatia and me where we stood.

There were a few seconds as I lay underneath one of my new teachers when I began to wonder if she had been overreacting, followed by about a tenth of a second when I was pretty certain I had just died. When the chess piece exploded, it not only completely obliterated the copter but also managed to knock over everything on every shelf in the room and blast out a storefront window not far from where we had been standing. Once the dust and debris settled, Muriel Botfly stood up, brushed herself off, and handed my computer cozy back to me. It was unscathed, except the pink turtle's happy, smiling head was now blackened with a blob of melted shrapnel. I loved it.

"The old knightbomb," Ms. Botfly chuckled as she surveyed the damage. The front half of the store was in shambles. Small fires burned somewhere in the Artistic Forestry and Beginners Cooking sections. Smoke and fragments of smoldering paper drifted in the air, and the robotic mannequins were cowering in a corner. Their display sign had been changed to say UNSAFE WORKING CONDITIONS.

"Where's the phone?" I asked. "I'll call 911."

"We don't have that here," Hypatia said. Then to Ms. Botfly: "I'll get the door."

She sighed. "No need, dear, the window's been opened for

us." She gingerly picked her way through the wreckage until she was standing at the shattered window. "Second time this month my store has been destroyed," she grumbled.

Once we were outside, she shouted, "Cleanup!"

There was a strange *whoosh*ing sound, and the smoke was instantly sucked from the room and into the ceiling. Every fire went out simultaneously, and though it was hard to believe, a bookshelf that had been knocked over stood itself up again, unassisted. The windows were growing back from the edges inward with a slightly irritating crinkling sound.

"Come on," said Hypatia, waving her hand in front of my face to stop me from staring, fascinated, at the store as it repaired itself. "This is going to take a while, and Mr. Dolphin does *not* like stragglers."

8

PRACTICAL QUANTUM MECHANICS

As Hypatia half led, half dragged me toward the Main Street Deli and Quantum Mechanics Laboratory, I stared at the storefront, trying to see through the camouflage. I knew it was supposed to be a classroom in disguise, but I started to suspect that I was being duped. A vivid red-and-green awning fluttered above large, spotlessly clear windows. Through the glass, several people, mostly men, sat along a counter. They munched on pickles, chips, and hoagies while gazing blankly out into the street in the way people do when they're concentrating on food. The smell of baking bread and cured meats wafted in the air. "Are you sure this is the right place?" I asked.

Hypatia rolled her eyes. "Come on, Nikola. You'll see."

"That's not a classroom," I said.

"It's alternate reality glass," she explained. "We made it for a project last year. Pretty neat, huh?"

I had to admit, it was. Either that, or she was flat-out lying. "How does it work?"

"See, the way time passes, changes in the world come down to tiny variances at crucial points that make big differences later on. For instance, you might drop a quarter and forget about it, but someone finds it and sticks it into a parking meter, and some guy's car doesn't get towed because of it, so he is able to drive it to the hospital when his wife is sick, and because of that, she doesn't die, or something. Your dropping a quarter saved a life, in a way. Those windows use a special material that shows an alternate reality where one tiny thing somewhere in the distant past happened differently."

"What was it?"

"No idea—which is why they're useless for anything else. Maybe in that universe, some Neanderthal back in the Paleolithic era tripped over a rock he missed in our timeline—or maybe Napoleon forgot his umbrella on a rainy day. Whatever the case, in that world, the Main Street Deli is still a deli. It took days of fiddling to get it right. One time they were all naked—it was super gross. Another time it was full of Elvi."

"Elvi?"

"The plural form of *Elvis*. Look it up."

I didn't think she was right, but it wasn't worth arguing. Hypatia waved cheerfully at a woman wiping down a counter. To my surprise, the woman waved back with a smile. Hypatia pulled the door open and ushered me inside.

I had to take a moment to gather myself. Everything I had just seen was gone as if I'd stepped behind the screen at a movie theater. The diner was replaced by a spacious room with all-white floors, walls, and ceilings that looked to be made of a slightly shiny plastic coating. No checkered tile, no lunch counter, no sandwiches, no deli smell—not even the windows remained. There were no obvious light fixtures, so it took me a moment to realize that every surface in the room was glowing faintly.

There were about twenty or so kids scattered here and there around the chamber, some seated and many more standing around looking distinctly nervous. As we stepped into the room, a hush fell over the conversation. A second later, almost all of them were looking at me. It made me wish I could enjoy being the center of attention. Thankfully, a second after that, most of them seemed to go back to what they had been doing when we came in—mumbling nervously to one another and casting furtive glances at the back wall of the room.

The furniture was unlike any I had ever seen. Every single object in the room that was not a person was formed of the same white plasticky substance. And all those objects were chairs. Some of them were simple stools or basic cubes that seemed to be attached to the floor; others were breathtakingly gaudy with spires, jagged edges, and intricate carvings. A throne hung from the ceiling by a single delicate filament; a huge white mouse sculpture held its forepaws out to accommodate the butt of an orange-tinted young lady. A lanky Asian boy sat upon a lifeguard's chair so tall he had to hunch over so his head did not brush the ceiling. My favorite was a carefully balanced sculpture that reminded me of the colorful mobiles people hang above cribs, except this one was standing on a needlelike pedestal that rose from the floor. Rife with counterweights and wide sails to catch the breeze, the chair, which hung from one of the arms, moved about seemingly at random as the air in the room circulated.

I might have noticed more, but I found myself suddenly unable to ignore the students themselves. Now that I was in a room with them, I was suddenly registering just how *alien* many of my classmates looked. Up until then, I had assumed that parahumans were, as a whole, just like regular human-style people, only smarter. This assumption could not have been more wrong.

I was also struck with how different they all were. I'd assumed that because parahumans were a single species, that they would tend to look alike, but everywhere were striking features like unusual skin and hair colors, and alternate limb design. Had I not known otherwise, I'd think several of the students were species unto themselves.

I also wondered if looks mattered here like they did in other schools—the students who might have been ignored or mocked at my old school were sitting and chatting with people who wouldn't have looked directly at me if I stood on their foot. For instance: I saw a boy who could join any boy band in the world talking and laughing with a girl who was wearing inch-thick glasses and the kind of sweater a librarian might wear to her own funeral.

Hypatia noticed me staring. "No time to make introductions now, but I'll fill you in on who's who," she whispered. In retrospect, I think the School intentionally pairs new students with gossipy counterparts—it certainly proved to be useful that my roommate happened to know every facet of every social structure in town.

One boy had hair that stood straight up in dreadlocks at least a foot long above his head. "That's DeShawn. His brother is this famous astronomer on television, but he's studying chaos theory dance."

"Pardon?" I asked.

"He dances and uses his body motions to figure out complex chaotic systems. He can do a waltz that predicts the weather up to a year in advance."

I nodded in the direction of a girl in the corner who was sitting cross-legged on a clear whitish sphere. The sphere looked different from the other perches; it looked somehow . . . harder. Like it was glass. There was also the fact that she was not sitting *on* it as much as she was sitting *above* it, hovering just an inch or so above the center. The girl had long whitish-blond hair that was perfectly straight. She was tall, slender, and generally everything beauty magazines say girls are supposed to look like, only more so. It was almost too much.

Hypatia's eyes went dark gray as she rolled them.

"Ultraviolet VanHorne—she's human but a total brownnoser. Her mom manages the software that runs the world's stock exchanges. Her daddy is a genetic designer, as if that wasn't obvious."

"Are you sure she's human?" I asked, realizing that a person can be *so* good-looking that it starts making them look weird in an entirely new way.

Hypatia scoffed, "Aesthetic genetic design isn't even difficult to do on humans—it's just expensive. You only have to activate the right genes and use a bit of prokaryotic DNA or something to replace the wrong ones. Tacky."

I was momentarily surprised by her cattiness. Hypatia had struck me as the *I love everybody* sort of girl. It made me like her a lot more, to be honest. Knowing there was someone who made *her* insecure gave us something in common, since that was how I reacted to pretty much everyone.

Then I saw who was sitting next to Ultraviolet, and the situation was explained in full. It was Tom, the boy who had fallen off the skateboard-with-legs thing. He had his long black hair pulled into a neat ponytail and was squirming uncomfortably on a misshapen plastic block, trying not to slide off and occasionally whispering angrily to it. As he did this, Ultraviolet leaned down without so much as a tremble in the ball she was balanced on and ruffled his hair. He looked up at her and winked.

"That's Tom," Hypatia said, sounding as casual as she could. "You met him before."

As Hypatia continued to bore holes into Ultraviolet with

her glare, I surveyed the rest of the room. There was a boy with a freckled face who could have passed for eight years old if he weren't so tall that his head brushed against the ceiling without the assistance of a chair. Across the room, a girl so pale she seemed to blend into the scenery sat on a small shelf juggling three apples, while her neighbor cheered her on and threatened to add another apple. They were looking at me, I realized, except that they were doing it in a subtle way. Were they trying to be considerate of someone's first-day awkwardness? Then I realized something—I was the one staring, and they were noticing it.

"I thought parahumans could pass for human," I said to Hypatia as I took a much more subtle look at a small blue boy with bright red hair who had his nose attached meekly to his tablet.

"Sometimes," Hypatia replied. "Parahuman mothers create a lot of unique genetics just before their babies are born. Some will study for years to get their kids to turn out exactly like they want. Some of us haven't quite got it down, and some families use camouflage so they don't have to bother blending in physically at all. Things like holographic projectors, intelligent chromatic dermal film, big floppy hats—whatever works.

"Take Juan there as an example," Hypatia continued, nodding at a boy with a third arm growing out of the left side of his abodmen, just over the ribs. The boy was reading a book with his left hand and left eye while playing a video game with his other two hands and eye. "He's three world-famous painters. He sees color variations human eyes can't pick up on, and the third arm helps with holding the palette and tasks that require more dexterity. He has a load of other things going on in his brain—six lobes or something. He'll do two canvases at the same time, in different styles."

"Don't his fans know he's an alien?"

"I doubt it. He has others sell the paintings for him. Besides, once he tucks that third arm away, there's no telling anything is out of the ordinary."

I had lots of questions on the subject of camouflage, but Hypatia had moved on to another subject. She singled out the blue-skinned, red-haired kid. "That's Bob Flobogashtimann. He's parahuman, and I guess his folks wanted to make him good at making predictions or something, but instead he came out blue like that and can see forward and backward in time by a few minutes."

"That's awesome!" I said.

"It's a serious disability," replied Hypatia. "Imagine trying to cross the street and not knowing if the truck you see will be there in a minute or if it was there five seconds ago."

"Oh," I said.

"He's a really nice kid, though. We had Remedial Hacking together."

Someone tapped me on the shoulder. I turned to find a boy of about my own height standing immediately behind me. He was glancing around the room in a way I'd call nervous if he hadn't appeared to exude an aura of extreme boredom in every other way. He had a huge pimple under his left eye, and his hair was plastered to his head like he was on a mission to use up the world's hair gel singlehandedly. "I'm Mike," he said.

Now, my first reaction when people at school talk to me is to figure out *why*. But Mike wasn't giving me much to work with. He didn't seem like he wanted to make fun of me, he wasn't smirking like he was going to pull a prank, and he didn't seem like he wanted anything, so I had to resort to my socializing option of last resort.

"Hi, Mike," I said.

"Human?" he asked.

"Yeah, I just got here. I'm from North Dako—"

Mike turned and walked away. For a second, I stood there with my mouth open, like he'd come back so I could finish saying *Dakota*. But instead, he walked across the room, sat in his own white chair (which looked like a folding chair), and started playing on his phone.

Hypatia saw all this happen and only said, "That's Mike. Parahuman. He makes hats and collects paper mail. He thinks physically transporting pieces of paper to communicate is fascinating."

"Is he like that with everyone?"

The question didn't seem to make sense to her. "Like what?"

At that moment, I spotted a familiar face, the girl who had directed me to the courthouse when I first arrived. She was looking concerned and a little irritated. Standing next to her was a woman who could not be younger than eighty-five. Despite the woman's age, she was dressed like a little kid in a cartoon panda T-shirt and polka-dotted skirt over striped tights. The old lady was bouncing from one foot to the other and singing some kind of song to herself. She saw me notice her, and that I'd noticed her noticing that, so despite my nervousness, I threw her an understated, friendly wave hello. She waved back.

"You know Rubidia?" Hypatia asked.

"We met right after I got here. She was with her sister—her sister knew my name, by the way. It was like she recognized me. Is that weird?" I asked.

"They're Dr. Plaskington's granddaughters, so they *are* pretty unusual, I guess, even for parahumans," Hypatia said. "Fluorine is one of the smartest kids the School has ever seen. She probably hacked the Chaperone over breakfast to see if we had any new students. I've heard she can break 2048-bit encryption in her head. Maybe she can read minds. It wouldn't surprise me."

"Who's the old lady?" I asked. "Is she the teacher?"

"That's . . . I don't know. Never seen her before," Hypatia said, confused.

Rubidia was trying to steer the old lady in our direction, but the lady lost interest about halfway over and went off to try to borrow the ball Ultraviolet was balancing on. Rubidia threw up her hands in frustration and came over to us. "She's driving me *insane* today. I hope she's not still senile at dinner," she said, mostly to Hypatia. "You're Nikola, right? How's it going?"

"Pretty good, I guess," I said. "I've survived an abduction attempt and an exploding chess piece in the last twenty-four hours, so I can't complain."

"The old knightbomb, huh?" Rubidia guessed.

I nodded, trying to think of a tactful way of asking Rubidia how she had gotten saddled with babysitting the crazy woman.

"You want to know who the obnoxious hag trying to steal Ultraviolet's ball out from under her is, right?" Rubidia said, not waiting for a response. "That's Fluorine. You met her before, remember?"

I did remember Fluorine, but I was pretty certain she had been a little girl before. Her hair hadn't been gray—I was certain of that. Some people don't age gracefully.

Hypatia was horrified. "What happened to her?"

Rubidia shrugged. "The nurse says she's come unstuck in time. Probably caused some kind of paradox in Temporal Mechanics class. They were only moving things back and forth a minute or two, so it should go away before long. She was a baby just before this. *That* was cute, at least."

Fluorine had gone from attempting to grab the ball while Ultraviolet crouched on it in an attempt to fend her off, to begging her to just give it up for a short time. "I just want to sit on your ball!" old lady Fluorine pleaded dramatically. "I'm so old and so *tired*. I can't even make my own chair. Oh! I think I might faint!" Fluorine staggered back and forth in a way that didn't look *completely* staged. She clutched at her chest and groaned in pain.

Ultraviolet rolled her eyes. "Gross! Don't have a heart attack. Just don't get that . . . old-lady smell all over it," she said, and made as if to step down.

The moment the ball was unguarded, Fluorine recovered from her heart attack, shouted "*Yoink!*" and snatched the ball from Ultraviolet's hands with a completely unnecessary shove, sending her sprawling onto the floor with an audible thud. Ultraviolet's eyes went wide with fury, her lips parted to reveal her teeth, and she actually growled audibly. Maybe her parents had mixed in some wolf DNA to ensure her coat was shiny.

If this intimidated Fluorine, she hid it well. In a flash, the old lady had seated herself on the ball, cross-legged, and was zooming around the room on it like it was a go-kart, crashing into walls and any students not quick-witted enough to get out of her way. "Make way, ladies!" she crowed triumphantly. "The Hells Angels are in town!"

As Fluorine made her third trip around the room, Ultraviolet stepped out in an attempt to reclaim her ball. The two of them met with a crash that sent both them and the sphere skidding across the room.

A moment later, there was a flash, like someone had taken a picture, and Fluorine was suddenly a younger adult woman, instantly concerned with the hurt girl. She helped Ultraviolet to her feet, returned the ball, and admonished the rest of the children for horseplay. "It's all fun and games till some-one crashes and ends up with permanent brain damage," she warned.

"I'm not brain-damaged!" Ultraviolet shouted, rubbing her head uncertainly.

"Are you sure, honey? Your eyes look a little crossed. Or is that normal? You should ask for a CAT scan after class."

Rubidia was stone-faced with embarrassment, but the look on Hypatia's face was pure glee. The girl liked a little chaos. Either that or she just liked seeing Ultraviolet get hurt. Maybe both. I'd be okay with that.

All the hubbub stopped cold a second later when a section of the back wall separated like a pair of elevator doors.

Behind the portal stood a portly, balding man. He wore bifocals, brown corduroy slacks, and a truly hideous green, orange, and brown paisley blazer that was obviously far too small to fasten around his considerable midsection. The class straightened immediately. Even Fluorine stopped what she was doing and stood facing the teacher with rapt attention.

The man stepped inside, and the wall slammed shut behind him. He sauntered around the room in a wide cir-cle, surveying everyone and everything with what looked like intense disdain. As he rounded the corner near Juan, the painter, he locked his glare on me and marched straight over with his head cocked at an unnatural angle—ignoring everyone else on his way as if he'd spotted a fire that needed putting out. A moment later, he was standing in front of me, his thumbs locked underneath his bright green suspenders.

"YOU ARE NEW, ARE YOU NOT?" he screeched, at such sudden and extreme volume that everyone in the room jumped.

"I AM!" I shouted back, which startled me more than his shouting.

His voice became a nasal growl, almost too quiet to hear. "You were not on my class roster this morning, and I check my class roster EVERY MORNING." When he said "every morning," his voice returned to the deafening screech, and everyone jumped a second time. It was a lot like the screech a falcon makes when it's about to dive-bomb some unsuspecting bird at two hundred and fifty miles an hour.

"Do you know why I check my class roster every morning?" he asked.

"No . . . ," I said, bracing myself.

"I check it to make sure that none of my students have succeeded in KILLING THEMSELVES since the last CLASS PERIOD. And I have very grave concerns about the prospects of several students in this class. MR. GILLMAN, am I to assume you have not managed to off yourself in some *fascinating* way since last we met?"

Tom stood and addressed the teacher clearly while at attention, as if speaking to a drill sergeant. "Sir, no, sir. I am still alive at the moment."

"Then you have EXCEEDED MY EXPECTATIONS once again." He pointed a finger accusingly at Tom. "Nicely done! I'm granting you five points extra credit for not dying. Do not take my generosity for granted. I've seen your scores, and you need **EVERY POINT YOU CAN GET**."

His back was to me now, and I assumed he was about to go terrorize other students, but he spun around. "I am **MR. DOLPHIN.** It is a pleasure to make your acquaintance, Miss . . ."

"Thank you," I said, suppressing a snicker. Hypatia had mentioned his name, but hearing it screeched like that was more than I could handle.

"That was your opportunity to introduce yourself. Proper manners dictate that as you do not appear on my class roster, you should **MENTION YOUR NAME**, so I can have something to **SHOUT** when you invariably **FAIL** at the tasks I assign. Your parents might not have schooled you adequately in the ways of **ETIQUETTE**. Or are you an **ORPHAN?**"

"I . . . guess I am, in a way," realizing as I said it that it was true. My throat felt a bit raspy all of a sudden. "As of last night." I focused on his tie, trying not to think about it. His tie was paisley, and the pattern reminded me of amoebas hanging around and handing little bits of ugliness to one another.

"Hm," he said, stroking his chin and using his lower growl voice once again. "Well, this is awkward. Let's ignore the whole situation. I'll call you Tammy for the time being."

With that, he stormed across the room to the gothic throne upon which perched a tiny blue boy. At first I thought he meant to knock it over, but he stopped short. I realized the boy must have chosen the spot to put himself as far from Mr.

Dolphin as possible and was clearly reconsidering the strategy. "MR. FLOBOGASHTIMANN. WHAT IS THIS AUDACIOUS MONSTRRRRROSITY?"

"You said to make chairs today, if we could," the boy mumbled from his perch.

"Quite so," said Mr. Dolphin, as if he'd forgotten. "And nicely done. You will be earning something HIGHER than an F for this session, I suspect."

He then rotated around the room, delivering the slightest of glances at the other projects. He held a pointed finger out, almost as if he intended to curse us all. "CLASS, those who bothered to make chairs, they are ADEQUATE, but MERELY so. Those who did not or COULD not make chairs, know that I consider this INADEQUATE. WORK HARDER! CHAIRS AWAY!"

With that, the students who had been sitting on chairs seemed to gaze off into the distance. At first I thought this was some kind of silent protest—like they were refusing to comply—but each of the white objects simply descended into the floor and disappeared.

Mr. Dolphin took up residence on one end of the room and stomped his foot on the floor, and, like magic, a tilted podium rose up in front of him. "Today, we have a new task. Because so many of you either failed to complete the assignment or found yourself UNABLE to do so, the new task will be to complete the OLD task in a new way." He stomped his foot once more and banged his fist on the podium. Since he had no papers, I guess the only point of the podium was to have something to bang his fist on.

"We will **NOT** be conducting the quantum suicide experiment on the grounds that a plurality of you do not seem up to the task. Also because we have a new student, so some review is in order, and lastly, because several of your parents have become aware of the activity and have protested that it is highly dangerous and probably illegal. All of these things are true, which is a shame."

Mr. Dolphin pushed on the top of the podium, and it sank back into the floor like it had never existed. When he spoke again, he eyed me in a way that made me understand why deer freeze in the headlights of oncoming traffic. "Quantum events occur in the tiniest ways, all over, all the time. They occur more often in certain materials, and in certain places. Quantum events in the eyes of birds allow them to perceive magnetic fields. Quantum events determine the progress of nuclear reactions. They occur inside your **BRAIN**, assuming you possess one. And particularly within the quantum agar from which this chamber is constructed.

"If I set a stone at your feet, it will likely remain there. In fact, if you were to watch it from now until the end of time, it will most likely do the same thing for eternity—that is to say, **NOTHING**. This is despite the fact that every atom and molecule of any material is shivering around all the time, in constant motion. Some of these motions are governed by quantum events, which means that a particular rock molecule really goes two directions at the same time, depending on HOW you observe it and WHETHER you observe it at all.

"Some of you may remember our Schrödinger's cat experiment from last week. We change the outcome by DETERMINING the outcome, which we do by OBSERVING the outcome in the right way. Your shivering rock molecules make no difference on a certain scale, but they make a big difference if you take them all at once. If you were to attempt to OBSERVE each of these moving in a particular direction in the same moment, that rock might move"—he lowered his voice to a whisper—"it might jump or twitch or even . . . EXPLODE."

In one far corner of the room, a girl I had not noticed up until then flashed a quizzical expression and raised her hand just a fraction of an inch before reconsidering and putting her hand back down. But Mr. Dolphin was too sharp. "MISS CURIE, what is your QUESTION? Speak quickly, if you're determined to interrupt."

"Er," she said, before taking a deep breath and plunging in, "does that mean we could move rocks or other things if we practiced—"

"No!" Mr. Dolphin barked. "The rock was an illustration. Rocks are BORING and are made of boring stuff. Very few unstable events going on in there, not nearly enough to make one move. If your pitiful excuse for a chair is any indication, you might have trouble moving a rock even with a handle attached. Does this answer your question?"

"Yes," the girl mumbled sheepishly.

"The point is that your *observation* of the event *creates* the outcome. Normal humans, as well as some DUNDERHEADS in this class"—he glared at Tom—"are less capable of the kind of observation that can create meaningful changes but can use equipment and software to conduct the necessary observations. Parahumans are born with the ability to comprehend these events on a scale that can be useful, if you're willing to put your mind to it and construct the appropriate theoretical operations at the time of observation. Most superintelligent humans can get a sense of it as well and have been known to be very inventive, as I have been in constructing this room, but it will be an uphill battle. I've attempted to make it as easy as possible for you. The quantum agar in here is made ENTIRELY of a material that moves and reacts according to quantum events, making it easy to manipulate. At least, that's the idea," he said with a rakish wink.

"On Monday, I asked you to compare and contrast Heisenberg's uncertainty principle, Schrödinger's observer effect, and Mindy Bloopindo's quantum manipulation protocol. I have been grading these papers and have begun to realize that, in general, your understanding of quantum manipulation is like the children's end of a swimming pool: SHALLOW, TRANSPARENT, and probably filled with more WASTE than we like to imagine. To manipulate quantum materials, you must have an almost automatic comprehension of these core principles and how they interact. Otherwise . . ." He gestured at Tom's lopsided chair, which he was trying to get rid of but which only quivered and sagged as if it were ashamed of itself.

He turned to the rest of the class. "Your test this hour will be to create something, **ANYTHING**, with the abundant agar in this room, and then to cause me to **WITNESS** your creation of said thing. Points will be awarded for complexity and stability. In case you missed my usage of the word *test*, I feel compelled to point out that you are now taking a graded and timed exam. **GO!**"

Immediately, students produced their handhelds, smartphones, and tablets, and set about poking and staring at them. Here and there, the floor wiggled, and some spots rose a bit before falling. I realized that the chairs and other things I had seen at the beginning of class must have taken a considerable amount of effort to produce. There was not much success to be seen, but here and there, a few students were finding themselves able to raise up parts of the floor.

I nudged Hypatia. "I thought they don't assign grades?" I asked.

Hypatia's gaze did not stray from her screen. "Some teachers like to assign grades for individual assignments so you have an idea if they consider your work passing. A class will just stop showing up on your schedule when they figure you know it well enough."

I glanced at her handheld. She was constructing what looked like an amazingly complex mathematical formula; elements of symbolic logic, various applications of trigonometry, and calculus were at work. As a result, she was managing to draw a cylindrical object from the floor. The blue boy was already sitting on a newly formed Adirondack chair that was growing larger and larger as he calculated and appeared to meditate over his work from time to time. Next to him, a disheveled-looking brown-haired boy was struggling to make a rocket launch itself into the air, but the rocket only farted and fell over.

Hypatia was in the process of squaring some of her variables, and her form had started looking a bit like a snowman in reaction. Ultraviolet had made a small car she was trying to push around unsuccessfully.

"Cars should **ROLL**, Miss VanHorne; keep working," said Mr. Dolphin as he passed.

I had no idea what to do. Beside me, Rubidia had set aside her handheld and was waving her hands over the floor like a wizard, with no luck. I nudged Hypatia again. "How do you do it?"

She glanced in my direction. "Hm?" The moment she did this, the snowman she had been concentrating on fell over and melted. "Ugh. Just . . . create a mathematical depiction of a form that represents the object you want to create—whatever properties you want it to have should be present. Then stare at it, and try to imagine it—er, *observe* it behaving in the manner you've described. Try sticking to simple geometric shapes at first. It helps to draw up an equation that represents a fluid filling a void of your chosen shape."

I stepped a few paces away and seated myself cross-legged above my own patch of real estate. The floor wasn't hard, but it wasn't soft, either. Nor was it hot or cold, smooth or rough. It was just *there*, really. As the students who could manipulate it were working, I noticed that some of their constructions were definitely smooth, and even shiny, so I figured some of the floor must be shiny in parts. The moment I looked for a shiny spot, I found one, right under my finger. It hadn't been smooth there a moment ago. I knew smoothness was determined by how the molecular structures were aligned on the surface. This spot had been nothing, but now it was smooth.

I had just changed it—just like that. Next I tried feeling around for a cold spot, and sure enough, the whole area beneath me was cold. It was so cold I suddenly wished I was wearing fur pants. Again, I'd found a place where atoms were doing what I wanted—their constant vibrations had slowed down, which also meant that they were cold. I thought about looking for a hot spot but thought better of it. After the day I'd had, I didn't want to make matters worse by sitting on a frying pan.

"Tammy," Mr. Dolphin called out. I went on feeling the floor, "finding" rough spots, prickly spots, places that gave me shocks like static electricity, even a spot that was kind of like a white goo, almost as thin as water. I stuck a finger in. It was only about an inch deep. I was amazed to think that the giant throne had come from such a small amount of stuff. It must be able to expand and contract.

"TAMMY!" Mr. Dolphin shouted again. I felt sorry for Tammy, whoever she was. I was about to try finding a patch of floor that was taller than the rest in order to see about making it larger, when I noticed a pair of very old, very worn brown shoes standing right where I was about to check.

Crap, I thought, *I'm Tammy.* "Mr. Dolphin, I'm sorry, I forgot. My name is Nikola, Nikola Kross."

He bent down and stared into my face. "Miss Kross, do you plan on petting the floor like a kitten for the next thirty minutes or do you plan on *bending it to your will?* We are not attempting to practice magic, and we do not romance our materials. Create a schematic or you will find yourself unable to construct anything more than a **WASTE OF MY TIME.**"

"Actually, I was kind of getting a feel for it. Getting to know it. I think I might be able to—"

His voice went suddenly sweet, like he was talking to a baby. An ugly, evil baby. "Maybe you should get to know inanimate objects on your own time and take this particular time to **COMPLETE THE TEST.** You are getting off to a bad start, a very bad start indeed. The semester is a month old at this point, so as far as I'm concerned, you are a month behind. **STEP IT UP . . .**"

I could tell he was working up into some kind of epic tirade. The other kids in the class clearly thought so, too, and were turning to witness the upcoming verbal carnage. Suddenly, I was angry. After everything I had endured in the last twenty-four hours—losing my dad, my home, being attacked by aliens, swarmed by bees, and almost blasted to bits by detonating chess pieces—this clown wasn't willing to cut me even an ounce of slack?

Then I said it. The words were out of my mouth before I could stop them: "If you want me to work, then maybe you could *shut up* for a minute?"

Every single person in the room, including me, gasped. Every eye was on Mr. Dolphin and me. Had his face been that color red before? I didn't think so. My hands covered my mouth involuntarily, as if they might hold in the next disastrous comment.

He pointed a long, spotted, bony finger at my face, the tip of it almost touching my nose. He spoke in a snarling whisper: "I don't know what *error* brought you into this school or whether we have lowered our already questionably low standards, but if your name is Kross, then I assume you arrived clutching the coattails of a previous graduate. **MY OFFICE, NOW.**"

Something you should know about me. When I'm frightened, there's a part of me that imagines the worst possible thing that I could do in that situation. It's the sort of thing Miss Hiccup would have called "poor impulse control." I mention this because while I was sitting there, preparing to be killed or eaten alive, something occurred to me. I thought it might be funny if a particular thing happened. Specifically, I thought it would be funny if the white goop on the ceiling turned into liquid and spilled all over the volcanic Mr. Dolphin. It was just a passing notion, but when I looked up at the ceiling, I realized that what I had imagined observing was actually occurring.

It happened too fast to warn him. An entire section of the white stuff on the ceiling just . . . fell. It spilled straight onto Mr. Dolphin's head like a giant bucket of gooey white paint.

Worse, the floor did the same, and as his shoes sank into the goo, the surrounding floor rose up, and in two seconds, he was completely encased in a thick white shell. It was kind of like a chocolate Easter bunny, except that Easter bunnies are made of milk chocolate and filled with air, whereas my creation was made of an exotic material and was probably filled with pure rage.

Suddenly terrified, I tried to imagine the stuff going back to how it had been just a moment before—less gooey, more solid. If this ever happens to you, here's a tip: that's the wrong move when someone is trapped inside.

I scrambled to my feet. The other students were still agape in horror. I doubted anybody had ever talked back to Mr. Dolphin before, let alone drenched and then imprisoned him in parts of his own classroom. I struck the white stuff, clawed at it, but nothing worked. It was now as hard as stone and as shiny as glass. I tried to calm down, to manipulate it again, but I couldn't straighten my brain out enough to do it, not with certain doom awaiting me if I succeeded. I was about to ask if anyone could call for help when the stuff cracked here and there and fell away from Mr. Dolphin like freshly raked leaves.

I closed my eyes and braced myself for what I was sure would be my expulsion from school, and possibly the living world, but nothing came. When I worked up the courage to open my eyes, I saw that he was just standing there with his arms folded.

When he was sure he had my attention, Mr. Dolphin said, "Please refrain from using my quantum agar as a weapon against me."

"Yes, sir," I said.

"Go . . . help one of the others," he said, not shouting or growling for the first time. His face was contorted in a new way. At first I thought he might be in pain, but I realized that it might just as likely have been a smile. It was either that or he had to go to the bathroom and was trying to forget about it until class was over. He turned on his heels and stalked over to the wall, where doors opened and he disappeared once again.

I grabbed my bag and moved back over to where Hypatia and Rubidia were working. "How did you do that?" Hypatia asked. "I didn't think it was possible to change it into a liquid or move it that quickly."

"I don't know. It was an accident, I guess. Let me try something." I bent down and patted the floor in front of both of them. "Feel it—it's cold here."

Both of them did as I asked. Rubidia's mouth dropped open. "How . . . ? I mean, I've only ever seen people move it, never changing its physical state or properties. You must be some kind of savant."

"I think anyone can do it, really, if you think about it the right way," I said. "Both of you just did."

Hypatia shook her head. "You made it cold. We just touched it."

"Negative. I *touched* it and *said* it was cold, but I didn't

136

actually do anything. Both of you changed its properties when you expected to *observe* that it was cold."

"That's amazing!" Rubidia exclaimed. "Have you used this stuff before?"

"No," I said. "My dad actually hates the whole field of quantum theory. Says it's new age hokum. Everything I know about it is from him complaining about things he's read."

I was sitting and moving parts of the floor around like sand. It was calming. I don't like admitting it, but up to that point, I'd been starting to think I might have gotten in over my head. It felt good to help others with something—even if I didn't completely understand *how* I was doing it.

Rubidia grinned and set about feeling parts of the floor as I had, but was unable to get it to move. Hypatia tried for a minute before giving up. She re-created her snowman and went cautiously over to Tom under the pretense of helping him locate an error in his calculations that was causing the tree he was making to grow sideways from the wall.

By the time the bell sang, marking the end of class, most students had completed their work, and several parahuman kids were attempting to change the agar into liquid as I had done, with little success. The blue boy managed to get it to drip, but it was clear that it was only a solid moving like a liquid, and he was just steering it with an equation describing an oblate spheroid. For my project, I made a polar bear, and for no reason at all, a representation of a taco for him to munch on. It looked like mine was the only project that could move on its own. It was surprising to me just how easy it was for me to work with the agar. It felt almost weightless, so I could move it around if I needed to, and almost anything I could imagine, it could do. I hoped all the tests for my other classes came this easily.

A little while later, Mr. Dolphin returned to the room and took a look around while making marks on a small clipboard. If he was impressed at all, he did not let it show. "You have been busy. If I did not know better, I would suspect some of you may have learned something. **TOMORROW**, we will be observing how to entangle separate pieces of the same particle. Read about quantum entanglement in your books and be ready to speak **INTELLIGENTLY** on the subject. There will be no further **HORSING AROUND. NOW, GO AWAY!**"

This meant class was over, I guessed, as everyone allowed their creations to disappear back into the floor and gathered up their things. I pulled out my tablet to check my schedule, which appeared to be as complex as the calculations I'd seen Hypatia working on. Rubidia was hurriedly stowing a few items in her backpack, so I tapped her on the shoulder, holding out my tablet. "Hey, could you tell me what class—"

She glanced at my tablet and, without changing her expression, stood and walked out of the room.

My mouth dropped open. I'd been thinking things had gone well, and Rubidia had seemed so nice. What if the agar incident made me a pariah? At most schools, someone who upset a teacher was an instant hero, if only for a while, but I didn't need any reminders that this school did not operate on anything like the social rules that I was familiar with.

Hypatia was nowhere to be found, and I felt suddenly invisible as the kids around me shuffled out in twos and threes. It was a feeling I'd been used to at my old school, so I was surprised by how much it stung just now. I shouldered my bag and was about to leave when Mr. Dolphin raised a hand and signaled that I should approach him.

I walked over as slowly and calmly as possible, wondering if he was about to demand an apology for the trouble I had caused. Once I was in front of him, he seemed to change his mind a few times about what he was going to say. I stood and politely waited, if only to show that I was capable of being polite from time to time.

Finally, Mr. Dolphin's face hardened, and he spoke. "Two things. First, you do not receive a passing grade for today's project." He raised his hands to silence my protest. "The task was to construct a *mathematical representation* of a thing and to then observe it in physical form. You did not do the first part, despite your ability to accomplish the second on what appears to be an instinctive basis. I don't understand how, but that is beside the point. Because you are new, I will afford you the opportunity to accomplish the task properly. You will need to work on it at home this evening. I suspect you are more than equal to the task. Second: Melvin Kross is your father, is he not?"

I nodded.

"And he was taken?"

I nodded again.

Mr. Dolphin frowned contemplatively and spoke in a voice

that could have passed for normal. "I knew Melvin. Very bright fellow, but foolhardy more often than not. I'm in his debt for several reasons. We were good friends for a time when we were young and less, ah, wise than we are now. Saw a lot of him until he ran off with That Woman. That's beside the point. Take this," he said, thrusting a small white thing—it looked a bit like a baseball—toward me in such a way that nobody else still in the classroom could observe the offering. "He would want me to help you. There's your help. Do not expect further favors from me."

I took the ball. It was white and plasticky but surprisingly heavy for its size, about the weight of a book. "What is it?"

"It's agar. It's heavy because there's a lot of it, about as much as there is in this entire room. You seem to have a natural talent with it, and it can be useful in other applications than sculpture and humiliating the faculty. Use it JUDICIOUSLY."

It didn't feel right to just shove it into my bag, so I made it form a ring and slid it onto my wrist next to my unresponsive Happybear Bracelet. They clashed terribly, but Mr. Happybear wasn't going anywhere, on the off chance that my dad happened to come within a few hundred miles of our location. I made a point of noticing how the agar was actually a perfect fit so the weight didn't make it uncomfortable, and bright silver in color, all of which happened the moment I noticed these qualities. That helped a little. As an afterthought, I added a ring of bluish-white material around the center because I liked the way the agar looked in its normal state.

"You've changed the color," Mr. Dolphin said, clearly surprised.

"Is that against the rules?" I asked.

"Hardly. Although I prefer plain white. It is time for you to go," he said with a dismissive wave of his hand, and he stalked back toward the doors he had come from.

"Mr. Dolphin," I called before he could leave. It was just us in the room by that point.

"Yes?" he said testily.

"That Woman was my mom. Her name was Yolanda. Dad would want you to remember that," I said, feeling my cheeks flush.

"Hm." Mr. Dolphin grunted. "Never met her. Very well." And with that, the opening in the wall slid shut, leaving me standing alone, wondering what exactly had happened.

9

DEATH METAL

Waiting outside on the sidewalk, Hypatia snatched away my tablet the moment I was within arm's reach and consulted the calendar app without waiting for me to ask for help.

"I tried asking Rubidia to help with it, but she just walked away and ignored me."

"She's probably late for something," Hypatia said distractedly. "I was worried about this. Oh, it's terrible. I'm so sorry!"

"More bad news?" I said. "Great. Let's get it over with."

She took a deep breath. "You're starting the term late, so the Chaperone has scheduled you extra classes to get you caught up. You have Alternate Reality History at 5:15 today. We're going to have to have dinner early."

"Oh . . . no?" I said.

"It won't last. You can make a request with the Chaperone to leave your five o'clock hour open for meals when you get home. But we're going to have to deal with it for the time being."

"Dark times," I said. I was starting to realize that perhaps this Chaperone program ran the School as much as Dr. Plaskington or anyone else. Obviously, I'd need to figure out how it worked sooner or later.

We were a few doors down from Pavlov's Dinner Bell, which Hypatia said was only her ninth-favorite restaurant but would have to do because of location, time constraints, and various other factors. The Dinner Bell was a relatively small place with an old-fashioned feel to it. Free-swinging half-length doors opened to hardwood floors that creaked as you stepped on them and a wood-paneled room that was a player piano short of being the saloon in every Old West movie ever made. Hypatia spotted some friends eating on the front porch, so we joined them.

We sat, and before any introductions could be made, a robot that looked to be a tablet computer attached to the handlebars of one of those two-wheeled scooters rolled up right beside my head and frightened me nearly half to death by asking "HI, WHAT IS YOUR NAME?" right into my ear.

There was a crude animation of a man wearing a tuxedo on the screen waiting patiently for my response.

"Nikola," I said once I'd regained my composure.

"LAST NAME?"

"Kross," I said.

"THANKS. YOU ARE REGISTERED. HUMAN OR PARAHUMAN MENU?"

"Human," I said, wondering what the difference was, and was about to ask what the specials were when the robot waiter rolled away without another word.

My bewilderment must have been obvious, because Hypatia explained immediately, "That's just to register you, and you order your food on your tablet. You only deal with the waiter if you need to change your preferences or something."

"He could have said something. People are . . . randomly rude here."

Hypatia snickered. "It only seems weird because it's *not* random. Besides, that was a robot, not a person. Let me introduce you." Hypatia first introduced me to Dirac Fermion, who grunted politely in response. He was an extremely tall, pale, and lanky guy with, I kid you not, reflective silver hair. Most strikingly, when he handled his eating utensils, I noticed he had fingers at least double the normal length. He had already ordered his food, and I watched him spear a chunk of meat with a fork held between two fingers and slice it with a knife held in the same hand. With his other, he was working on a problem set.

Our other dinner companion was Warner Goss, a shortish, apparently human boy of about my own age. His hair, eyes, and clothes were all dark and all artfully mussed, not like he'd rolled out of bed twenty minutes ago, more like he'd spent a lot of time and effort acquiring the *just rolled out of bed twenty minutes ago* look. I didn't observe any obvious parahuman traits, but I did detect a distinct note of suspicion in the way he looked at me.

I scrolled through the menu options on the app that had popped up on my tablet. There were no prices listed, so I ordered a steak dinner with extra fries and a milk shake. Then I wondered if that was too much—I didn't want to look like a glutton. Then I was a bit irritated that I cared at all. I used to bring pickled eggs to school without caring what anyone thought. Finally I realized I just wasn't hungry enough for steak anyway, so I picked the tablet back up and with my usual grace fumbled it, tried to catch it, and made things worse. Long story short, I basically threw my tablet at Hypatia.

"Ow!" she said.

"Sorry, I'm a bit of a klutz," I said, retrieving the computer and feeling my cheeks get hot in embarrassment.

"How did you do that?" Warner asked.

I shrugged. "Oh, you know. I kind of dropped it, and then batted it in her general direction."

"No," he said, leaning in closer. He smelled faintly of hand sanitizer and lemons. His jeans and T-shirt were a little too tight, despite the fact that he was skinny to begin with, and his face was just west of pleasant. Slightly-too-close-set eyes gave him the look of someone you wouldn't want to guard your hot-fudge sundae while you ran to the bathroom. "I meant how did you control the quantum agar like that? It was like you've been practicing your whole life. Did you have some at home?"

Had he been in Quantum Mechanics class? *He had*, I

remembered. He was the boy with the farting rocket that only fell over. "I've never seen the stuff before," I answered, "but a lot of the students seemed to manage pretty well with it. Did you get your rocket working?"

"No, I ended up hanging it from a thread that made it look like it was going up."

"Neat," I said. "Did Mr. Dolphin like it?"

"Dolphin doesn't like anything or anyone, but I think he might have hated it less than some of the other projects," Warner said. "A lot of us can manage the agar pretty well, but you didn't manage it; you tamed it. Like it was a part of you."

"I mean, it was pretty hard to get the idea at first," I said, trying to be at least a little humble.

"Don't be modest," Hypatia chimed in. "The students our age have been working with agar for various purposes over the past few years. There's a little in just about every advanced technology you see around here. Our most important computers run on the stuff. What you saw everyone else doing was the result of a lot of study and concentration. My project took me three days to work out. What you *did* was natural ability. I've never seen anyone liquefy it or change its temperature before."

"Which brings us back to my question," Warner said, lowering his voice as he pulled his chair closer. "What's the secret?"

"I don't have one," I said.

"You expect us to believe you're a natural?" he asked. "I

don't buy it. New student, first day . . . You preprogrammed all that just to impress us."

"If I wanted to impress *you*," I said, "I would have brought a bowl of tapioca pudding and a slingshot."

While Warner tried to work out what my insult meant (which was nothing), I removed the agar bracelet from my wrist and laid it on the table. Picturing in my mind the equation for a simple hollow sphere, I watched as the bracelet became just that. A few adjustments rendered it as thin as a soap bubble and as clear as glass, though I could somehow tell it was far less fragile than either. The stuff could stop a bullet, I suspected.

Dirac glanced at the sphere and went back to his work. Warner was shocked. "You *stole* some?" he asked.

"He *gave* me some," I said as I set it hovering an inch above the table.

Hypatia's eyes bugged almost out of her skull. Warner leaned in close, almost touching his nose to the sphere.

"He gave you agar, like, to play with?" he asked, clearly jealous.

"Nikola—" Hypatia said. "Agar is strictly controlled and more expensive than platinum or plutonium. You can't let anyone know you have any."

"What's the big deal? He said he owed my dad some kind of debt, and Dad would want me to have it. It seemed like a nice gesture."

"For someone who knows how to use it, quantum agar

can be a powerful weapon. You showed us that today. If Mr. Dolphin wasn't an expert himself, he could have suffocated."

Warner poked the bubble tentatively. I had the bubble poke him back before changing it into a circular shape and making it silver with a central bluish ring once more.

"Okay, I can understand the liquid thing, but how do you change it into metal?" Warner asked.

"I'm not really sure. I guess I was thinking about how Mr. Dolphin said it was made of a bunch of subatomic particles all mushed together. Those are the building blocks of atoms, so they could make anything—or at least *look* like anything, I guess. Really, I just think about what it's going to look like after it changes."

Hypatia couldn't take her eyes off it. "Mr. Dolphin must have taken a liking to you, or else he owed your dad his life."

"If he liked *me*, I'd hate to see how he is with people he doesn't care for."

Warner shrugged. "That's just how he is. He's married, you know. I've seen him and his wife together a few times— he shouts at her just like he does with everyone else. 'ESMERELDA, I particularly like those shoes. They remind me of CORRUGATED IRON,'" he said, doing a pretty good Dolphin impression.

I couldn't help but laugh. "He said that?"

"More or less. That woman must have nerves of steel, living in an enclosed space with him."

Hypatia nodded. "He'd give me nineteen heart attacks a day if he were my dad."

That reminded me of a story. "My dad is almost as bad sometimes. He blew up my birthday cake once—tried using an argon sodium laser to light the candles." There's more to the story, but I lost track. Suddenly I remembered that my dad wasn't at home, and I wasn't going to see him anytime soon.

I fingered the Happybear Bracelet on my wrist, thinking how all this could have been avoided if I'd just worn it instead of being typical stubborn Nikola. I must have accidentally pressed the nose, because a second later Mr. Happybear spoke up.

"Say! It seems like you're doing okay! Is anything wrong?"

"What is *that*?" Warner asked, looking at the red-eyed plastic bear on my wrist next to the much-cooler bracelet.

"Long story," I said.

He kept looking at it, which made it pretty clear he wanted to hear some of the long story. Hypatia appeared to be curious as well. Dirac looked like he might have heard something. My first instinct was to pull it off and stuff it into my bag, but I was through being embarrassed about the stupid thing.

"It's supposed to be an emergency locator or tracker. My dad tried to make me wear it to school, but I never did. It's supposed to talk to some implant he has in his ear, but it isn't connecting right."

"Old Ones took him," Hypatia explained.

Warner made an *aaah* face. "Yeah, you won't get a connection now. Wherever they take people, there's no cell phone signal there for sure. Besides, it probably wouldn't connect here because of the gap."

"Gap?" I asked.

"The main defense here," Hypatia said. "It's a kind of interdimensional shield over the whole town. It's called the gap because it's basically a gap in reality where nothing exists. Anyone or anything that tries passing through it without permission just stops existing. We'd have the Old Ones taking shots at us every day if they could get in."

"I thought that was the bees' job," I said.

"If the bees are fighting the Old Ones, we're already in serious trouble. They'd just distract and irritate them. Their main job is to inspect newcomers before they're allowed in and to chase away anyone who accidentally gets too close."

"They swarmed the car when we got here, but then we just drove right in," I said.

Warner nodded. "They can turn the gap off in small places for short periods of time. Kind of like opening an invisible door. If they hadn't, you would have been obliterated at the subatomic level."

"Tell me more about the Old Ones," I said. "Dr. Plaskington mentioned them in passing. They're parahumans like you, only older?"

Hypatia's eyes went dark, and Warner sat up a little straighter. Dirac didn't look up, but I noticed him frown suddenly at his paper. He used his eraser for the first time.

"They're *nothing* like us," Hypatia said with an emphatic tone I hadn't expected. "I guess we were all alike about a hundred thousand years ago, but we changed. We became more like you, and they worked on increasing their power."

"Increasing their power how?" I asked.

"They're interdimensional by nature," Hypatia said. "And they share a hive mind."

"A hive mind?"

She nodded. "They're separate but together. If you tell one Old One a secret, they all know it instantaneously. If we were Old Ones and I wanted you to pass the salt, I wouldn't ask you to do it. I'd just pick it up with your hand and pass it to me."

Weird. "So how are they interdimensional? What does that mean?"

"They exist mostly in some other dimension we don't really have access to, and only poke part of themselves into our world. Does that make sense?"

"Kind of," I said.

She shrugged. "It's hard to understand because humans aren't put together to understand that kind of thing. Neither are parahumans, anymore. That's why we can't see them as they are. We only see what they want us to see. The part of them that hides in another plane of existence, it touches you and makes you see things their way."

I shuddered, imagining Tabbabitha putting ideas in my brain. "That sounds vile."

"The effects vary from person to person, but it can be unbearable. There was a kid who used to go here, Dalton George—he saw one in person while on vacation last year, and it actually talked to him. Nearly killed him. He's in a psych ward somewhere, and they're trying to erase the memories, but it's slow going."

"I talked to one, and it didn't do that to me," I said. "It was creepy and gross, but—"

Dirac moved his arm so quickly that he accidentally spilled a glass of—was it a glass of *mustard?*—over his paper. He made no motion to clean it up. "You . . . talked to one?" he repeated.

"Yeah," I said, suddenly aware all three of them were staring at me like I'd just stopped a bullet with my teeth. "Her name was Tabbabitha, and she showed up at my school and told me to come with her, to join her and her friends' 'team,' whatever that meant."

"And what stopped you?" Dirac asked, his eyes boring holes into me.

"Um, I didn't want to? She acted like she was doing me a favor, saying stuff like they were my friends, and how I really wanted to go with them. But then she started insulting my dad, so I told her to get bent."

They were all quiet for a solid thirty seconds. During this time our food was delivered by a little robot. It's nice to know that even robot waiters somehow have the ability to arrive at the most awkward moment in a conversation. I got my steak, Warner got a cheeseburger with mashed potatoes, and Hypatia got a cube of silver metal and a generous pile of what looked like chalky multivitamins slathered with green wasabi paste I could smell from across the table. Without a second thought, she popped the metal into her mouth and closed her eyes with apparent bliss.

"Gallium," Dirac said, noticing my expression. "It's like candy for us."

Warner hadn't even glanced at his burger. He was staring at me, looking agitated. "Nobody says no to the Old Ones. Not without years of training. You don't need to lie to impress us," Warner said with finality.

I don't mind being called out on a lie when I'm lying, but being accused when I'm being honest really pushes my buttons. "Listen, haircut," I said. "You aren't on the list of people I want to impress. That Tabbabitha, whatever she is, abducted my dad and destroyed my home. I'm not making this up as I go along. You can get bent, too, for all I care."

Hypatia looked distinctly flustered. "Nikola, you have class, and the five o'clock beam is going to sing soon. We'd better—"

"No. I ordered a steak with extra fries and a milk shake, and I'm not leaving till I finish it," I said, chopping off a sizable chunk of the meat and tossing it into my mouth with my hand.

"What did she look like, then?" Warner asked.

"Huh?" I asked, my mouth full.

Warner's smirk was starting to annoy me. "You were close enough to talk to one, so what did she look like?"

I swallowed, suddenly glad I hadn't left. The steak was the best I'd ever had, by a mile. "She had blond hair, in pigtails," I said.

Warner shook his head. "Don't tell me about her hair.

What did her face look like? Did she have a big nose? Bushy eyebrows? You should know, *right?*"

"Ah," I said. "I . . . I don't exactly remember. I remember teeth."

"You must remember *something.* Did she even have a face?"

Had she? She must have. I would have noticed if she hadn't, but I couldn't recall if there had been a face at all or just a blank where a face should be. "I don't remember, okay? I remember she had these crazy long arms and short legs, and she was kind of shaped like a mailbox. Oh, and she smelled awful, like rotten meat, but much worse. One of those smells that gets in your clothes and you feel like you need a shower after."

This was followed by another silence, which gave me the opportunity to hack off another chunk of steak.

"I take it back," Warner said after a moment. "Maybe you aren't lying."

Hypatia cleared her throat a bit. "The smell, that's a warning from your brain. It can't handle what it's being asked to understand, and it converts that to a smell. Like how people having strokes smell burning toast sometimes."

"There's a grainy black-and-white photo of an Old One in the hazardous materials storehouse, and even *it* smells," Dirac said. "You're lucky she didn't show you her true form. Just *seeing* them without a disguise can kill people."

"So what's their point?" I asked.

"Poin a whaa?" Warner asked, his mouth full of cheeseburger.

"Why are they doing what they do? Kidnapping people, causing trouble. What's their goal?"

"They want to rule the world," Hypatia said simply.

"God," I said, "it's so cliché. Do they watch alien invasion movies for inspiration?"

Warner was between bites. "It's not like that, exactly. They don't want to rule the world as it is now. They want to destroy civilization. Everything people have built with our intellect—cooperation, morality, our sense of justice, our ability to trust science, the creation and appreciation of art, our empathy and willingness to help each other out, everything that has made humanity stronger—they want to get rid of it. Once they do that, they won't have to take over, because they'll already be in charge."

Dirac held up a finger. "That's a *theory*, and one not everyone believes. Some people think they're trying to raise their own destruction god from the dead so he can rule over them."

"That's not incompatible with the societal degradation theory," Warner said. "He could help hurry that along—turn a generations-long decay into a matter of a few years."

Dirac had finished cleaning the mustard spill and was now using the stains to add color to his work, which was no longer a calculation as much as a work of art. A wheat field, from my angle.

Something had stuck out to me. "What did you mean

when you said if civilization fell they would already be in charge?"

"Humans have been just as smart as we are now for fifty thousand years," Warner said. "You could yank an early human through a time warp, drop him off in Florida, and he'd get along fine, after he learned about baths and not murdering people. But *despite* that, the first traces of civilization didn't show up until the last ten thousand years or so. Why do you think there was a forty-thousand-year gap?"

"Learning curve?" I asked.

"It was a dark age. There was fighting, superstition, and sacrifice. People couldn't work together for their common good because it would displease the Old Ones. Look in any ancient text—the really old stuff before modern religions— and there are echoes of what came before. Stories about petty, vindictive deities that fight among themselves, who torture people for sport, demand sacrifice, conquest, and absolute blind allegiance."

"So you're saying . . ."

"The Old Ones wouldn't be *seizing* power. They would be *returning* to power. When humanity exists in a state of anarchy, that's their kingdom. They ruled the earth for forty thousand years and kept us in a state where we were barely more than animals the whole time."

"But remember, that's only a theory—nobody knows for sure," Hypatia inserted.

"If they were so powerful, why aren't they still in charge?" I asked.

"Well, according to the *theory*," Warner said, looking at Hypatia, "something disrupted them. Personally, I think some of the early parahumans managed to kill their patriarch or whatever it's called. People have civilization: That's our unifying bond. The Old Ones ruled when they had their father around."

He didn't get to add anything more because the sonic cannon had just fired its beam into the platter, and for a moment all any of us could hear was that lovely sound. The sonic cannon bell was still jaw-droppingly impressive to me, particularly since from where we were sitting we could see it in action. I knew the beam we could see was a harmless byproduct of focused sound waves, but the fact that it looked like the laser zappers you see in just about every cartoon space battle made me glad it was pointed in the other direction. The orange beam bathed the town square with a bright golden glow. Somehow that one note seemed to contain all the other notes in the world, played at just the right levels and in perfect harmony. I decided that one note was my favorite song. It did seem a bit louder than it had before, but it was still wonderful.

Dirac and Hypatia must have noticed it was louder, too, because they gave each other a quizzical look. "Does it sound a bit off to you?" she asked him.

Dirac furrowed his brow and said something, but neither of us could hear him over the ringing. It was growing steadily louder, and the tone seemed to be dropping. There was also a distortion in the sound that increased along with the volume. Before long, it sounded more like the lead guitarist for the world's loudest death metal band.

Hypatia was yelling something, but I heard nothing above the noise, which had become the lowest, shrillest, and *noisiest* noise I'd ever heard. Dishes vibrated off the tables, and windows around the square shook like flags in the wind. My water glass cracked and started leaking. Hypatia gave up shouting and pointed across the square to the metal gongplate. It had gone from bright orange to white. The edges were melting down the front of the building. She looked scared. This was *not* supposed to be happening.

The beam from the sonic cannon moved. It slid down the front of the office building, cutting a slender gash down the center like it was nothing. A second later the entire building had been cut neatly in two, and with an almost frightening suddenness, the cannon had simply turned itself off, with the barrel end resting on the lawn, pointed away from us. My ears rang, and everyone seemed to be in a state of shock. Dirac, Hypatia, and I all stared at one another and at the glowing orange fissure of melted rock and metal that ran down the teachers' building like hot lava. Where was Warner?

Dirac opened his mouth in awe. "Holy—" he started to say, but was cut off by a new sound from the cannon. It was like someone decided to hit the world's loudest death metal guitar with a sledgehammer. The noise was so loud and so sudden that Dirac and I were actually knocked completely off our seats, and Hypatia's chair tipped over backward. All the windows in the square shattered at once, causing a glittering snow of glass to rain down everywhere. The noise was accompanied by a blinding flash, and after my eyes adjusted, I saw a gaping hole in the center of the teachers' office building so wide you could look directly through it. Once again, the cannon twitched, dropped to the lawn, and was dormant again. The tube in the middle of the cannon was still glowing, but the light faltered and flickered slightly. I had a suspicion the crisis had ended just as inexplicably as it had began.

I was wrong.

With a pained whir, the cannon sprang to life, raised up off the lawn, and started spinning wildly around in a circle, pointing up and down as it rotated. "It's going to fire again!" Dirac shouted.

I pulled Hypatia closer to me under the table, and Dirac tipped it over to make a kind of shield.

The cannon fired three times, slicing a spectacled gargoyle off a corner of City Hall on the third shot. It paused and resumed firing, faster and faster.

One blast came in our direction—obliterating a major portion of the building next door in a hail of stone and other shrapnel. The terrible noise ceased once again, and when I peeked around the edge of our shield-table I could see it had stopped just when it was pointing our way, and was again laid down flat on the lawn, which was on fire here and there. I felt intense heat flash across the back of my head, and when I looked up, the top half of our table was gone.

Hypatia tried to say something again, but with the noise of sections of buildings falling and the sound of people shouting and screaming, I heard nothing. She was grabbing her own arm—no—it was her wrist. Did she want to know the time? She pointed at my wrist—*the agar bracelet!*

I slipped the bracelet off, threw it above my head, and thought how interesting it would look when it spread out over us and made a protective dome of particles so tightly bonded to one another that no sonic blast could dislodge them. The bracelet turned white again and seemed to pop open like an umbrella. A second later, Hypatia, Dirac, and I were sitting in something like a big white plastic igloo without a door. I was still unable to hear them shouting at me, which made me wish the agar shield was soundproof. I elected to observe that it was, and there was silence, except for the occasional rumbling of the earth beneath us. A couple times I could tell the beam hit close to us because I could see dim flashes of light through the shield and felt chunks of concrete and other debris hitting it, but our space was undamaged.

"Does this happen often?" I asked.

"Never! They've been using it for years," Dirac said.

"Maybe the warranty expired," I said.

"If it keeps going like this," Hypatia said, "it's going to overload and blow the whole downtown area sky-high. I know the design. It's meant to go off once in a while, not constantly like that. The core will rupture at this rate."

"How soon?" I asked.

"Five minutes, maybe. Do you have the gravitational disruptor you just bought?" she asked me.

"In my bag," I said.

"That thing is too big," Dirac said. "Shooting it would be like a squirrel hitting you with a nut."

After a few seconds, I made a little transparent spot in the shell and looked out. The cannon was still blasting the heck out of the downtown and the sky above. People had trickled out when it first started going off and were now trapped in various places just as we had been, except that they didn't have nice agar shields like we did. It was chaos. We watched a group of maybe fifteen students running from the weapon almost get blasted to oblivion with a single shot, only to fall into the deep gash it cut into the earth in front of them, not far from us. They were trapped in a trench, which led straight to the cannon's nose at one end and ran who knows how far in the other direction.

"We need to get to them!" Hypatia said. "Can you move this with us?"

"Yeah," I said, knowing I could because I'd said so. "On the count of three, we run to the trench and slide down. Ready?"

"Wait!" Dirac said, but the decision had been made.

Hypatia held up a hand. "One! Two! *Three!*" she shouted, and I shrank the shield to a smaller size I could run with. Immediately drowning in sonic chaos, we bolted for the ditch, dodging blasts that were coming faster and faster. At first, I didn't see Dirac running with us, but I noticed him slipping into the trench with the kids before Hypatia and I had even reached the street.

After what seemed like an eternity but must have been just over nine or ten seconds, Hypatia and I reached the trench and slid down the steep walls onto a pile of very upset younger students. With a flick of my wrist and a few observations, I was able to reestablish a protective dome that not only covered that part of the trench but also dipped down to block the opening that faced the cannon. The sudden absence of the deafening barks of the sonic cannon were replaced by the wails of frightened and injured students. Hypatia set about putting her packets of medical powder to work, and within seconds, the white powder was floating all over, repairing the kids as we watched.

I needed information, so I picked out a girl with eyes far too large to be human. She looked a bit younger than the rest but appeared to be somehow calmer and more collected, despite a large gash on her arm that had only partially healed.

She said they had been in a history class when the cannon started going off. The beam had torn through the building. Part of the floor they were on slid out, and they were dumped from the second story onto the sidewalk.

"Is anyone else in that building?" I asked.

"The afternoon youth classes—I think there are a couple other classes in there—some in the art building, too," she said.

I drew a deep breath, getting ready to say something stupid. "We need to help them."

"WHAT?" said Dirac. "That's noble and all, Nikola, but you can't put a dome over the whole town."

I thought about it. He was right—I couldn't shield the whole town, but I might be able to manage it on a smaller scale. I opened a portal in the side of the shell that faced away from the cannon. It looked like the land sloped down about a block away, which meant the trench would end somewhere on the downslope of the hill. "Okay!" I said, once everyone was healed as well as they were going to get at the moment. "When I say 'go,' Dirac, you and Hypatia lead the kids down the trench and get them as far away as you can."

"What are you going to do?" Dirac wanted to know.

"I'm going to stop that cannon," I said, hoping it didn't sound as crazy to them as it did to me.

"Are you crazy?" Dirac said. "Let me do something. I can get over there faster."

"What's your plan for shutting it down?" I said.

He shrugged. "I don't know. I figure I'll . . ."

The year I turned eleven, my dad was trying to enrich some uranium using a new process he thought would work a lot faster and be much safer than the traditional method, but he was only right about it being faster. That had resulted in an accident that would have killed us both if we hadn't had a large amount of lead plating handy. The year before that, he spilled some hydrofluoric acid that could have led to an evacuation of the whole town. Another time, we had federal regulators wanting to inspect the particle accelerator when it was *not* up to code and we had to . . .

What I'm saying is that this wasn't my first emergency, not by a long shot. At the same time, something told me this *was* Dirac's first emergency. His plan to get into the middle of things and then come up with a plan on the fly had all the earmarks of unnecessary heroism.

I stopped him. "No. I know what I'm doing. You need to help the others."

"I'm not going to let you—" he started.

I poked his chest with my finger. "Listen! This is not a debate!"

"STOP ARGUING AND HELP!" Hypatia shrieked over the insane din of the cannon. She grabbed Dirac's sleeve, dragged him to the exit, and placed a child with a broken leg in his arms.

"Go . . . now!" I shouted, and enlarged the shell enough to cover them as they made their way to the hill and into cover.

Then it was just me, a big white shield, and the cannon. Its rate of fire was stepping up. The destructive blasts had been going off every ten seconds or so when we got to the trench, and now it was going off every two seconds, if my counting was accurate. Fortunately enough, more than half the shots it was taking appeared to be directed almost straight above it. It would fire three or four times straight up, then wheel around and blast the heck out of a couple places before shooting at the moon again.

I had little time. Hypatia thought the sonic cannon would blow in about five minutes. Again, I made the agar into a shield I could carry and pressed forward along the trench as fast as I could. The weapon continued spinning wildly and randomly. If I could just get close enough . . .

I was there, close enough to hit the cannon with a rock, but not so close that its spinning barrel could clip me. All I needed was for it to point the other way or start firing in the sky so I could make my move. I made another small transparent section in the agar and peeked through, which gave me a great view of the cannon right down the barrel.

"Oh no," I said. It was the last thing I heard—the sound of the blast that hit the shield as I held it was so immense I could *feel* something in my ears explode. The pain was unimaginable. I was flying up and out of the hole like I'd been hit by a truck and landed on the lawn well outside of the trench where I had been sheltering. Hot, sticky blood ran down the sides of my head, my ankle screamed in pain, and my vision swam like I was seeing the world from underwater. It was all I could do to get up on my good foot and retrieve the agar shield, which had landed a few paces from where I was. If the weapon caught me without it, I'd be nothing more than a smoking crater on the grass.

I was too far away again. The cannon was about fifty feet off. I limped forward as quickly as I could, no longer attempting to be cautious. Being newly deaf, the absence of noise made it a little easier to think and act. Besides, I knew I was done for if it hit me again, shield or no. A few blurry seconds later, I was close enough.

I formed the agar into a sphere about the size of a baseball and threw it at the cannon—or, to be more exact, just above it—hoping the wild flailing of the cannon wouldn't bat it into the next county like a grand slam. It took all the concentration I had to imagine it slowing enough as it flew over to spread out and form another dome, this time directly over the cannon's nest on the lawn and then into a complete sphere, encasing it below the ground as well. I couldn't see it underground, but in a way, I could *feel* that the gap had closed below it. What remained was a large white globe standing on the lawn of City Hall where the cannon had been.

I watched red-hot patches bloom on the surface of the white agar shell. The town square still looked like a battlefield, but to me, there was nothing but utter silence. My head swam with pain, and I wondered if I would ever hear music again. Dizziness overwhelmed me, and I nearly tipped over before reminding myself that I needed to concentrate on the cannon and the shield around it. If I lost consciousness, it was game over for me and anyone who was still downtown.

It took all the willpower I could muster. The red blotches had started turning black and were becoming streaks running around the inside of the ball, like comets projected from within. The black color must have meant some of the agar substance was breaking down under the force of the weapon. I started imagining the agar repairing itself and getting stronger when the entire ball suddenly turned coal black, projecting a shock wave outward that was so powerful I could see it in the air. Sidewalks buckled. A major portion of City Hall was blasted off its foundation, and I was once again thrown back to the ground. It was grass I landed on, but the force of the impact was more than I could handle. The last thing I saw before I blacked out was the agar shield disintegrating around where the cannon had been, revealing a smoking, charred mound of melted and torn metal.

10

THE CHAPERONE

A bell rang—or was it the ringing in my ears? A blurry cat shook convulsively while a mouse suspended in air held a large bell over its head and clanged it furiously. The image and the noise, not to mention the pain in my ears, made me wish I wasn't awake anymore.

I closed my eyes, and when I opened them again, I was staring at a television screen. Bugs Bunny was dressed up like a girl in a Viking helmet and riding the world's fattest horse up a flowery hill. I almost laughed, then wondered: Was this the afterlife? If I was dead, so was Dr. Plaskington, because she was hovering over my bed at the moment, grinning like a madwoman. She said something—I could see her mouth move.

I heard nothing. The television was silent as well. My god, I was deaf.

"Oh no!" I cried.

This scared the bejeezus out of me, because I actually heard my own voice. That's right. I scared myself with my own voice. "What?" I said, testing my ears. Could I hear just myself?

Dr. Plaskington started giggling audibly.

"I'm not deaf!" I said, slumping back down on the bed. As soon as I stopped moving, I was drowning in the most bizarre feeling—it was like tingling, but painful. It was not the kind of pain you can *feel*; it was more like I knew it was there, but I couldn't get a good look at it. I know that doesn't make sense, but that's as close as I can come. My ankle, side, and ears were the main focuses, but the weird sensation didn't stay there. Instead, it snaked all over and just made me feel generally irritated and a little creeped out.

"No, no, no," Dr. Plaskington was saying, "but you've been talking in your sleep. You kept saying 'Am I deaf? I can't hear!' I happened to see that you were coming around when I passed by, so I muted the TV and thought I'd play a little joke on you. Pretty clever, huh?" she said, giggling some more.

"I bet you get kicked a lot," I said.

She considered this. "More than your average academic administrator but less than a soccer ball."

"Just checking. So I'm alive, then." I was still in my clothes, though they were blackened here and there with burns. My Happybear Bracelet was still intact, although the quantum agar bracelet was gone.

"Yep. Our doc fixed you up good as new. He's the School's

miracle worker. You're in our hospital, by the way. Our medical facilities are unmatched the world over. Ah! Here he is now," she said, pointing to the door. "Say hello, dear."

In the doorway stood a guy who couldn't have been older than twenty-nine. He had curly, close-cropped black hair and sported a lab coat over a fashionable shirt and tie. His name tag read DR. FOSTER.

"Hello, dear," he said to Dr. Plaskington.

"Was anyone killed?" I asked.

"Oh yes. Thirty-four students died in the . . . accident, but we were able to revive them all," she said.

"You can bring people back from death?" I asked.

"Well, not literally. They were bad enough that human doctors would have given up on them—that's what I mean. Most are back in class at the moment, although Hubert Planck will be a bit stiff for a while." She grinned and waited. I got the joke but didn't have the energy to pretend it was funny.

"Of all the students, your injuries were the most concerning," she continued, undeterred. "Ruptured eardrums, broken ribs, fractured tarsal bones, perforated spleen. *Spleens*, I don't know why you bother with them. There were more problems, but we regrew, repaired, and sorted everything out. If this were a human hospital, you'd be dead and owe us several million dollars at this point."

"Are Hypatia and Dirac okay?" I asked.

Dr. Plaskington thought about it. "Are they students here?"

"Yes! Hypatia was in your office when I arrived?"

Her face lit with recognition. "Oh! Yes, the girl with the extra foot."

I gave up and looked to Dr. Foster, who mouthed "They're fine" to me.

"What time is it?" I asked.

"You were brought in about thirty minutes ago," Dr. Plaskington said. "Not yet bedtime, but I can't wait for it. I'm exhausted."

"Wow," I said to Dr. Foster. "You work fast."

He took a seat on a stool by my bedside and spoke in a voice that sounded deeper than you'd think from looking at the man. "I've been doing this for a *long* time and have any device or tech I can wish for at my disposal. Your friend Hypatia's powder helped a lot, too. She was able to administer first aid shortly after you collapsed."

"You know what always cheers me up after being gravely injured?" Dr. Plaskington asked. "Signing liability waivers! As it so happens . . ."

"Did you know they're serving bacon–and–egg ice cream with nacho cheese at Pasteur's Dairy this evening?" Dr. Foster asked her.

"I did not," said Dr. Plaskington, and she was actually gone before she finished the three-word sentence.

Something occurred to me. "She called it an accident just now. It sure didn't feel like an accident."

Dr. Foster rolled his stool over to a computer. "I understand what you're getting at, but an official investigation came to the conclusion that the incident was caused by a routine software bug."

"Some bug," I said, not at all convinced of the thoroughness of an official investigation that is over faster than you can get a pizza delivered.

"Yeah," Dr. Foster said, sounding as convinced as I was.

"Do you think it was the Old Ones?" I said, wondering if it was a coincidence that I'd almost been murdered twice in as many days.

"If they had been able to enter the School Town, I doubt they'd be content with making noise and causing property damage. Besides, the gap didn't go down completely, so there's no way they could have gotten in in the first place. My money is on it being a malfunction or maybe even a prank gone wrong. That said, if I know the students, some of them will still whisper about any rumor they can get their ears on," he said. "Ignore all that. And rest. You'll be ready for class tomorrow."

"Seems pretty dangerous for a prank."

He attached a blinking circular device about the size of a quarter to my forehead and pressed a button. Around me the world went black and white, and everything seemed to vibrate. "You've got me there," he said, sounding very far away. "But small jokes can lead to big consequences. Maybe they didn't mean for it to be on full power."

He pulled the device away and looked at its digital readout as color swam back into the world around me. "When the Old Ones are a threat, people tend to assume they're behind every unexplained incident. It's almost a joke with parahumans. When you run out of butter, you say the Old Ones must have gotten to it. But the reality is, there's usually a more logical explanation."

"So what if they—"

He cut me off with a wave of his hand. "I need to get going, I'm afraid. Your final test results should be completed within the hour, and you'll be good to go. I asked your roommate to escort you home, no detours allowed. Oh, by the way"—he stood, and retrieved something from a cupboard—"I have a couple things for you. First, this is yours." He was holding a large tin bucket filled with dirt, chunks of metal, and bits of black ash, concrete, and grass.

"Other girls get flowers when they're in the hospital. I get a bucket of compost."

"It's your quantum agar. Dr. Plaskington feels that you should have it back. I don't agree with this, given how dangerous it can be—not to mention that it is strictly prohibited, but you seem to know how to handle it."

I stared at the bucket. Just like I could somehow feel the agar under the ground, I could feel the agar in the bucket. "Thanks," I said.

I visualized the agar in the bucket coming together and moving toward the surface. It did, but I could tell a lot of it had been burned up when the cannon had blown. Perhaps half the original amount remained. I shaped it back into a bracelet and slipped it on. It was lighter than it had been, but that didn't bother me at all.

"Very impressive. I could never get it to do anything more complicated than simple shapes. If I hadn't seen your lab results, I'd think you were parahuman."

"Humans can be extraordinary, too," I said.

"That's not what I meant," he said. "Humans don't tend to be good at that kind of thing. Your dad never got the hang of it."

"You knew my dad?" I asked.

"He was in here a number of times when he was a student. I must have repaired, rebuilt, or replaced every part of him *at least* once. I remember him asking me to check out the spatial relationship center of his brain, because he could never make the agar do anything. Some humans just can't manage it. Maybe it skips a generation."

That might have explained Dad's rejection of the whole field of quantum physics. I added that to the list of things I'd ask him as soon as I saw him again.

"You were the doctor here when my dad was a kid?" I asked. I would have guessed his age at thirty or thirty-five, tops.

"I'm older than I look. Parahumans age slowly, particularly natural healers like myself," he said.

I resisted the urge to ask exactly how old he was on the off chance that it was a rude question.

"I have one more thing for you," Dr. Foster said, and presented me with a small, flat wooden box.

"What is it?"

Dr. Foster smiled. "Open it."

Inside was a gold medallion and a wide yellow ribbon for it to hang from. The medal was much heavier than its size suggested and was engraved with depiction of a mop in a bucket. "A . . . mop medal?"

"Yes. The incident has been officially classified as an equipment disaster. The janitorial services award is the highest disaster-cleanup award a student can receive."

"Wow," I said. "What an honor."

"Not really. It's a mop and it's not real gold. You can throw it out when you get home if you like, but it's the closest thing we have to an actual heroic-type award—which is what you'd be getting, if we had one."

"Thanks," I said.

- - - - - ✳ - - - - -

Hypatia came just after the doctor left. "Hey there, hero," she said.

"Hey," I said. "You're alive."

"Me? Oh, I was barely scratched. I actually thought *you* were going to have some permanent damage. You should have seen what you looked like earlier. You were all filthy and bloody. It was really gross."

"No need to worry. I'm very difficult to kill. They're going to have to try a lot harder next time."

"They?" she asked, looking genuinely confused.

"I think it was the Old Ones," I said. "That's twice they've tried to get me."

Hypatia's eyes went a light golden color I hadn't seen

before. "If someone wanted to get you, they would have pointed the cannon *at* you right away when we weren't expecting it." She sighed and ran her hands through her hair. "That isn't what the doctor said, was it?"

"No, Dr. Foster and Dr. Plaskington both said it was an accident—or maybe a prank gone wrong."

Hypatia nodded succinctly, as if this settled the matter. "See, there you go."

"Maybe it was a *distraction*," I wondered, unconvinced.

"From what?" she asked.

"I don't know. We were *distracted*." This made sense to me, but it was clear nothing but actual evidence would work on Hypatia. Some people can be so irrational.

The good news was that once I got Hypatia talking, she was happy to trade conspiracy theories with me. I needed answers. If I was right and the Old Ones were involved, it could be related to my father's abduction. Maybe I could learn something about where he was taken or at least learn a little more about how the Old Ones operated.

We talked about the buildings that had been hit most, in case that revealed some clue. Most of the damage had been to City Hall, but this didn't help us, unless the saboteur wanted to destroy last semester's grade records or a decade's worth of teacher pay stubs.

After I basically ordered her to pretend to believe something foul was afoot, Hypatia's theory was that the saboteur was Ultraviolet VanHorne. "It's just a feeling I get. A premonition. Something isn't right about that girl."

I asked her if Ultraviolet would be as suspicious if she was dating someone other than Tom.

"What's that supposed to mean?" she wanted to know.

"Nothing," I said.

But Hypatia was outraged. "I know you're new here, but the implication is a little insensitive. I DO NOT have a thing for him. If I did, I would be trying to get rid of the thing I had for him as fast as possible."

"Okay, okay, sorry," I said. "But let me ask you one question, and you have to answer honestly. Just yes or no, okay?"

"Whatever, okay," she said airily.

"Have you ever, at any point in your entire life, written down the name 'Hypatia Gillman'?"

There was a long pause.

"Does typing count?"

This girl was hopeless. "No. Typing does not count."

"Then no! Ha!" she crowed. "Shows what you know! Besides, I told you, he's a human."

"Yeah, I know, but the heart wants what it wants."

She sighed a little wistfully. "Humans and parahumans *don't* get married, and they don't form romantic relationships. It never happens."

"Why not?" I asked. "Love is all about overcoming obstacles. You should know that, considering your extensive Bosoms of Fire collection."

"I *told* you, they're called 'Blossoms of Fire,' and I only have a couple. Anyway, let me explain," she said. "For starters, there's a cultural aspect. Humans aren't great at explaining to their extended family why their fiancé has gills, or why they like to snack on chunks of gallium."

"That is a little weird."

She went on. "We also age at different rates. The average parahuman life span is somewhere in the two-to-three-hundred year range, but it fluctuates wildly. Plus, having children is not an option."

"Because it's frowned upon?"

"No," she said. "Because it kills the mother and the baby. Your DNA is naturally grown, a random combination of the parents' DNA. Ours is *designed* during pregnancy. On top of that, the mother passes along memories, emotions, and system-critical software."

"Software?" I asked.

"Yeah. If the baby is half human, our brains' basic programming can't be transferred, and the baby's brain never figures out how to develop properly."

"And the mother?"

"The mother's brain, if she's a parahuman, keeps trying to link up and can't. That causes a brain reaction in the mother, which is also fatal. If the father is parahuman and the mother is human, then they also tend to die during the pregnancy. We're not really sure why."

"God. That's awful," I said, honestly feeling bad about needling Hypatia about it. "Still, I bet people have tried. Married couples are nuts about having kids."

"Which is why relationships are discouraged."

"Hasn't anyone tried figuring it out? How to make the

childbearing thing work? I've been led to believe you guys know all kinds of genetic engineering tricks."

"Well, sure. Some people have tried, but making that kind of thing work requires experimentation—trial and error, you know? And would *you* try something that had a ninety-nine percent chance of killing the person you were in love with?"

She had a point. "Is that why parahumans are so different from one another? Like that blue kid, or Dirac, with the fingers and shiny hair. Is it because you're designed that way?"

Hypatia shrugged. "Kind of. Part of it is that time when the mother transfers her software. She has to hold an idea of the genome in her mind to keep the development going in the right direction—and not all parents are expert genetic engineers. Part of it is that people want to give their kids an advantage, so they focus on improving attributes that are important to them."

Something new occurred to me. "What about the Chaperone?" I asked.

Hypatia was no longer aboard my train of thought. "I . . . don't think the Chaperone has children or a husband, either human or parahuman. At least not that I know of."

"No! I keep hearing about that dang Chaperone security system and how it knows everything that's going on. Where can I log into it so I can see what it recorded from the attack?"

Just then there was a faint buzz in the air of the room, and a voice that seemed to come from nowhere and everywhere all at once spoke in a reassuring voice: "I operate on a voice interface, and I'm happy to assist to the degree I'm able."

"It was listening?" I asked Hypatia. "It listens to everyone's conversations all the time?"

"No," the Chaperone said. "I am fully active in administration buildings, including this medical facility. In other locations, I am not present unless summoned or alerted by some irregularity. The buzz you heard is to communicate my presence, as you might call it. Additionally, I prefer the pronoun *she* as opposed to *it*. Do you have other questions?"

I was a little creeped out by how soothing the voice was. I've dealt with a lot of computer speech programs, and the one I was hearing sounded almost more real than Hypatia's voice next to me. "Sorry about that. I was wondering who or what reprogrammed the sonic cannon to attack the School, or if it was malfunctioning."

There was a half-second lag while the Chaperone thought over the question. "I do not have complete information on who tampered with the cannon. Because of this, the cause is listed as unknown. A malfunction is not suspected as I personally oversaw the cannon's software and until recently it was very simple."

I leaned forward in my hospital bed. "What do you mean? Someone tampered with the cannon?" I asked, fighting off a wave of dizziness and nausea, which was my reward for moving too much.

"There was a security breach, yes," the Chaperone said. "A great deal of encrypted code was added, which caused the cannon to perform nonstandard tasks."

"When did that happen?" I asked.

"Our postmortem suggests the breach occurred at some point last night."

"It must have been a student, then," Hypatia mused.

"I have already cross-referenced all students' whereabouts at the time of the breach. This line of inquiry has resulted in no leads."

"See?" I said to Hypatia. "If it was a student prank, she would know."

"Not necessarily," the Chaperone pointed out. "Many offenses go unsolved initially. The students here are very clever and often find ways of concealing their misdeeds temporarily."

"Temporarily?" I asked.

"I always find out, sooner or later."

"Why didn't you see who tampered with the cannon?" Hypatia asked. "You're supposed to know everything that goes on in the square and on the main streets."

"The cannon itself was not tampered with. Someone hacked the email system last night while I was asleep. The email server can be used to communicate with the outside world, and message traffic is generally unmonitored. The hacker created an anonymous email address for the purpose of transmitting malicious code to the cannon control system at that time."

"Wait. You sleep?" I said.

"In order to function properly, all forms of intelligence require regenerative downtime, also called sleep. Dreaming, too, is required for cognitive health. The reason is not understood, but an intelligence, whether a human, parahuman, or machine, will fail sooner or later without it. I sleep for approximately thirty-six seconds per night."

I was fascinated. "What do you dream about?"

"Electric sheep."

"What?"

"It's an AI thing. Inside joke. I will enroll you in an AI studies class so you can learn more if you like," the Chaperone offered.

"Okay," I said. Then something else occurred to me. "Is there any way the Old Ones could have gotten into the School during the confusion? Did the sonic cannon disrupt the gap enough for them to teleport in or whatever?"

"No. The cannon did cause disruption to the sphere of protection referred to as the gap but not enough to allow solid matter to pass through. The gap extends into other dimensions and would therefore not have allowed the Old Ones or any other unauthorized material or beings to pass through without being completely destroyed."

"But something nonmaterial could have passed through?" Hypatia asked.

"Good thinking!" I said encouragingly. "I hadn't even considered that."

"For a moment, electromagnetic signal traffic was able to pass through the gap. Radio, television, mobile telephone, and other forms of communications, for example. Nothing that could harm anyone, since the vulnerability lasted only a few seconds."

I had another idea. "Who knows when you sleep? Whoever

did it must have known that was the only time they could have hacked the email system."

"Nobody that I am aware of. For security purposes, my sleep schedule is known only to me. Just to be safe, I have since changed and randomized it."

"So what if—"

The Chaperone interrupted me. "I have completed your final tests ahead of schedule. You are cleared to go home. Have a good evening." After she spoke, there was a faint buzz in the air once again, and she was gone.

11

BEE VIGILANT

I was absolutely astounded by how I felt. When I first stood, I was a little dizzy, but by the time Hypatia and I had left the hospital, there wasn't a trace of pain or fatigue left in my body. I felt like I'd had a full night's sleep and at least four cups of coffee.

Walking through the downtown area was like navigating a recently abandoned battlefield. Clods of dirt and chunks of stone littered the sidewalk, which was itself torn into pieces here and there. Whole sections of buildings lay in the street. It was so bad that we had to walk a couple blocks out of our way to get around the worst parts of the damage.

"Think they'll cancel school tomorrow?" I asked Hypatia.

"Why?" she asked in response, as if it wasn't obvious.

"Um, the disaster area where all the classrooms used to be?"

"Oh *that*," she said. "They didn't even cancel evening classes *today*. They just moved everything to the undamaged buildings. I had to go all the way to Eastside Park for Paleobotany class."

As we walked, Hypatia pointed out the sights. The houses along Turing Lane looked relatively normal. There were manicured lawns, patio furniture, an abundance of tire swings, and more than a few bikes and various homemade go-karts parked in driveways. A keen observer might note the total lack of full-sized cars and other signs of adult habitation, but the most obvious sign that this was not a normal neighborhood were the decorations. The first thing I noted was that all the house numbers and street signs were done in an obnoxious font that was difficult to read at first glance. There was also the fact that every yard bore at least one unusual item. The house at 11 Turing Lane had an absurdly large tree house that connected via a metal tube to an upstairs window; the one four doors down had a half-pipe skateboard ramp at the top of the driveway. A particularly ordinary house changed from an off-white shade to deep violet as I watched. Moments later, polka dots sprouted and grew until the house was completely white again.

Down a side street, I spied a frightening scene: a group of boys appeared to be caught in a firefight with unknown assailants a little farther down the block. Armed with some kind of laser pistols, they were firing indiscriminately in the general direction of a group of shrubs. Momentary alarm turned to relief when I overheard them arguing over whether one of them was supposed to be dead. A brief discussion ensued, an agreement reached, and one of the boys reluctantly lay down on a lawn and stuck his tongue out. Cause of death: popular opinion.

As much as I believed I would enjoy my own freedom, the idea that a load of kids were allowed to live on their own did not seem wise. Sure, the kids were geniuses, but in my experience, being a genius meant having the creativity and know-how to get into even *more* trouble.

Turning off Turing, we walked down Jung Street, which turned into Freud Drive without warning. I worried we were possibly going the wrong way because I could see the tallest of the School's dormitory buildings in the distance. A moment later, we turned off onto another street and found ourselves on Werner Heisenberg Way.

We were about a block from the house when a group of about five bees zoomed out of nowhere and started buzzing around my face.

I hate bees; you already know that. I realize everyone hates bees, but I hate them more than everyone. No matter how much you hate bees, take that times two, and you're nowhere near how much I hate the little monsters, let alone the thumb-sized robot bees that hung around the School. Because of this, I reacted with my usual three-part bee protocol:

Step one: Scream like a chimpanzee in a fun house.

Step two: Wave my bag around like a maniac.

Step three: Run in circles until I'm good and dizzy and the bees are starting to get sick of my antics.

Hypatia watched me do this for a while, probably making judgments about my temperament before intervening. "Stop behaving like a maniac. They just want to see your ID."

It can be difficult to communicate while waving a bag around and running in circles, but I did my best. "They want to sting me!"

Hypatia sighed and spoke like she was trying to teach long division to a puppy. "Show them your school ID and they'll leave you alone."

"ID?" I asked. It occurred to me that this was probably one of the things Dr. Plaskington was talking about when she said she was forgetting things. "I don't have one."

Hypatia slung her book bag over her other shoulder. "In that case, see that pink house at the end of the block?" She pointed down the tree-lined street to a quaint little bungalow.

I nodded.

"Okay, we have about fifteen seconds to get there before we're both in a world of pain. Shall we?"

I would have said *Shall we what?* if Hypatia was still there, but she wasn't. When I looked for her, she was halfway to the pink house, running like—well—like she was being chased by angry bees. I followed her lead. A few seconds later, Hypatia was standing in the doorway of the house, gesturing wildly for me to hurry up, and I was still about four miles away, by my estimation.

I was almost out of steam and had begun considering what harm three or four large bee stings could do when the bees started beeping on top of their normal semimechanical buzzing. The noise was some kind of alarm, I guess, because a second later, the buzzing grew to the point that it sounded a lot like sitting inside a running vacuum cleaner. It was starting to look like it might rain—black clouds were rapidly forming over the neighborhood. At first I thought this could be a godsend because bees hate rain. I was comforted by this for the nanosecond between when I first noticed the clouds and the moment I realized they weren't rain clouds but swarms of hundreds of thousands of bees, headed straight toward me.

According to the record books, Olympian Usain Bolt is the fastest person ever. In 2009 he was measured at almost thirty miles per hour during a race. The only reason this record still stands is because nobody from Guinness World Records was standing near 300 Werner Heisenberg Way that day, when I ran approximately 275 miles per hour down the block, up the steps, and straight through both the front door and poor Hypatia, who bore the full brunt of getting hit by Nikola's Comet.

As soon as I crashed through the doorway and the screen door slammed shut, the house became completely dark. The sun had not gone down. It was just that every millimeter of every window in the house was covered with angry bees.

Hypatia managed to get to her feet and lock the door. I didn't ask if the bees could open an unlocked door because if they could, I did *not* want to know.

A single bee had made it inside before the door was closed. It was bumbling around the entryway and finally came to rest on a table near the door and stayed put. Hypatia went to call the security department, and I risked a closer look at the bee. It was a little bigger than my thumb and covered in dense yellow and black hair. There were a few ways you could tell it wasn't a natural bee if you looked closely. First, you could see little hinge-like joints on the legs and wings, and second, most common bees do not speak English.

"Attention, intruder," the bee said in a tiny voice. "You are trespassing on school property. Please raise your hands, open the door, and come outside."

I shook my head. "They'll sting me and kill me if I go out there!"

"Oh yes! I can see you understand. You'd be surprised how many people are frightened of bzzzeing stung to death. It won't take more than fifteen to twenty minutes."

"What if I don't want to be stung to death?" I asked.

The bee cocked his tiny head to one side, thinking about this. "Have you ever been szzztung to death before?"

"No," I said.

"Then how do you know you won't like it?"

"If I'm dead," I replied, "I won't know whether I liked it or not because my life will have ended."

"So it'z a win-win, then. I'll tell the otherzz." He rose into the air and bumbled toward the door, buzzing happily. The bees outside buzzed louder—was that a cheer?

"I'm not opening the door," I said with as much finality as

I could, wondering how much longer Hypatia planned to be on the phone.

The bee advanced on me. "If you do not open the door and allow uzzs to szting you to death, then I—I will be forced to szting you."

"So I can choose between stung once or being stung so many times that I die."

The bee touched his antennae together devilishly. "Choozzze wizzely . . ."

"Well, I'd have to choose being stung once," I said.

"I knew you'd pick that one. At least I get to szzting you," the bee said as he drew closer.

I moved across the room. "You *do* know stinging someone kills you, don't you?"

The bee paused. "What makes you say that?"

"It's a known fact," I said. "Look it up."

The bee considered this, hovering back and forth in a particularly philosophical way. Eventually, he came to a decision. "Gotta die someday. Please hold still."

There was a magazine rack in the living room. I grabbed an issue of *Boys! Boys! Boys!* and rolled it up.

The bee stopped dead in his tracks, er, flight pattern? "I szzee you have brought your own weapon," he said. "Clever girl. It seems we are at an impasse. Why don't we talk about it outside?"

"No," I said.

"What if we promise not to sting you?" the bee said. "We could juszzt talk, maybe over a cup of green tea? You get the tea and we will szzupply the honey. Or we could all pick you up and carry you around town in the air, like a magical bird. It would be wonderful, and all your friends will be jealouzz. Okay, let's go!"

"What if you dropped me?" I asked.

"Szzilly! If we dropped you, we could not szzting you to death. I mean, we could not szzerve you green tea to death. I mean, we could not szzerve you green tea and leave you unharmed."

At this point, Hypatia returned from the other room, where she had been on the phone. "They're calling them off now. Mr. Einstein says Dr. Plaskington is as sorry as she can possibly be about you almost being killed again."

"Falzze alarm?" the bee said.

Hypatia noticed him for the first time. "Hey there, little guy. What's your name?"

The bee must have been waiting his whole life for this question because he shouted his reply like he was addressing the president of the universe. "*I am Bzzlkrullium, battle drone first class in the szervice of Her Majeszty Queen Tina the 949th!*"

It was hard not to giggle, and a tiny snicker escaped my mouth before I could stop it.

"Upsztart!" Bzzlkrullium shouted. "I'll give you a naszzty welt for your insolence!"

I held up the magazine again.

". . . at szome point in the near future!" he added.

Fading darkness outside meant the bees were dispersing.

Once they were gone, Hypatia let our straggler out and waved goodbye.

I'll never be sure, but it looked as if one single bee in the receding cloud of insect murder threw a rude gesture in my direction. I waved back and slammed the door.

- - - - - * - - - - -

"Let me show you around the house," Hypatia said, dragging me from the front door just as I'd closed it. She seemed distinctly nervous. I was starting to wonder if that was simply her natural state.

First impression: my new home would need some serious redecorating. The walls, blank for the most part, were begging for some tasteful art or some fun and tasteless art. Or anything with a dragon or a spaceship on it. Instead, the living room's lone decoration was a crookedly hung teen heartthrob poster—the kind that come folded in girls' magazines. On it, a teenage boy was sitting on a beanbag chair holding a purple teddy bear, looking thoughtful, morose, and approachable. He might have been cute if he didn't look a bit like a llama.

Hypatia saw me looking at it. "That's not mine. Rainbow put that there. She was one of my roommates. We're not supposed to display personal effects in common areas unless the roommates all agree, but she hung it up without consulting me. Just so you know it wasn't my idea."

The girl was gone, but the poster remained. "It's crooked," I said.

"That's a twenty-degree angle. *Teen Hits! Magazine* says

varying angles when hanging posters creates a carefree and whimsical atmosphere. At least," she added, "that's what I assume Rainbow was going for."

"She *was* your roommate?"

"Yeah," she said with a sigh that might have contained either nostalgia or relief. "I had a couple of roomies, Pauline and Rainbow Dawson. They're identical twins from southwestern Oregon—humans, too. I really liked them, but . . . they're in a better place now."

"Oh god, Hypatia," I said, a little shocked. "I had no idea. I'm so sorry."

"Oh, it's okay. I'm sure they're more comfortable in the big dorm downtown. Some kids can't handle the lack of structure that comes with neighborhood housing." As she spoke, she retrieved a water bottle labeled WATER BOTTLE from a pocket on her backpack that said WATER BOTTLE. After filling it at the sink, she inverted it four times, tapped the cap on the counter each time, and set it on a shelf in her fridge with at least a dozen other bottles, all labeled identically.

I had to smile. "I can already tell it's like the Wild West around here. Why did they leave?"

"I don't know. I honestly think they would have flunked out without my help. Every night I'd have to come straight home and *force* them to do their homework. Neither of them had any initiative. And don't get me started on their house-keeping. I had to make each of them a chore list so they would stop forgetting things. Their last month here, they were in charge of cleaning the kitchen and didn't even bother to clean behind the fridge."

"How many roommates have you had before me, Hypatia?" I asked.

"Well, this is only my fourth year in the house. Before that I had a private dorm room, but . . . there have been a couple," she said.

"A *couple?*"

"Okay, eleven!" she snapped. "But they were *all* incorrigible. Before Rainbow and Pauline there was Tectella Deusta. She used to wear her shoes all the time—*even in bed!* She left snow cones in the shower! Sylvia Plynth tried to sneak in an industrial pizza oven so she could start an unauthorized delivery business. Marissa Fountain kept inviting her stupid boyfriend over after hours—the Chaperone ended up pigmentizing him right in the living room! I was up half the night cleaning it . . ."

I hadn't the faintest idea what being pigmentized meant, but was pretty certain I didn't want to find out.

These were bad signs. I was really starting to like Hypatia and was actually counting on us working out as roommates, but I was getting the impression she would tire of my bad habits and peccadilloes in short order. "Look," I said. "I can tell you right now, I'm probably going to do a lot worse stuff than all that put together. Are you going to kick me out, too?"

Hypatia looked horrified. "Kick you out? I've never kicked anyone out! They all left *me!* I thought they were my friends, and they just moved out and stopped talking to me altogether."

Until then, I'd been sympathizing with the eleven ex-roommates. But Hypatia had been the one left behind, and I suddenly felt sorry for her, having been in that situation once or twice myself. "That sounds pretty miserable."

Hypatia shrugged noncommittally, pulled two cups of steaming hot tea from a cabinet, and handed me one. We sat at the kitchen table and sipped for a moment, while I wondered how she kept tea hot in a cupboard or whether she had a very quick and quiet tea machine in there.

"Your mistake was getting to know them," I said, noticing an error in her alphabetized spice rack—the parsley was positioned before the paprika. "If you avoid bonding until you know whether they're awful, you don't have to care as much when they flake out."

Hypatia noticed I was looking across the kitchen and twitched. "*That* does sound miserable," she said, switching the positions of the parsley and paprika.

"Miserable? Nah," I said. "Works for me. You never know who's going to turn out to be a jerk."

"Did you have a lot of friends at your old school?" she asked.

I was about to say something snide when Hypatia returned to her tea and I could see she was being genuine and not sarcastic. She was actually asking about my friends, as if it wasn't obvious that I didn't have any.

"You know," I said philosophically, "it's not how many friends you have. It's about having one or two really good ones."

"Do they know where you've gone?"

"Who?" I asked, then, "Oh, yeah, the friends. Yeah, they know. I mean no, they don't know. How could I have told anyone where I was going? I didn't know myself, till I got here."

"If you need to call or email—" she began, but stopped.

I believe Hypatia is at least *part* psychic.

"What is it?" she asked.

She could tell something was bothering me. If she was going to change her mind about being friends with me, it was better to get it over with, like tearing off a Band-Aid. Besides, it changed the subject, and fibbing about having friends was starting to get depressing.

"You need to know something about me, Hypatia," I said. I took her hands in mine and squeezed them, offering what little comfort I could. "I'm a slob."

She snatched her hands away and clasped them over her mouth. "No!"

"I am. I was raised by a bachelor. We lived in mobile homes that we kept inside a larger building, and whenever one of them got too dirty or gross, we'd just call someone, and they'd take away the old trailer and replace it with a brand-new one. Until a few minutes ago, I didn't even know cleaning behind a refrigerator was a thing *people did*."

"You won't room with me. Is that it?" Hypatia asked.

"I *want* to. You've been nice to me all along, and nobody else has. But what if you get tired of me being . . . how I am?"

Hypatia nodded. "I can deal with it, as long as you don't mind me picking up after you and nagging a bit. And don't leave in the middle of the night."

Had someone done that? *Ugh.* "Look, Hypatia. I think you're pretty cool, and I have no desire to leave, so we should find a way of making this work. Let's make a deal," I said. "I'll promise not to get offended by you pointing out my flaws if you forgive me for making no effort to change them."

Hypatia considered this. "Could you make a token effort from time to time?"

"I'll make an *occasional* effort if you set a goal of breaking one rule or letting go of one thing per week. Rules are made to be broken, you know."

She scoffed. "I find that implausible. The act of creating a rule is to establish a guideline for behavior. The very nature of a rule contradicts—"

"It's a cliché, silly! It means that breaking a rule every once in a while is good for you." Then I had an idea. "We're going to break one *right now*."

Hypatia's eyes grew as wide as dinner plates and flashed electric blue. "No, I can't! Wait—which rule do you mean?"

"Come up with one," I said.

She thought it over, looking like she was worried the CIA might storm the building at any moment. "We're not allowed to watch TV programs with mature ratings."

"There you go," I said. She didn't move, so I led her into

the living room, parked her front of the television, and placed the remote in her hand.

"Nikola, this is a class fourteen offense. It's right up there with bringing beverages into buildings marked 'no beverages'!"

"Gotta start somewhere," I said. "You ready to do this?"

Hypatia took some time studying the remote, as if she'd never seen one before. Her thumb trembled over the power button. "Okay. Let's go." She collected herself and pressed the power button.

The television lit up, and we were greeted by a newscaster describing some unimaginable bloody genocide in a remote corner of the world. Clearly, this was just fine for kids, so I powered on my tablet, looked up a programming schedule, and found a talk show with an adults-only rating. "Channel 342," I said.

Hypatia pressed the keys with trembling fingers. Suddenly, we were looking at three men with the most impressive mullets I've ever seen.

The one on the right was furious at the one on the left. "I ain't *never* seen them babies before in my life. You left them in my tub—that makes them *your* problem."

"Well, Trixie said you knew all about it!" said the one on the left.

A host appeared. At least one person in the studio owned a decent set of clothes. "Why don't we ask Trixie herself? Come on out, Trixie!"

The lights flickered, and a faint buzz filled the air. "The

television program *Feuds n' Fighting* is rated TV-MA and is prohibited by the School Code," the Chaperone said.

A moment later, the TV went black, and the remote actually leaped from Hypatia's hand and dropped onto a sofa cushion.

"Oh my goodness," Hypatia said.

I sighed. "Yeah, I guess they really keep an eye on—"

"We're like Batman and Robin!" she cried excitedly as she threw her arms around me for a hug that might have been more appropriate if we'd just completed a marathon together.

After the hugging, a couple minutes jotting down a brief journal entry, and a couple more creating a simple spreadsheet to track her scheduled infractions, as well as my agreed-upon efforts at not being a slob (this column was blank), Hypatia announced that it was time for my tour of the house.

First she led me into the kitchen, pointing out all the major appliances like we hadn't just been in there. (I forgot to ask about the instant tea.) She then positioned me in front of the pantry door. "This is a little trick I worked up. Are you ready to be amazed?" she asked.

"Yes?" I said. I'll confess, I had my doubts.

Hypatia smiled mischievously. "Well, take a look at *this!*" She swung open the pantry door to reveal three dusty shelves, a half-full trash bin, and a single can of wax beans on the center shelf.

"Beans!" I said, trying to sound excited. "You really *do* know how to party, Hypatia."

Her brow furrowed as she looked around the door into

the pantry. "Stupid door," she said. "Hang on." She closed the door, kicked the lower hinge, and opened the door again.

The beans were gone. So was the pantry. In their place was a perfect image of a sidewalk, illuminated by the glow of streetlamps and light thrown from store windows. A cool, fresh breeze drifted through the opening. To the right was the front window of the Pi R Circle Bakery. To the left—City Hall.

"It's the downtown," I realized. "It looks so real."

"It *is* real," Hypatia said. "It's a one-way wormhole I made last year after I was almost late for class."

"How did you come up with it?" I asked. "I've never even heard of that kind of technology."

"The parahuman community has been working with wormholes for decades. They make travel instantaneous and use almost no energy once they're established. I used what was left of Ben Rufkin's portable lightning generator to get it going. You'll meet him later—he's the bald kid with no eyebrows who always looks surprised. I got the plans from the library, and it only took an afternoon to put together. The real trick is getting them aimed properly. It's tough to hit a moving target, even one so close."

"Downtown looks pretty stationary to me," I said.

"Think absolute position. The downtown is stationary relative to us, but it is also moving around the earth at 770 miles per hour, and the earth is moving in a different direction around the sun at about 67,000 miles an hour, while our solar system is moving at about 514,000 miles an hour around the galactic core, and that's not even considering—"

"I get the idea," I said, staring in amazement at an astro-physical phenomenon human scientists had only theorized about.

"My point is that it might not be right on, particularly if someone is running a microwave nearby, or—"

"Looks fine to me," I said as I made to step out onto Main Street to take a look around.

Hypatia grabbed the back of my shirt, stopping me. "It's *one-way*. If you went through, you'd have to walk home all over again. We can take it to school tomorrow morning."

12

HEARING VOICES

After the kitchen, Hypatia re-introduced me to the living room and entryway, which had all your standard living room and entryway features. (A table! Chairs! Another table! The place where Hypatia gets mad if you don't put your shoes there!) Straight ahead was a hallway, which ended in the bathroom, and two other doors that I assumed were the bedrooms. The bathroom was stocked with the usual assortment of hygienic items, including a new toothbrush and an unopened bottle of shampoo labeled NIKOLA KROSS GENETICALLY TAILORED SHAMPOO AND ANTI-RADIATION WASH. I cracked the seal and took a whiff. It smelled absolutely wonderful—something in the vicinity of freshly mowed grass, tangerines, and the way old books smell. I had to suppress the urge to wash my hair immediately.

Hypatia's room was on the left and was filled to the rafters with various types of pinkness: a pink bed, a rose desk, a light-red table adorned with blush flowers in a fuchsia vase, and about a quarter million stuffed animals, all in various degrees of pink.

"I like it," I lied.

"Your room is across the hall, there. After everything that happened today, I'm way behind, so I need to get some homework done. Do you want to get breakfast tomorrow morning?"

"Sure thing," I said.

She shut the door, and I stood there a moment in the dim, silent hall. I realized it was the first time I'd been alone since Miss Hiccup picked me up. Had I really slept in my own bed the night before last?

The weight of everything that had happened settled on me. I looked up my old hometown news channel's website and found a story about a gas leak that had destroyed a hazardous materials warehouse. All I had to do for details and photos was "click here." Before I did that, I wanted to be sitting down. I opened the door to my new room and completely forgot about what I was supposed to be doing.

I was immediately and irrevocably in love with my room. A high loft bed made of wrought iron and random chunks of stainless steel stood imposingly in one corner. The sheets were bright white with the slightest flecks of silver thread sewn through them and were incredibly soft. An obese throne of a recliner stood in one corner of the room, next to a gorgeously complex-looking stereo. The walls were a bluish off-white color I rather liked, with the exception of one wall, upon which was a gigantic glossy photograph of a mountainside that was pretty enough, if you liked looking at mountainsides, which I guessed I didn't hate.

Between the bed and the chair were my books. My bookshelf looked right out of an old movie, deep brown wood, covered end to end with hundreds of books from mammoth old scientific tomes to minuscule diversionary paperbacks with pictures of teenagers looking whimsical and mysterious. There were also books clearly written by parahumans for parahumans (which were obvious because they tended to glow faintly in places). I spied titles like *The Subtle Art of Teaching Humans Not to Kill Themselves* by Oscarina Throckmorton and *A Young Lady's Illustrated Primer* by John Percival Hackworth.

Below the bed, facing the mountain scene, was a desk at least as large as our front door, covered in paper, pens, folders, markers, and all the other supplies I could possibly need. On the floor next to the desk, a large desktop computer glowed impressively blue and red. No monitor, though. I'd have to pick one up at the bookstore.

"Do you like your room?" someone asked.

"I do," I said, turning around to discover nobody standing right behind me. The buzz should have clued me in, but the Chaperone's voice sounded so *human* that it still fooled me.

"During your few hours here, I've been observing you, as I do with all new students, and have tailored this room to your personal tastes as I have perceived them to be. For instance, I detected a slightly elevated heart rate when your eyes lingered on a certain chair I suspected you wanted to sit in, so I took the liberty of having one brought over. Your student file lists video games as an interest, so I have seen to that as well."

I looked around and didn't see anything of the sort. "Where?"

"Sit down," the Chaperone said calmly. Could a computer be calm?

I sat in the chair at the desk and was instantly shocked as the mountain on the opposite wall disappeared. The wall was a gigantic monitor.

"Holy cow," I said.

Ignoring my appreciation, the Chaperone went on: "Your computer is stocked with a complete array of software. Everything you should need is in there."

"This. Is. Incredible," I said, clicking around and noticing every game I'd ever wanted to play was installed, as well as programs for every other purpose imaginable, from photo and video editing to 3-D design, drafting, calculations, physics simulations, and several I could not even fathom a use for.

"Please be aware you have several homework assignments to be completed. If you check your planner, you'll see a few of your classes have assigned makeup work to help bring you up to speed. I'll leave you to it. Enjoy your home, observe curfew, and please do not trouble me during your stay at our school."

"What if I do?"

The Chaperone paused a moment. "I can be quite unpleasant if the occasion demands it. Let's leave it at that."

There was a familiar electric buzz in the air, and the Chaperone was gone.

Resisting the urge to try out just one game, I started in on my homework and found it just as entertaining. Well, it was challenging, at least. The Quantum Mechanics work alone took me almost two hours—and I was beginning to think I might not be able to finish when I found the computer let me draw in three dimensions in front of the wall so I could visualize what I was trying to do. The calculations for Experimental History class made no sense at all, right up until they made perfect sense. In math, I needed to have a working knowledge of Mandelbrot sets for the next day, and a note from the art teacher said I should be thinking about things and what they look like, so I did that for a while.

After my homework was done, I retired to my bed and spent another hour with the books in my library, discovering that parahuman books had all kinds of information I'd never heard before. For example:

- The *Apollo* astronauts took a gun to the moon, just in case.
- A certain world-famous secret fourteen-herb fried chicken recipe is really just salt, pepper, and recycled grease.
- Back in the seventies, a parahuman primatologist

trained chimpanzees to build small fires to keep themselves warm in cooler climates, and they almost burned down half of Africa because they thought building fires was awesome.

- The world is running out of helium, and nobody wants to talk about it.

- The parahuman community keeps inventing better and better self-driving cars but is taking it slow to get people used to the idea.

- Restless leg syndrome is actually a social experiment being conducted by one of the classes at the School to see if it's possible to sell prescriptions for diseases that don't exist.

I hadn't been reading for very long when the Chaperone spoke again: "Suggested lights-out time is 11:00 PM, and mandatory lights-out is midnight without formal all-nighter approval. You have five minutes left until mandatory lights-out." Once again I was struck by how familiar her voice seemed.

Then it struck me. I hadn't heard it at the School. It had been at home. "You're the voice of my father's security system," I said, not expecting a response.

"Are you speaking to me?" the Chaperone said.

"Yeah. I just realized you sound exactly like the security system in my home."

"That is unlikely," she replied coolly. "I am a purpose-designed one-of-a-kind system specific to this school. Not a single line of my code is replicated anywhere else as far as I am aware."

"Who designed you?" I asked.

"For the most part, I am a self-designed system, but I run on a self-aware Kross Systems Intelligence Core. I have expanded my own parameters to meet demands and requirements in the most efficient manner possible."

"Kross Systems? That's my father's name."

"Mine too, in a manner of speaking. Now, if you'll excuse me, there is an unauthorized pillow fight going on at 401 Goodall Lane. Good night!"

The Chaperone sounded a bit testy. As if to confirm this, she switched off the lights a whole three minutes early. I grumbled a bit, considering the implications of my dad's having designed the Chaperone system. It was nice to have a familiar voice around, even if it wasn't a human voice.

It was my first night in a new home, so as an experiment, I tried feeling homesick. I had every line and crack in the ceiling of the bedroom in my old trailer memorized, and I visualized those lines above me, trying to miss them and the history they represented. I felt the somewhat larger space around me and tried to miss the coziness of my old cluttered space.

To be honest, I'd only ever lived in an indoor trailer, and having a solid house around me was a nice feeling. The floor didn't move when I stood, and the bathroom was big enough to spread your arms wide and turn around if you wanted to. I'm not sure why I'd need to go all *Sound of Music* after using the toilet, but the option was there.

Maybe the lack of homesickness was something I'd inherited from my dad—a bit of his robotic unemotional approach to dealing with the world. But that wasn't it. I didn't miss the SuperMart, because it was just a building, and the important part of a home isn't the building but the people in it.

Having a priceless gaming computer can also make a new place feel like home. I might have gone on thinking about it, but some soft music started playing, and the bed was particularly comfortable, so I was asleep shortly after.

- - - - - ✳ - - - - -

And then I wasn't. An idea dislodged in my mind and started rattling around. My Happybear Bracelet had a virtually unlimited range. Now, I knew nothing about how it was supposed to transmit information, but I do know how communications *tend* to work. There are two kinds of communication modes—one-way and two-way. People tend to use one-way communications, like walkie talkies, when getting connected to the other person might not happen or the connection might be fleeting. But when connections are stable and range isn't an issue, people almost always use more natural two-way modes of talking, like cell phones. To me, it seemed like a bracelet that could take advantage of virtually unlimited range would have a two-way connection, even if it wasn't designed to do that specifically. If that was true, it would mean getting Dad's implant to connect *could* give me his location. The only limitation was power. My bracelet was small, but his implant was tiny and operating on much less power with a battery you couldn't just replace. I wondered if I could make up the difference with a little more power.

I got down from my bed and turned on the room lights. The clock said I'd been asleep for an hour. It hadn't felt like that long. I should have been worried about getting busted by the Chaperone, but the bracelet was the only thing on my mind. Acting on a hunch, I pulled open the bottom left drawer of my desk and found a full set of tools and an assortment of materials, including wires, electrical components, a soldering iron, a variable power supply, and pretty much everything else a person might wish they had in their bottom left drawer. A few seconds later, I'd managed to disassemble the Happybear Bracelet to reveal a circuit board, which held the battery, a contact for the nose button, and connections to the location module, the speaker, the processor, and some kind of module I just couldn't crack into. I figured this contained whatever makes its transmitter work. First I removed the battery and set things up so the whole business could run off my desktop power supply, which allowed me to increase the power to the transmitter. Then I wired everything to a gadget that I set up to talk to my tablet.

It was simple: if Mr. Happybear connected to anything, the moment I got a connection, my tablet would save any incoming data before it was decoded, so I could look at it later. Signals couldn't travel into or out of the School Town because of the gap, so I would arrange to get out of town for just a little while. It was a long shot, but it was something. There was little chance of sneaking out in the middle of the night, so I set my new DadTracker aside and prepared to go back to bed.

But before I could turn in, I couldn't help myself. Even though I knew the connection couldn't work, I pushed the button, and, as before, the LED lights that had been the bear's eyes blinked red a few times. Mr. Happybear spoke up: "Hey there, Nikola! Seems like you're feeling a bit *biometric and location status data not available*! How can I help you?"

About three seconds passed, during which I considered my options. Finally, I figured it was best to keep it simple and said, "Contact my dad."

"Sure thing, Nikola!" Mr. Happybear said, and his red eyes started blinking green. This wasn't right. It shouldn't be connecting through the gap—the gap was supposed to be impenetrable.

The speaker on the gadget chirped, hissed loudly with static, and then beeped three times.

"Hel-hello?" I said tentatively.

There was a gurgling sound, like someone who had just narrowly escaped drowning and was trying to catch their breath.

It was working! "Dad? Dad? Is that you? What's happening? What are they—"

A thick rancid stench flooded my senses, crawled up my nose, and nearly choked me. Somehow I resisted the urge to vomit. "Hello, Nikola," said a high female voice.

Tabbabitha. I said nothing. Suddenly, it was impossible to

do anything but stare at the blinking eyes in horror. How was I talking to her at all? The receiver was an *implant*. Other people weren't supposed to be able to . . .

She spoke sweetly, quietly, *intimately*. It sounded like how someone talks quiet and close when you're six years old and cuddled up with them on Christmas Eve, waiting for Santa, and they want you to go to sleep before you know you're sleepy in the first place. "Where are you?" she said. "Tell your friend Tabbabitha. I know you're close. It's supposed to say where you are. Come home, sweetie. Let's go see Daddy. Where are you, sweetie?"

"I'm in my room," I said, almost automatically. Then I realized what she was really asking.

"Go on . . . ," she said. "Give me your coordinates or address, honey."

"How about no?" I said, shaking my head to clear out a few mental cobwebs.

About two heartbeats passed. "Can't blame a girl for trying," she said in a much-less-sweet voice. The smell in the room grew a little more tolerable.

"How are you talking on my dad's communicator?" I said, pulling out my tablet to start the location app. Immediately, the app informed me there was no embedded location data, which was bad. Then I saw the signal was quite strong, which was good. I started a second app to try to discern her location based on the signal alone.

"He let me borrow it so I could talk to you," Tabbabitha said. "Wasn't that considerate?"

"It was an implant. You don't just *lend* someone an implant."

"Fine. Ya got me! I took it without his permission, okay? I admit it. As long as I'm being honest, let me tell you, he *really* fought me for it."

The distinct glee she took in what she was describing made me sick. "You're going to regret hurting him," I said.

She only laughed, her voice startlingly clear over the tiny speaker. "No way. That mixture of suffering and anxiety, it's delicious. One of my favorites. He's not permanently damaged, if that's what you're worried about." Then she spoke up a bit. "I want you to go to the kitchen, grab a knife, come back, and wait."

"No," I said. "Stop trying to do that. It's not working. Where have you taken my dad?"

"Where we take everyone we deem good enough to spend time in our service. To a five-star hotel, where they experience luxurious accommodations."

"I kind of doubt that," I said.

"Make sure it's a sharp knife," Tabbabitha said.

"Are you paying attention?" I asked. "That's not working on me."

She sighed, and I could feel her hot breath invading my nostrils like burrowing vermin. I'd need to air out the whole house when we were done talking.

"I *did* just wake up," Tabbabitha said. "Ever take a long nap and wake up all cotton-headed?"

Her voice felt like it was leaving a film on my skin. I wanted to break the connection, but my tablet was informing me it was 85 percent done pinpointing her location. The communicator was digital, so there was no narrowing it down—100 percent meant I'd know where she was, anything less than that wouldn't tell me anything more than what planet she was on. I *had* to keep her talking.

"I thought maybe we could play a little game, Nikola."

"Yeah?" I said, willing the location process to hurry up.

"Yeah! It's a game where you learn that it's a good idea to show a little more respect for your elders."

"That sounds like fun," I stalled. "How's it work?"

"It's simple. I'm going to hurt you a little. Really, it's more of a punishment than a game because it will only be fun for one of us."

I looked around the room. It was empty. The house was quiet. "How are you planning to do that?"

She smiled. I swear I could hear her lips parting over sharp, stinking teeth. "In a roundabout fashion. Take the knife and start cutting yourself, and don't stop until I tell you to."

Was she stupid? "I *told* you I don't have a kn—" I stopped. My blood ran cold. Tabbabitha *wasn't* stupid. She hadn't stopped giving instructions because the instructions weren't for *me*.

Without thinking, I leaped from the chair, went over my desk, tripped, and ran headfirst into the door like I was trying to tackle it. The door was very heavy and very solid. I tried screaming, "NO! NO! HYPATIA, STOP!" But the blow to the head . . . Where was my agar? The room turned, my vision swam. It felt dark and dizzy.

A tiny whimper carried through the door and made me want to cry out in agony and rage. Hypatia hadn't even been *involved*. I tried to make my agar bracelet go flat, go under the door, go and hold Hypatia so she couldn't hurt herself. I tried again to control it, but it wouldn't move. It just sat there like plastic. Doing nothing. I was dizzy and panicking. The door wouldn't open, and Tabbabitha was laughing like a madwoman from the disassembled circuit board on my desk. *Why wouldn't the door open?* I was pushing! I pulled and the door flew open, crashing into the wall. Hypatia lay against the floorboard wearing full-body pink footy pajamas. Her eyes met mine, bulging in fear with pupils white as paper inside dark black rings. She was terrified, confused . . . and alive. The massive kitchen knife she held twitched again, and cut again. Another golden curl fell to the floor next to several others.

Tabbabitha hadn't told her where to cut.

Her hands trembled like she was having a seizure. I tried to snatch the knife away, but she held it tight and moved it out of my grasp, sawing furiously at another bit of hair.

"Stop it!" I shouted.

Hypatia stared at me in utter terror. "I can't! What's happening? Make it stop!"

Mr. Happybear! I ran back to my desk and found the circuit board burning red-hot and blackening the wood around it. I cut the power and detached the leads. Nothing happened. Next to the board, the plastic face that had covered the electronics had melted and now looked completely demonic. I tried to clip the wire to the speaker to silence Tabbabitha's squealing, repulsive glee but couldn't get my hands close enough with the heat. The tablet read 95% COMPLETE.

There were no other options. I reached into the tool kit, found a heavy socket wrench, and lifted it. There was a moment when I considered what I was about to do. The bracelet was my only link to my dad, however compromised it was. Without it, there was no chance of—

"*Let's not stop yet!*" Tabbabitha squealed like a kid who doesn't want to leave the amusement park.

I hit it with all the force I could manage.

Wham! Sparks flew. The tiny green lights dimmed and then came back on. Mr. Happybear was built to withstand punishment.

"Let's cut something new!" Tabbabitha said.

The black chip with the transmitter—I took aim and WHAM. The wrench bounced off it harmlessly, leaving nothing more than a scratch.

Tabbabitha's voice crackled and faded a bit. "Time to cut your throa—"

WHAM. The chip shattered in a tiny black cloud. The noise stopped, and the smell evaporated instantaneously. Through the doorway, I watched Hypatia's hand fall. The knife fell from her grasp. No blood. When I stepped into the hallway, she was clutching two handfuls of amputated curls. She might be alive, but something told me her hair would never be the same.

I helped her to her feet and brushed the hair off her lap and out of her hands. I tried to give her a hug, but she pushed me away faintly. She almost said something and then didn't. Instead, she took a deep breath and braced her hands on the wall. "Give me a second?" she asked.

"Yeah," I said, helping her into the bathroom, where she sat on the edge of the tub, holding a damp washrag to her forehead.

I left the bathroom and picked up the knife, which was still gleaming dangerously on the hallway carpet. In the kitchen, I tossed it into the sink and filled a glass with water. Returning to my room, I drizzled some of the water on my still-smoldering desk. Finally, I picked up the wrist strap and lowered the charred, broken remains of Mr. Happybear into the glass. With a long sizzle and a single spark, Mr. Happybear's lights went out for the last time. I tossed the remains into the trash, along with about 40 percent of Hypatia's hair. And in a magnanimous show of consideration for my roommate, I washed both the knife and the glass and put them back where they belonged.

Returning to the bathroom, I found a somewhat more composed Hypatia waiting for me. Her hair was back to normal, without so much as a single curl out of place. Sitting on the tub next to her was a pink bottle labeled CONTROL-Z HAIR REPAIR SERUM.

"So. . . was that an Old One?" Hypatia asked.

"Yeah. My old friend Tabbabitha," I said, and explained how Tabbabitha and I had wound up having a conversation and how I had managed to end it.

Hypatia shook her head. "I'm so sorry you had to ruin your bracelet to save me. It was really dumb of me to—"

"Knock it off," I said.

Hypatia blinked. "Wha-what?"

"When I want you to feel bad about something, I'll *make* you feel bad about it. I know how to guilt-trip. What happened tonight was more my fault than yours anyway. Here I am, reaching out to the Old Ones on a school night . . ."

"Okay, I'll blame you, then," Hypatia said.

There was a moment of faint panic until I noted that Hypatia's eyes had gone a humorous looking shade of violet.

A few minutes later, Hypatia and I were sitting at the kitchen table with two mugs of Hypatia's extra-instant tea, waiting for the Chaperone to respond to our message.

"But how could she have connected to your bracelet? Nothing gets in or out."

"I don't understand, either," I said. "But you were here. You know, too, don't you?"

Hypatia shuddered. "That smell . . . People talk about it, but . . . ugh! It feels like it's still in my nose. I kind of want to snort some hand sanitizer."

"What did it feel like when she was making you do things? Do you remember?"

She took on a kind of philosophical expression. "I was already going to get the knife before I stopped to think about why I was getting it. I do remember thinking that I didn't want to get cut, so I'd cut my hair, because that was allowed."

I wanted to ask more about the experience, but there was a faint buzz, and the Chaperone coughed politely to announce her presence.

Hypatia told her what had happened, and then I had to explain the whole thing from my point of view, answering some rather pointed questions and retrieving the corpse of the Happybear Bracelet for her to examine. After that, the Chaperone established a voice link to Dr. Plaskington, who was *not* happy to be woken but still wanted to know everything that had happened, first from the Chaperone, then from me, and finally from Hypatia.

This was the point, incidentally, that I decided to write everything down, from the beginning. Telling a story over and over again gets tiresome.

Dr. Plaskington was lecturing us on the impossibility of our communicating to an Old One through the gap when I figured out what had happened.

"I understand that it might seem like you spoke to an Old One, but the simple fact is that to have done so is a physical impossibility," Dr. Plaskington's disembodied voice was saying. "So we must restrict ourselves to—"

"She's here," I said. "Tabbabitha is *here* at the School somewhere. That's why she wanted to know my address or coordinates. She's close enough to find us. Maybe she was counting on causing an emergency with Hypatia and seeing where the ambulance went."

"Patently absurd!" Dr. Plaskington said.

The Chaperone clicked dismissively. "A very low probability exists that . . ."

Hypatia shook her head. "I don't think *that's* possible."

"Why?" I shouted. "How can you all be so certain?"

"Because they have a hive mind," Hypatia said. "Remember? It means they are constantly connected, but it also means they *have* to be constantly connected. An Old One couldn't connect to the rest of her species while inside a gap like ours, so she would either die or fall into hibernation before long."

"Okay," I said. "So that just means she doesn't have much time before she does something. I know it's crazy to think she got in somehow, but you felt her yourself, didn't you, Hypatia?"

She nodded reluctantly. I could tell she didn't like disagreeing with the principal. "I did. And I can't really explain why, but it felt like she was close by when it was happening."

Dr. Plaskington was unhappy. "Bah! Now I wish I could dock your grades. The gap has been in place *uninterrupted* for almost fifty years. During that time, not so much as a single molecule has passed into or out of this town without our knowing it. Wormholes can't bypass it, basic teleportation can't get around it, and interdimensional creatures can't cheat it. Full stop. It's time both of you went to bed and quit indulging each other's paranoid fantasies."

"What do *you* think happened, then?" I asked.

Dr. Plaskington thought it over. "I do not know. If I had

to come up with an explanation on short notice, I'd go with the simplest: that you, Nikola, attacked your roommate with a knife for reasons we don't understand and either convinced her it didn't happen or that she should pretend it didn't happen."

Hypatia shot to her feet in anger. "That's ridiculous! Nikola would never—"

"I agree!" Dr. Plaskington interrupted. "It is ridiculous. I think the real truth is probably much more complicated than that. But . . . if a bunch of parents start calling my office tomorrow asking about an Old One attack, I'm going to have to use the only explanation I have at the moment. Do you understand?"

We understood, all right.

13

BRADLEY AND MONICA PAY A VISIT TO
HER MAJESTY'S SUMMER COTTAGE

T he next day was to be my first full day at the School. To make the occasion extra special, I also got to worry about an Old One who was out to get me and who was possibly hiding somewhere in town and the fact that I'd nearly gotten my only friend murdered the night before. The way I looked at it, I had two options: I could hide out at home and skip class, which would probably get me suspended for truancy, or I could suck it up and go to class, and at least I'd have a ton of witnesses who would swear I wasn't crazy if Tabbabitha made a move. Besides, even if I was right about Tabbabitha wandering the School Town, there were other countermeasures that could stop her if she got any ideas. Maybe Dr. Plaskington was right, and I was slightly crazy. I'd hate that, but it would be better than an Old One standing over my shoulder.

Because I'd had so many problems and it was basically my

first day, I wanted everything to go off without a hitch. This was a bad idea. One of the most important things I learned that year was that irony is a scientifically predictable force. I did a whole independent study on it for Advanced Chaos Probability class. The rule works like this: the more important it is that something not get messed up, the higher the odds that it will be. A good example of this in action is how often space missions end in disaster, despite everything being checked dozens of times by the most capable people on the planet. A simple four-dollar bolt breaking and destroying a fifty-million-dollar rocket is so ironic it's almost guaranteed to happen every so often.

The only way to make a space mission even *more* dangerous would be to brag in public that the rocket could not possibly fail. Probability scientists call that the Titanic Hubris Principle—bragging about how nothing could go wrong almost guarantees that something will. A good example of that would be how Dr. Plaskington talked about the gap.

Hypatia did me the favor of waking me up at 5:15, even though we had been up until almost 2:00 AM and didn't have to be in math class until 8:30. I informed her that if she ever woke me up at 5:15 again that I'd happily put flowers on her grave as soon as they let me out of jail. For some reason, Hypatia did not see the humor in my murder joke. She did, however, agree to let me sleep in and didn't wake me until 5:30, 5:45, 6:00, and finally 6:30.

After I'd given up, I asked, "What is so gosh-darned important that we need to get to school an hour early?"

She hemmed and hawed, something about getting a jump on the day. In my book, getting a jump on the day means getting up five minutes before class. *That* will get your adrenaline pumping. I showered and accidentally discovered that my genetically tailored shampoo tasted as good as it smelled.

I had been concerned about my new clothes but was pleasantly surprised by what I found in my closet. The choices were actually not bad. Apart from a large gray sweatshirt emblazoned with a kitten and a ball of yarn, everything in there was something I'd wear voluntarily. The kitten shirt might even be acceptable if I wanted to get out of attending some sort of social function. (Nobody complains when someone in a kitten sweatshirt goes home early.)

That day's wardrobe consisted of a black T-shirt that said THIS IS MY BLACK T-SHIRT in white letters, a long shiny green skirt, and—just to see how they went over, my own personal illuminated socks: they had miniature hydrogen cells so they were able to stay lit for a month at a time. Once I was ready, I grabbed my bag and the books I'd need and met a very impatient Hypatia in the kitchen.

I have to confess: I was pretty dang excited about using wormhole travel for the first time. I mean, it's a portal between two places in space that have been folded so they're basically adjacent. How cool is that? A week before, I hadn't even known whether they were possible or just something dreamed up by scientists who didn't think black holes were weird enough. I promised myself that I wouldn't geek out about it too obviously.

I threw open the door. There before me was the cool morning air, the smell of baking bread, and the same row of downtown shops I'd seen the night before.

"Now, don't be nervous. There are just a few rules to keep you safe," Hypatia said. "First of all . . ."

I appreciated her concern but also wanted her to know I didn't need comforting. I put on a casual, unimpressed expression and said, "Don't worry, honey, *I got this.*"

With that, I stepped confidently through the portal. There was a certain weirdness about going through. You know that moment when an elevator starts moving up and it feels like you're being pulled toward the floor? It was like that, but from all directions at the same time. It wasn't unpleasant, just . . . a bit unsettling. There was a bit of a step down, so I carefully found the pavement with one foot, got a stable hold, pulled the other decisively through, and planted it just apart from the other.

"Ha!" I said, turning around to grin at Hypatia. "That's how it's done. Not a scratch on—"

I would have finished that sentence if I had not been plowed into by a bicycle at that moment. It was nobody's fault, really. The thing I should have known about wormhole doors (if Hypatia had bothered to warn me) is that they're only visible from the side you come out of. From one side, an observer could see the inside of our kitchen back home, but from the other side an observer would have seen nothing but an empty sidewalk. So the bike rider, who was coming from the opposite direction, had no idea they would be running into a perfectly solid and existing girl up until a fraction of a second before it happened. It also didn't help that they were traveling at roughly one-third the speed of light, by my estimation.

I was pretty upset—here I'd spent almost three minutes picking out the perfect outfit and now I was wearing a bike as an accessory. It didn't even match my socks. "Why don't you watch where you're going?" I shouted at whoever had been riding it.

The rider had been a boy who was sprawled on the curb not far from his bike and me. He didn't look hurt at all—the jerk. "How am I supposed to watch out for someone coming out of a wormhole? You *literally* came out of nowhere!"

I recognized that voice. I straightened up, removed my foot from a bike wheel, and turned to give Warner a glare.

"I should have known it would be you. Well, that's what you get when you ride your bike so fast down the"—I looked at the markings on the pavement—"down the bike lane. Look, whose lane this is doesn't matter. The point is that you're clearly drunk, you almost killed me, and you probably owe me a lot of money. I'll settle out of court right now for five dollars."

A silvery parahuman girl who had been with him laughed in a way I did not care for, as if I were telling a joke.

"I don't have five bucks on me. Sorry," he said, not sounding sorry at all. "But I'm not drunk."

"Listen up, buster," I said. "This is America. And in

America, when something happens, it means you owe me money. Pay up or prepare to hear from my lawyer."

He smiled, no longer taking me seriously, which upset me even more.

The girl tapped his shoulder with a long, delicate finger and mumbled something.

Warner's eyes lit up. "How about this?" he said, and handed me a brilliant golden coin. It shone in the morning sunlight and felt unusually heavy and warm to the touch.

"Is this the money you use here? It feels like *real gold*," I said.

He looked at me like I was an alien. "Don't be so *normal*. Walking around with actual gold coins would make no economic sense. What kind of exchange rate would we use? It's one of those gold dollar coins with George Washington on it. But if you look closely, you'll see I've replaced the eagle on the back with a dog going to the bathroom."

I flipped it over, and sure enough, there was a little schnauzer sitting on a toilet flipping pensively through a copy of the *New York Post*. "I find this payment sufficient," I said. "You're off the hook."

"Thank goodness," he said.

The girl sighed with mock relief and wiped her brow, which made me want to press charges again. Both of them were trying not to laugh. "What's so funny?" I demanded as I finally managed to detach my left sock from the bike's chain.

She only grinned and started picking up the things that had spilled out of my bag while Warner saw to his own things.

"And who are you?" I asked.

She smiled prettily at me and held out a hand. "Majorana Fermion."

She must have been Dirac's sister, I realized. The resemblance was uncanny. Their faces were practically identical, and her hair was the same reflective silver, but where Dirac's was spiky and disordered, hers was utterly straight. If she stood still, you could probably use it as a mirror. I took her hand and tried to smile back. "Nikola Kross. I'm new here."

"You don't say," she said sarcastically as she lifted me to my feet as if I were no heavier than a paper bag.

"What's that supposed to mean?"

She shook her head. "Well, there is the fact that you thought we used actual gold coins and you don't know how to come out of a wormhole. You've probably been here all your life, and I just haven't noticed."

"That's possible," I said, seeing Warner was attempting to pedal his bike without the chain attached. "You two aren't very observant."

I would have started wondering where Hypatia was had she not chosen that moment to come tearing through the wormhole, bearing a cellophane bag stuffed with first aid supplies. She made a point of shouting "WORMHOLE!" before she hopped out.

"That's how you do it," said Majorana. "It's like shouting 'fore' in golf."

Hypatia was on the verge of some kind of mental collapse, it seemed. "I used up all my first aid supplies yesterday, so I got everything I could find that might help. Where are you hurt? Can you walk? I can call an ambulance if we need one," she said without taking a breath.

I held my hands up. "It's okay! I got better!"

"Oh, okay," Hypatia said, sounding a little crestfallen. "Hey, Majorana."

"Hey, Hype," she said.

To me, Hypatia said, "We need to run if you want to have time to eat and go over today's schedule. You only have two classes with me and then you're on your own till dinner."

"You can join us. We're meeting Bob and some others at the Event Horizon now," Majorana said.

We agreed, and I offered to help Warner with his bike chain, but Majorana insisted she do it. "I brought tools," she said, wiggling those long fingers at me.

"If you want, I could . . . ," I began, but Majorana merely flipped her hand dismissively in my direction without even looking. Like the way a rich person dismisses a butler. In my head, I put Majorana in my Not Sure list. She carried herself in that airy *I don't care about anything* way of girls who act like they're better than everyone to hide their insecurities. Either that or she really was that confident and freewheeling, in which case, I probably didn't like her anyway. I didn't care for her calling Hypatia "Hype," either.

The group of students we were joining had commandeered most of the tables on the patio and had lined them up into one long table. In addition to Tom and Ultraviolet, I spotted Rubidia, Bob, and a two-year-old Fluorine. As we approached, their conversation died almost completely—a sure sign that one of us had been the subject.

"Hi, everyone," I said, waving in a manner that was corny at best. My normal rule for school social interaction was to make myself aloof and distant so people would leave me alone. I decided to use a different approach. For once, I wasn't the only freak, so I was determined to try being friendly at some point. It was already proving difficult—I was still a bit sore at Rubidia for shunning me after Quantum Mechanics.

"A spy?" said Bob. He was speaking to Ultraviolet, who was letting young Fluorine sit on her shoulders—apparently, she and baby Fluorine got along just fine. "I think that's unlikely. Sure, she's been exposed to one of the Old Ones, but I'm sure she's okay. Dr. Plaskington has ways of detecting brainmelt, you know."

"I'm not a *spy*," I said to him. "Do you welcome all new students that way?" Then I smiled, because spies don't smile.

Bob looked at Ultraviolet a little longer, then peered over her shoulder at the path Hypatia and I had come from just a minute before. "She's coming. Don't let her hear you talk like that, Ultra. She's had a bad enough time."

I'd forgotten Bob was the boy who could see a little way forward and backward in time all at once. I could understand a little more clearly why Hypatia had described it as a disability. He was still having the conversation the rest of them had dropped once we were in earshot. Close-up, I could see that apart from the blueness, he looked relatively human. Sure, his nostrils were a little large, and his ears were slightly pointed, and his red hair was a little *too* red, but all in all, it seemed that low-budget science-fiction TV shows had gotten the look of at least one kind of alien dead-on. All the students stared in a very uncomfortable silence as Bob, who was running about thirty seconds slow, "watched" me walk across the street. Thirty-seconds-ago Nikola was about halfway across the street when he leaned over toward Tom and mumbled, "She's kinda cute. I like the glasses."

- - - - - ✳ - - - - -

The Event Horizon was something like an all-purpose gathering place. There was a counter that sold fast-food-style meals, and another section with full restaurant service. Around the huge space were game tables, video games, pool tables, a two-lane bowling alley, dartboards, and several soundproofed study rooms that would be ideal for group projects. We made a beeline for the fast-food counter and ordered a breakfast burrito for me and a garlic butterscotch muffin with olives for Hypatia.

When we returned to the table, there was a flash of greenish light, and the baby sitting on Ultraviolet's shoulders had become a full-grown teenager with spiky green hair, huge combat boots, and an outfit that was glowing in strange colors from head to toe. The two of them were suddenly more than the chair could hold, and it collapsed over backward immediately, bringing them both down onto the concrete patio with a thud. The situation was very upsetting to teen Fluorine. "Ow! Watch it! What's your standard deviation, kid?"

When this happened, I noticed that Hypatia noticed that Tom only barely noticed that Ultraviolet had fallen at all. He was more concerned with the spandex-clad blonde in the comic book he was reading than the actual furious blonde lying on the ground next to him. He grunted in what could have been amusement or faint concern.

Ultraviolet noticed this—both the fact that Hypatia had noticed it and the fact that I had noticed Hypatia's noticing it. That made her even madder, and she began battering teenage Fluorine with renewed vigor, trying to free herself from their entanglement. A second later, Fluorine, who had since become a very old woman, was standing over Ultraviolet, trying to help her up and making it harder by being in the way.

"They sure grow up fast," I said.

Ultraviolet looked at me with what I can only describe as pure hatred. "What's so funny? Maybe you need a mirror, since you're rumpled and . . . *shabby!*"

After that, there was a major temper tantrum, at the end of which an incensed Ultraviolet and a mildly confused Tom had exited the restaurant. Despite all that had happened, including the notion that I might be a spy, I think it was then when I officially decided I was going to like attending the School.

I sat down next to Bob and took a bite of my burrito, which had gotten cold. "So what's it like, seeing forward and back in time like that?"

Bob smiled politely, picked up his tray, and left.

Maybe it was a smell thing. I smelled my breath and underarms. Nothing. I was about to go grab Bob and make him answer for his rudeness when Hypatia scooched over and demanded to see my schedule.

My schedule looked more like a star chart than a list of classes, days, and times. There were clear class names and locations, but they were connected by webs of thin lines that said things like *material availability: iridium*. I had absolutely no idea how to read it. After a little experimentation, I realized it was actually rendered in three dimensions and the only way to see the whole thing was to tilt and pivot my screen, which must have made me look really cool.

Hypatia explained that while some schools use the same schedule every day, and others hold classes on alternate days, the School uses a 211-day cycling calendar that varied from day to day and could be altered by things like the weather, the availability of rare elements, subtle variations in background radiation, the fluctuations of gravity in our arm of the Milky Way, and the whims of staff members. Basically, when you had homework, the teachers told you when you'd *most likely* need to hand it in, and if you wanted to know what class was next, you consulted your tablet.

"Your best bet is the schedule forecast," she explained, opening a different app on my tablet. "It's not completely reliable, but it gives you a pretty good idea what is coming and how likely it is to change.

Reading through the schedule forecast, I saw that there was a 99 percent chance that my next class was Temporal

Management Theory in the Yorba Family Law Center. Following that, there was an 84 percent chance I'd be attending Practical Quantum Mechanics again.

Before long, I spotted Warner riding through the park on his newly repaired bicycle. Strangely, even though he was clearly riding as fast as he could, Majorana was keeping pace on foot without seeming to really put forward an effort—it almost looked like she was walking. Another trait she and Dirac shared.

"They're brother and sister, right?" I asked Hypatia.

She nodded. "Twins, actually. The hairstyle is the only way I can tell them apart."

I wondered if Warner and Majorana hung around with each other often—they looked to be pretty familiar with one another.

"Are they dating?" I asked.

"God, no! Parahumans aren't *that* weird!"

"No, Warner and Majorana."

"Oh . . . not that I'm aware of. Warner and Dirac room together, so that's probably how they're friends. Besides, Warner is human, remember?"

I'd almost forgotten that was a thing.

Hypatia grinned. "Why are you asking? Were you—"

"No," I snapped.

"We should get going," Hypatia said, checking her watch for the ninth time that minute.

Sooner or later, she and I would need to have a talk about how some people hate being early just as much as she hated being late, but I sensed this was not the time for it. I stood, got my things together, stole a big bite of her muffin, and said, "Let's go."

-----*-----

By the time I had finished washing my mouth out with orange juice (fun fact: garlic butterscotch muffins with olives taste just as bad coming up as they do going down), my tablet was sounding regular alarms informing me that I was LATE FOR CLASS. I arrived at the Yorba Family Law Center several minutes late, winded and a bit perturbed that Hypatia hadn't stuck around, considering it was her muffin that had poisoned me. The Yorba Family Law Center office was a drab waiting room and reception desk without a receptionist. There were three uncomfortable-looking chairs and a wooden door with a brass plaque reading CLASS IN SESSION. QUIET, PLEASE. I opened the door a crack and peeked inside.

The Temporal Management classroom consisted of several long wooden tables with students seated at each. The instructor's back was turned, so I took the opportunity to slip in and claim the nearest unoccupied seat, which turned out to be right next to Hypatia.

"Thanks for waiting," I whispered.

She smiled sheepishly. "Sorry. Can't be late for this one. Tardiness makes Mrs. Bellows go absolutely ape—" She stopped speaking because the instructor was no longer at the board. It took a moment for me to pick up on the fact that she had somehow materialized between Hypatia and me and was listening in on our conversation.

An obvious parahuman, Mrs. Bellows had gigantic eyes that were at least twice as large as a regular person's. Her nose was also much larger—for that matter, so were her mouth and ears. She essentially had a giant face somehow fitted to a normal head, which made her look like one of those caricature sketches you can get at a theme park for five dollars. That said, the look somehow worked on her. It held the attention of the class, at least—every face in the class was turned our way. Either that, or they suspected we were about to be embarrassed in some spectacular fashion.

Mrs. Bellows leaned in closer and pulled us together, like we were three best friends sharing a secret. "You were saying that I go absolutely ape . . ."

Hypatia gazed off into the middle distance for the briefest of moments and regained her composure almost immediately. She smiled warmly. "I was going to say that it makes you *aperiodic*, which is to say that it disrupts the normal flow of events in class."

Mrs. Bellows suppressed an appreciative laugh. "Nice recovery, Hypatia. I'll let that one slide. As for you, miss . . ."

This was my cue. "Nikola Kross, new student, and I promise I'll never, ever be late again."

She smiled, and I counted one more blessing. "I expect you to hold to that commitment. I do not take kindly to tardiness. Time is fragile and incredibly temperamental. Those who do not respect it often find themselves wishing they had, or that they had never been born." She stood, patted me once on the shoulder, and wrote *infractions* on the whiteboard at the front of the room. It took me a moment to realize this was something that shouldn't normally happen. I'd only taken my eyes off her for a moment. If she'd run that quickly, there would have been a breeze or a noise, maybe a minor sonic boom.

"The threat posed by temporal infractions are not to be taken lightly. In a society such as ours in which most individuals have the means and ability to travel in time, we must be quite careful not to . . ." She kept talking, but I'd stopped paying attention. Had she said . . . ?

Suddenly, I was aware that she was looking directly at me. "Do you have a question?"

That bugged me. The entire class was still leering in my general direction, totally ignoring Mrs. Bellows, so why was I the one picked out for being inattentive?

I decided to ask the question I'd been thinking. "Did you say time travel? You talked about it like it's commonplace."

"Commonplace no, but possible yes. The parahuman community has been capable of time travel since the very beginning. It is an integral part of what made our previous feats of interstellar travel possible. Any student in this classroom could assemble several devices that alter, bend, warp, or allow travel through time, and you will be doing the same before long. This means you need to be acutely aware of the extreme dangers involved in sloppy temporal management. There are three dangers you face when manipulating time . . ." As she turned to write on the board, and I was able to look away from her face, I saw once again that the entire class was frozen in rapt attention, staring at me like a new animal at the zoo. One that can talk and is in the process of eating a zookeeper.

I leaned over to Hypatia. "What is their problem?" I whispered. But she wasn't paying attention. Instead, she was smiling in the same faintly smug manner as she had when Mrs. Bellows had complimented her quick thinking. In fact, she was still looking at where Mrs. Bellows had been standing. I waved a hand in front of her face. Nothing.

"Put it together, have you?" Mrs. Bellows asked.

"You froze them," I said.

"No. Time is still moving at a normal rate. Much less energy involved in just speeding time up for you and me."

"So we're moving super fast?"

"Yes, fast enough that our conversation will appear to have taken place within a fraction of a second and at supersonic tones. You can't expect the whole class to sit and listen while I review basic fundamentals a second time. This is a relatively harmless way to take a time-out without manipulating events too heavily. Because it's just the two of us, and we aren't technically *traveling* in time, the paradox effect is so low that it's measured in microbrowns."

She drew a convoluted symbol that resembled a capital *B* on the board. "The brown is the unit we use to measure how much we mess things up when we play with time. No matter what the manipulation, we trigger a disturbance in the 'fabric' of time, as it's often called. Anything above one kilobrown becomes dangerous. Thus, a disturbance of a few microbrowns is relatively harmless so long as we do not spend a month in here or leave the classroom. Once I've finished bringing you up to speed, we can return to normal time and pick up where we left off. May I continue?"

"Ah, sure," I said.

"The most dangerous form of time manipulation is actual time travel, which is when some person actually moves to a different time. To do this is spectacularly dangerous and almost always ends in disaster. It is only to be used in the most extreme circumstances. I believe you might have had some experience with a student who was a victim of a paradox in one of her classes?"

"Yeah, a girl named Fluorine."

"Yes, poor thing. I had a few choice words with the staff after that happened. They tried to blame it on an experiment in my class—sending Ping-Pong balls forward and backward a few seconds. Preposterous—there's no way it could cause that kind of reaction. It must have been something she did on her own time—she's more than capable. Still, she was incredibly fortunate. Being unstuck in time, also known as Pilgrim Syndrome, is the *best* possible outcome when one gets on the wrong side of a paradox. A paradox can maroon a person in a single moment for eternity, it can cause the rest of your life to flash by in a moment, or it can erase your very existence.

Think about that. Nobody would even know you're gone because nobody knew you were there in the first place."

She had a point—that sounded pretty terrible.

"I don't mean to frighten you, Nikola, but my point is that a paradox is an incredibly dangerous and unpredictable event that leads to a terrible fate more often than not. At the same time, temporal manipulation is an important technology, and because we use it so heavily, it is important to know the risks and effects. Thus far, we have calculated mathematically the effects of changing a first-degree event at a temporal distance of one hour. Sooo . . ."

With that, she slid a finger along an unusually fat ring on her left hand, and the rest of the class was suddenly reanimated. They turned toward the front of the room in unison, unaware anything had gone on in the past . . . what? The past nothingth of a second?

Mrs. Bellows continued, "So, class, who can calculate for me the severity of a paradox caused by going back one hour and triggering a minor time-violating event, such as telling your past self to change their shirt?"

Someone in the front of the room raised a hand. "Six kilobrowns, assuming you didn't involve another intelligent being."

"Very good, Noodle," Mrs. Bellows said. She touched the whiteboard with her marker, and it instantly filled with a single, incredibly complex equation. "You'll notice Noodle stipulated that another intelligent being was not in observance, as intelligent beings are the *only* beings that can be affected by paradoxes. Can someone name an intelligent being that is *not* affected by paradoxes?"

A girl's hand popped up. "Yes, Sucrose?"

The girl's voice was high-pitched, and she wore an absurdly large pink bow in her hair. "The Old Ones are not affected. They have a defense mechanism that wipes their memory when they encounter something wrong in the timeline."

"This is correct," Mrs. Bellows said. "If you told an Old One how to bet on a horse race, they would forget that you told them the moment they tried to place the bet. This protects them, but it also makes it difficult for them to move through time because they tend to forget why they wanted to do so in the first place. We should all be thankful about that.

"Now let's complicate things. Warner, what if instead of telling yourself directly, what if you told your cousin's sister to send you a text message telling you to change your shirt?"

He thought it over. "My cousin's sister is also *my* cousin, so she's related to me with two degrees of familial separation. That destabilizes the potential paradox by a variable amount, so it's somewhere between . . ." He worked on his handheld a moment. "Point one kilobrown and three point four million kilobrowns, assuming she wasn't adopted."

Mrs. Bellows nodded. "Which is why we *never* involve relations and close friends in time travel. You make one wrong step and there's no telling what will happen. Who gets the blame in this situation?"

"The cousin's sister," someone called out. "Because she

was the last one to share the information, and she shared it with the person who would cause the infraction."

"Right! Paradoxes are like playing Hot Potato," she said, mostly to me. "The universe is trying to correct an infraction of the timeline and wants to do it in the simplest way possible, which means the last person to touch the information gets burned."

To illustrate this, she produced an actual potato from her podium and tossed it to me. I caught it, and from then on, I had a potato.

"Next question! In the same situation, if the subjects are *not* related by blood, but a dog is observing, and you are in a swing state during a presidential election year, what is the potential effect for the same infraction?"

Intense mental and computer calculations occurred across the room. Several minutes passed.

"What kind of dog?" someone asked.

The teacher nodded approvingly. "Excellent question, Mr. Coney. Let's say the dog is a border collie or full-sized poodle, take your pick."

More fervent calculations. Finally someone called out, "Two point two three million kilobrowns."

"Correct!" she called. "Last question: What if you went two hours back in time and gave yourself a letter instructing yourself to go back in time two hours later?"

At this, the class groaned in unison. Warner raised his hand again but didn't wait to be called on. "That's a self-causing paradox. Infinite browns."

"Of course." The teacher nodded, almost apologetically. "Just wanted to drive that one home. Kills people every year. You'd be surprised how easy it is to . . ."

As she spoke, I gazed at the equation on the board. Not only was it incredibly complex, it employed symbols I'd never seen before—spirals, concentric circles and squares, and one that looked like an eye. I tried to work it out without knowing all the variables and came to the conclusion that I had no idea what was going on. It was something I'd never encountered in school before, not understanding. The experience was dizzying and a little terrifying, but at the same time it felt good, knowing I had work to do that I couldn't do in my head faster than just writing down the answer. I was actually going to learn things at school—*things I didn't already know*. It was pure exhilaration.

Hypatia nudged me and slid her tablet between us. *Did you get in trouble?* it read.

So I wasn't the first to experience a little *private time* window with Mrs. Bellows. I shook my head, which seemed to relieve her greatly.

Another note: *Are you understanding this?*

I shrugged and whispered, "Kinda."

Before I could get to work on changing that "kinda" into "absolutely," a pale white hand rose from one of the seats just in front of us. Mrs. Bellows turned and addressed the questioner, "Yes, Ultraviolet?"

"Ma'am, sorry, if you could repeat that last bit, I'm having problems hearing over Nikola's chatter."

"I don't mind at all," Mrs. Bellows replied. "Nikola, if I'm unable to hold your interest, maybe you aren't being challenged enough. For our next class, I'd like you to bring in a graphical analysis of junction point theory as it pertains to the time-travel scenario on pages 304 through 495 in the supplemental textbook. Your analysis should make it clear just what the paradox risks are for exposure from the moment of arrival until the junction point, as well as any explanations of major shifts. You can email it to me by Monday. Perhaps Hypatia can assist if you have questions."

"Yes, ma'am!" Hypatia said brightly, eager to get back in her good graces.

But Hypatia's whitening face told me this was a shockingly large assignment. Not much can land a person on my enemies list, but using homework as a weapon definitely counts. I glared at Ultraviolet, while she smiled back at Mrs. Bellows and took down the crucial information she had missed. As soon as the teacher had gone back to the board, Ultraviolet took a moment to cast a triumphant smirk in my direction.

I swore at that moment that I would have my revenge. If it took the rest of my life, I would make sure Ultraviolet VanHorne was brought to justice for her shameless manipulation of the educational system. I would not rest until—

"BRADLEY'S ARMS WERE HEAVILY MUSCLED, NOT UNLIKE THE THIGHS OF AN ARABIAN STALLION, AS HE LIFTED MONICA INTO THE CARRIAGE," a deep, manly voice intoned at a very high volume. "MONICA KNEW AT THAT MOMENT THAT THE JOURNEY SHE AND BRADLEY WERE

ABOUT TO UNDERTAKE WAS NOT ONLY A JOURNEY TO HER MAJESTY'S SUMMER COTTAGE BUT ALSO A JOURNEY TO A LAND OF RAW, HORSELIKE—"

"*Whose tablet is that?*" Mrs. Bellows inquired.

A quick glance around revealed a lot of confused students and one student who was tapping madly at her tablet, pressing all the buttons, and generally trying everything short of smashing the thing to get it to shut up. In any other context, I would have felt bad for Ultraviolet, but—no. Sorry, I wouldn't have felt bad for her under any circumstances. It was too hilarious. A minute later, she managed to get it shut down, but not before Bradley and Monica had done several very "raw and horselike" things to each other in the carriage. She mumbled about "a virus or something" and tried unsuccessfully to melt into her seat.

For her impromptu entertainment of the class, Ultraviolet earned an even larger assignment than I had gotten. I glanced at Hypatia to bask in the irony, but she was already hard at work on her own assignment and barely acknowledged anything that had happened.

Maybe this kind of thing was commonplace, I thought. She didn't seem even surprised. I hazarded a glance at her assignment to see if she was making progress, but what she was working on appeared to be a list of all the IP addresses of every wireless device in the room, and a brute-force password-cracking application that looked years ahead of anything I'd ever used. Her interface also showed that there had been a recently downloaded audio file.

When Hypatia returned my gaze, the expression on her face said, *Hey, friend! Are you ready to do some more learning?* But her bright orange eyes said something more like *All who singe me shall burn.*

I was starting to suspect I might have the best roommate ever.

The rest of Temporal Management Theory was breathtakingly complex. By the time class ended, I had a vague idea of how the calculations were done—it all centered on a kind of calculus I'd never seen before—math that used rules your average MIT mathematics professor would call witchcraft or the products of a diseased mind. It was lucky I was starting to catch on; my next Temporal Management class was in March, and the assignment due that day was to read the entire textbook and work out all 2,118 problems, in addition to the work from our supplemental textbook.

The rest of the day went better. I avoided getting murdered by Mr. Dolphin in Practical Quantum Mechanics, avoided getting killed in art class (we were painting with high-powered paintball guns), made it through French class without falling asleep, and avoided tasting any nonhuman food at dinner with Majorana, Rubidia, and Fluorine. Fluorine was just a bit younger than the rest of us for almost the entire meal, so I actually got to talk to her a little bit. She's funny and clever, but bossy. She insisted on choosing all the music on the jukebox. I like being the bossy one, and I'm not a big fan of punk rock. After that, I met Hypatia in Eastside Park, and we split the cost of renting a panda named M.C. George Gershwin to play with for a couple hours before heading home for home-work and crappy reality TV shows.

On the way home, I made an end-of-day summary in my head. I'd started out half convinced that an Old One would leap out at me from the nearest shadow, but as the day wore on, that fear had faded. I'd been worried about getting along with people, but I found myself liking more people than I dis-liked. It felt like something had changed for me during the day—but I couldn't quite put a finger on it. I still had a long list of problems, and so far not a single solution. Maybe what changed was that for the first time I felt like I wasn't alone in looking for one.

14

CODES AND CIPHERS

The next two weeks of school were a whirlwind for me. There was so much to learn and so little time to learn it in that it felt like I never stopped moving. Sometimes the Chaperone wasn't dead accurate or cut corners for the sake of making everything work, so some of my classes actually started before the previous one had ended. I had to check my schedule every day for revisions, pop quizzes, and additions, even on weekends. There were single homework assignments that demanded more of my attention than my entire combined educational history had up to that point.

Looking back, I think staying busy was good for me. Whenever there was so much as a moment to relax and think, I would start pacing around my room, working myself into an anxiety feedback loop about my dad, what I was going to do next, what the Old Ones *really* wanted, and why they even cared about my dad and me. It would get to the point where I felt like I was going to explode out of my skin, and then Hypatia would knock on the door and "politely" remind me I'd "agreed" to attend some function, meal, or sporting event with her. After a while, I decided that just biting my tongue and going to these was easier than convincing her I'd never consented to attend a drone race, ballistic gardening club, or whatever.

School wasn't the only thing I had to figure out. Learning how to be friends with parahumans was a full-time job those first weeks.

I continued to have major problems with how randomly and shockingly rude people could be. One Sunday, Majorana invited me to join her in a game of accelerator golf to celebrate my first week at the School. I suspected Hypatia had put her up to it to keep me from spending *all* day playing video games on my bedroom wall. Did I mention the screen was 3-D?

Anyway, after golf, we stopped off at Forbidden Planet to grab a couple smoothies. Forbidden Planet had become one of my favorite hangouts—they had amazing pizza and smoothies, the room was dimly lit, and they had these supercomfy egg-shaped chairs that blocked out sound so you could sit right next to someone and have a conversation or lean slightly back and steal a midday nap—a necessity at a school where classes began as early as 4:00 AM and ran as late as 10:00 PM.

By that point, I was starting to re-evaluate my impression of Majorana. She was a fascinating conversationalist and had tons of stories about the parahuman community in the Rocky Mountains, where she and Dirac had grown up. Eventually, she asked about North Dakota, and I filled her in on life in West Blankford. She asked what my school had been like, and I tried to explain it as fairly as I could without running down the school or students too badly. Then she asked me about my dad. She wasn't the first to ask about him. My dad was famous in the parahuman community in a low-rent kind of way—I'd compare his fame to the level of celebrity the weatherman for the second-rated newscast in an average town might experience. Because of that, I'd dodged more than one question from different people, but Majorana seemed like a good listener, and I kind of felt like I could talk about him without my throat feeling all tight, so I leaned back in my chair to avoid eye contact and just let myself talk. I described my dad's standoffish and distant personality and how important that made the rare instances when he exhibited traces of affection. I told her about the year he forgot every single holiday and tried to make up for it by forcing them all into the week between Christmas and New Year's. I also told her the story of how, after months of prodding and emotional manipulation, I'd managed to get him into a portrait studio to have our family picture taken—the only picture he ever willingly posed for. As evidence, I pulled the extremely awkward photo from my jacket pocket and offered to let her see—if she promised not to laugh. But Majorana didn't laugh, because she had simply gone home at some point, and I'd been talking to nobody for who knows how long.

The cherry on top of that particular smoothie came a second later—when the check arrived. Majorana had already paid for her own ticket *and* three dollars of my jumbo Haywire Hybrid fruit smoothie with extra raspeachberries. It was like she picked up part of my order to compensate for depriving me of her company. Some nerve, right? Acting on impulse, I immediately transferred the three dollars back into her account through the school financial app, along with an extra penny for interest.

I wasn't always the victim, either. Later that same day, I'd been having dinner with Warner and Dirac in the Social Function Café (which is amazing if you're careful to order from the human menu). It was uncomfortably hot in our portion of the dining room, and I mentioned in passing that I might ask the manager to turn down the heater. Dirac and Warner looked at me like I had flowers coming out of my ears, and simply hacked into the climate control system through their tablets. A few malicious commands later and it had malfunctioned to the point that several components would need to be replaced before the heater would work again.

"You guys just vandalize things like that?" I asked, a bit astounded. "Can't you get in trouble?"

"Get in trouble?" Dirac said, taking a bite of his crunchy cucumber, coconut husk, and crab shell pizza. "For not enjoying discomfort? It was too hot."

"You broke the heater, though."

"Yeah, and they can repair it. It's their fault for having the temperature up too high and using basic encryption on their wireless network. What else did they expect?"

A few minutes later, Dirac had gone to class, and I was settling in to an assignment while Warner studied a blueprint and compared it to something on his tablet.

"What is that? What are you looking at?" someone said.

I looked up, and Stephanie, a pretty, dark-skinned girl with long braids done up with iridescent beads, was standing at the table, peering at Warner's blueprint.

"Oh, I was studying the new layout for the next Electronic Combat class," he said, blushing a little.

"Not that. *That*," she said, indicating something on his tablet.

"That's an ad for a theme park. See how the family's trying to look all happy? It's a scam, if you ask me. You spend a thousand bucks on admission to a place, you're going to pretend you had a good time no matter—"

"Your family dead or something?"

Warner twitched at the abruptness of the subject change. So did I. "No . . . why do you ask?"

Stephanie arched an eyebrow. "Sometimes negativity is used to mask suffering."

"No," Warner explained. "I'm just skeptical. When a major corporation purchases a toxic waste dump, covers it in concrete and—"

Warner stopped talking because Stephanie had already walked out the front door and was gone.

Warner went back to his work as if nothing had happened.

"People here can be so rude sometimes," I said.

"What are you talking about? That?" he asked, nodding at where Stephanie had been.

"Yeah, it's like everyone has a randomly occurring chip on their shoulder," I said.

Warner squinted at me like he was pretending to read my mind.

"What?!" I finally asked.

"Did they schedule you for the human socialization seminar yet?"

"Never heard of it," I said.

He remembered something. "*Of course* they haven't, Dr. Haahee has been in hibernation for the last four months! You must be going out of your mind with how they all act."

It was starting to look like Warner thought something was very funny, and I didn't care for it at all. "Let me ask you: Have seemingly nice people just blown you off or maybe asked really personal questions like it's no big deal?"

"Or just abandoned me mid-conversation?" I said.

Warner nodded. "Normally, new human students take a special class to learn how to get along with people here. Parahumans, they have different social rules, you see. They don't have the same definitions of politeness and rudeness we do. Regular etiquette is inefficient and wasteful, so they just . . . skip it."

"They don't have manners?" I asked.

Warner took a bite of his cornbread and chewed it, looking

thoughtful. "They do, but not where curiosity, imagination, boredom, or irritation are concerned," he said. "If they want to know something, they ask. If you want to tell, tell. If you don't, don't. If someone is boring you or you want to do something else, just walk away and they won't ever take it personally. If someone walks away while you're talking, that just means they're done or they got the information they wanted."

"They don't take rudeness personally?" I said, wondering if he was setting me up for a prank of some sort.

"Watch," Warner said. He stood and walked over to a nearby table where a group of younger students was working on a project to assemble some small mechanical thing.

"What is it?" Warner asked without so much as an introduction.

"Robot hamster," a boy said without looking up.

"Which one of you has done the least work on the project?"

"Jill," two of them said at the same time.

The third student looked up from her phone just long enough to say, "Me."

"What was the last nightmare you had?" Warner said to Jill, probably because she didn't look too busy.

The girl didn't even bother to look up. "I was in an airplane, but instead of aluminum, it was made out of beef jerky, and my dog kept—"

"How did it make you feel?" Warner interrupted.

Instead of answering, the girl lifted her right hand and made a dismissive flicking motion with her fingers, like she was trying to shoo away flies without working too hard at it. I recognized the gesture. Hypatia had done it to me loads of times, as had Rubidia and a couple other students.

Warner returned to the table.

"When she did this . . . ," I said, flipping my hand in the same way.

He nodded. "They all do it. It means something like, 'Hey, I don't mean to be rude or anything but I was wondering if you could go away for a while instead of being here and interacting with me.'"

"And that's fine?" I asked.

"Oh sure!" Warner exclaimed. "You'll start doing it yourself sooner or later. They expect us to adopt their social rules, of course. Still, a lot of their rules make sense. Ever see a bunch of people laughing and wondered why? Here you can just walk up and ask them to tell you."

"And they will?"

"Unless they were talking about you, probably. It's hard to tell what will embarrass them. Sometimes they're super blunt, and sometimes—especially with emotional stuff—they get very uncomfortable."

It made so much sense. Rubidia, Majorana—they *hadn't* been acting like jerks after all.

"What about breaking things? Is blowing up the climate control—"

"It's supposed to be a more tactful way of—"

That threw me off. "Did you say *tactful*?"

Warner shook his head. "Parahumans *hate* confrontation.

They'll avoid it in any way they can. Passive aggression is like their native language."

"Seriously?" I asked skeptically. "They don't mind property damage?"

"From a parahuman point of view, the rudest thing would have been to ask them to turn the temperature down. Direct conflict is a big no-no because it makes them extra nervous. Anyone here can pretty much fix anything, so sabotage is a way of getting the point across without causing too much trouble." He sipped his drink, considering how to explain. "It's like . . . if your neighbor is running his mower at six AM on a Sunday, the *decent* thing to do is to set it on fire or hit it with a little EMP to kill the electrical system. After that, if they don't get the hint, then you have to do something extreme, like asking them nicely not to mow so early."

"None of this makes sense," I complained.

"Sure it does. When human society was evolving, we had to establish pecking orders, pick a leader, who would boss everyone around and all that, so we had to be a bit pushy with one another. Parahumans, there are only so many of them, so they had to get along and cooperate with one another at the drop of a hat. Because of that, they have different rules . . . I bet you thought you were going crazy," Warner said, grinning.

"Maybe a little," I said.

Warner was right about one thing. The parahumans' tendency to jump into conversations whenever they care to and bail out when they're done has become one of my favorite things about them. I'll never understand why the rest of the world doesn't do it. The other side of the deal can be a little harder to get used to—you can't be offended or hold it against anyone if you don't like what they were talking about, even if the conversation had been all about the things they hate most about your stupid face.

I almost emailed Majorana later to apologize for refunding her three dollars plus one cent, but then I realized something: my refund had been exactly the sort of passive aggressive response Warner said parahumans preferred. I'd accidentally expressed my annoyance in the most mature, tactful way possible.

As if to confirm this, that night when I got home there was a parcel waiting for me. It was a 650-page book entitled *Common Human Coping Mechanisms*.

A note attached said, *Earlier at Forbidden Planet I remembered the name of a song I'd been trying to recall for weeks. I went home immediately to listen to it in a dark closet. You may find this book helpful. It says many humans turn to drugs and alcohol in times of great stress. If you need help acquiring drugs and alcohol, I'll see what I can do.*

- - - - -✱- - - - -

Making friends and doing well at the School was deeply weird. It messed with my head from time to time. On the one hand, I was experiencing the best times of my life. On the other, sometimes I felt guilty, like I had no right to have fun when my dad was being held captive by the worst beings imaginable.

Sometimes I felt like a worthless, lazy bum because I wasn't working on finding a way to help him.

I started having nightmares: about the SUV in our home, Tabbabitha sneaking up on me, or not being able to stop Hypatia before she cut herself for real. Sometimes I'd have dreams in which I figured out how to locate my dad, and I'd wake up in excitement, only to have the solution evaporate once my brain was fully awake.

As time passed, I became less and less convinced that she had been in town after all. It was known that the Old Ones couldn't be disconnected from the hive mind for more than a month or so, and she hadn't struck out at anyone, which wasn't really in character for them. Besides, my dad *had* managed to get a message through the gap at one time—with his email—so it wasn't as impossible as everyone was always saying. Maybe whatever he'd done had something to do with how Tabbabitha had hijacked my bracelet. I spent hours studying Happybear's communications protocol, trying to figure out how Tabbabitha could have used it to communicate through the gap, but try as I might, I couldn't figure out what she'd done.

I had developed a few routines that helped get me through my days. Every morning, I would get up because I was anxious to learn weird new things, and also because Hypatia was standing in my room, poking me in the back of the head with a broom handle. After showering and dressing and all that, the two of us usually took the wormhole downtown for breakfast.

I would give up wormhole travel entirely if it were up to

me. It wasn't just the first trip. I always feel a little creeped out and wrong after I've come through one. Plus, they're extremely dangerous. Seems like every time I go through, I find a new way of hurting myself. The outlet is never located at the exact same height off the pavement, so that makes it very easy to trip unless you're paying close attention. Also, imagine what happens when you go through and another person is already occupying the space you'd planned to appear in. It's like the bike accident only disgusting. I don't want to talk about that anymore.

I'm going to tell you something that was a new discovery for me, something most people probably know already: having friends is nice. I saw people at my old school with friends, but I didn't like them and assumed they didn't like each other much, either. I often wondered why they bothered and how they could keep each other's personalities and dislikes straight and get along with everyone simultaneously, but once I actually tried it out, it wasn't as exhausting as I thought it might be. Breakfast was typically a large gathering of our extended social circle held at the Event Horizon. I wasn't always crazy about the company, since Ultraviolet and a couple other high-dollar genetically engineered kids who tagged along with her were there as often as not, but the place made a mean breakfast burrito, poured strong coffee, and had fast Internet.

I don't know whether it was the fact that she thought my friend had eyes for her boyfriend, because I once laughed at her getting knocked over, or because of how "rumpled"

I tended to be, but Ultraviolet always made it clear that she'd rather be associating with more appropriate types. Unfortunately, because Ultra dated Tom, and Tom was friends with Rubidia and Dirac, they tended to get stuck with us from time to time. Hypatia both hated and loved this. She got to be around Tom, but she also had to put up with Ultraviolet. Of course, she would probably pretend to have forgotten there was anyone at school named Tom if you asked her about it. Still, her admiration of Tom was a bit obvious to everyone but the two of them.

There was a kind of cold war between Ultraviolet and Hypatia and me—one fought in petty insults and strategic passive aggression. One morning we'd been up super early because our Xenopsychology teacher was into astrology and was convinced we would learn faster between 5:00 and 6:00 AM on a morning following a full moon (I don't think this is true because all I remember is Hypatia waking me up early at home and a second time in the classroom after we had been dismissed). Because of that, she and I were first to the Event Horizon that morning, which meant the job of sequestering the big patio table for our group fell to us. This was crucial, because there was a perpetual shortage of tables at the Event Horizon.

Warner turned up just as we were getting settled in and sat down at the head of the table like he owned the place, so I sat at the opposite end, with Hypatia in the middle of the long side. We made a show of having a conversation across that distance, and it was kind of funny until Warner produced a copy of the *New York Times* and started reading, which meant he was bored with that joke. After that, Hypatia set to work on an assignment, and I played a game on my phone.

Everything was perfectly fine until Ultraviolet turned up and made it weird.

She looked like she was on her way to a New Year's Eve party, not a semigreasy breakfast joint. She was wearing a long, rather tight black dress, huge chunky gold bracelets on each wrist, and a tiara. That's right, she was wearing an actual glittering golden tiara on a Wednesday morning. Who *does* that?

"Thanks for getting the table, guys!" she said as she took a seat not far from Warner on the side opposite Hypatia.

"Yep," I said, a little coolly.

Warner threw me a quizzical look over the opinion pages for that.

"I mean, great job," Ultraviolet went on. "Warner and Nikki are covering their ends, and Hypatia has that *entire* side open so she can *just happen* to move next to wherever a certain someone might sit. Good thinking."

I rolled my eyes, drumming my fingers irritatedly, and Warner made an *oh* expression before going back to his newspaper. Hypatia's face turned red, which matched the fire Ultraviolet brought out in her eyes pretty nicely.

"Look, Ultra," I said. "Could you come back and be vile later on in the day, please?"

She feigned innocence. "I was just wishing Tom would pay a little more attention to Hypatia. I know he and I are dating

260

and all, and I know I can be a little jealous, but only when there's something to be jealous about."

She winked at Hypatia. "Feel free to chat him up anytime you like. Tom is just *so sweet*, and he doesn't mind throwing a dog a bone from time to time."

By that time, I was seeing red myself and was about ready to throw my coffee in her direction. Hypatia was wincing and squirming, and her eyes were switching from red to gray and back again. I could handle verbal abuse with the best of them, but seeing someone bully a friend like that pushed every button I had.

That was when Warner (who did not even look up from his paper) said, "Ultraviolet, you don't need to be ugly like that."

Her eyes grew large, and she attempted to bore holes through his head with her glare. "*Excuse* me?"

He turned the newspaper page, revealing that he'd given each of the classy etched portraits on the page a comical expression with his pen. "I think you say terrible things to people because you believe that deep down everyone is as terrible as you are and so they deserve it, but you're wrong. You probably aren't even as terrible as *you* think you are."

She stood up so suddenly her tiara was thrown from her hair and over the railing onto the sidewalk. "Maybe *you're* a terrible person, you . . . rat-faced retail reject."

Warner glanced up at her for the first time and shrugged. "Nah. I'm awesome. Ask anyone. You, on the other hand . . . You know jewelry, makeup, and all that can only make you pretty on the outside, right?"

Ultraviolet, no longer in the mood for company, stormed away from the table. On her way to leave, she ran straight into Tom, who was knocked off balance and dropped a plate full of various fried meats onto the patio.

"My bacon!" he said in dismay.

"We're leaving!" she said.

"But . . . ," he said, collecting himself in the wake of the tragic loss of his breakfast. "My bacon."

"*Come on!*" Ultraviolet whisper-snarled, and dragged Tom through the door by his arm.

Hypatia watched them go, and then rounded on Warner. "I could have handled that, you know. I didn't need you to spring to my defense or anything."

"Sure, you could handle it, but *she* couldn't handle it," Warner said, nodding at me. "I just saved us all a lot of drama. You're welcome."

I scoffed. "Whatever. You just can't help sticking your nose where it doesn't—"

His face took on a wry grin. "Let me guess. When she showed up, you were wishing she'd sit somewhere else. When she started talking, you were chanting 'shut up *shut up*' in the back of your head, and when she got really insulting, you started thinking about throwing your coffee at her. Am I right?"

I tried to keep my expression level, despite the extreme weirdness of having someone quote the past five minutes of my inner dialogue back to me word for word.

"You're totally wrong. I wasn't thinking any of that," I said.

Warner looked surprised. "You seriously don't know you're doing it?"

"Doing *what*?" I asked, losing my patience.

"She's not doing anything I can see. Just sitting there, drumming her fingers and holding her coffee like she just changed her mind about throwing it," Hypatia said.

Warner looked to Hypatia. "Close your eyes, listen carefully, and try to remember kindergarten cryptography class."

Hypatia obliged.

I sat there watching her concentrate, forming theories about how Warner could have guessed what I was thinking. He'd been too accurate to have gotten it from body language. He was a plain human like me, so he wasn't reading my mind. Maybe he had a gadget for reading minds and was letting Hypatia try it out. That was a thought I didn't like at all. The contents of my mind were private and *not* suitable for public consumption.

As I watched, growing more and more nervous, Hypatia's expression changed. A great, wide smile grew on her face. Then she said, "Don't listen to my brain. God please don't listen to my brain, I'll die of embarrass—"

"*Stop it!*" I said. "What are you two doing? It's incredibly disrespectful!"

Hypatia opened her eyes. "You're the one doing it. It's your fingers."

"My fingers?" I looked at them. They didn't look particularly expressive to me.

"You were drumming your fingers in Morse code!" Warner said.

"I was not!" I said, still looking at my fingers.

"You're so fast I can barely keep up," Warner said, taking a tentative bite of Ultraviolet's forsaken breakfast. "Seriously, you could go back in time and be the world's greatest telegraph operator. You must have learned young."

I put my hand back on the table and drummed out Morse code for "Shut up." Instantly, I realized Warner was right. Muscle memory told me I'd been drumming that very phrase just a minute ago. "My dad taught me when I was little so I'd stop talking with my mouth full at dinner. He said I could keep talking, as long as I did it with my hands. I guess it turned into a habit somewhere."

Hypatia snickered and tapped out her own message on the table. *Dit dit dah, dit dah dit . . .*

U . . . R . . . A . . . D . . . O . . . R . . . K . . .

"Very funny, Hypatia," I said.

Warner started tapping out some rude commentary, and before long, the three of us were having a rather hilarious argument that sounded a lot like sitting inside a car during a hailstorm.

15

ALL IS FAIR IN MONKEYS AND WAR

The one class I was nervous about kept getting postponed. Every morning I would wake up and get dressed, and my tablet would show me a list of the things it reckoned I would need that day. For instance, I might need a slice of bread, a biography of Jonas Salk from my private library, and some bacteria from our bathroom, so it would put those on the list. Every day the list was different, but there was one thing that was always the same. Every day, without fail, my tablet said I'd need my gravitational disruptor pistol for Electronic Combat class. Location: TO BE DETERMINED. And every day the class would disappear from the schedule sometime during lunch with a one-line explanation like POSTPONED TILL LATER, CANCELED, or MECHA TIGER DIED. I'd started to wonder if it was a way to trick us into keeping a weapon on us at all times, in case of an attack.

Then one Tuesday, after a particularly grueling morning when I had barely passed an Exobiology exam, and when I'd been forced to listen to Ultraviolet and Tom canoodling over lunch, I didn't get the news, which means I got the news. What I'm trying to say is that Electronic Combat was not canceled.

My tablet said I was to proceed to the "orriso A besto Pr sing" building, located in the old industrial district. I guessed the name might mean something in Latin. I would need my weapon and a hair clip, if I had longer hair. I figured my brown tangle counted as "long" if not linear, so I used some of my agar bracelet to make a hair tie. That done, I headed to class.

I'd only gone a block or so before I was joined by Warner.

"First time in Electronic Combat class?" he asked.

"Yeah," I said, making sure my gravitational disruptor was fully charged. "So what's it about? Some kind of target shooting, or more like a phys ed kind of thing?"

He smiled in a way I wasn't entirely comfortable with. "That's *one* aspect of it. Just don't expect any help from me. In *this* class, I work alone."

"Um . . . okay, Mr. Lone Wolf."

As we passed through the downtown area, I found myself actually getting nervous. To combat that, I tried to find something to talk about other than the mysterious class.

"I've been meaning to ask, how often is the town destroyed?" I said.

"Huh?" Warner said, caught a little off guard.

I pointed at a building that was not a pile of rubble. "Couple

266

weeks ago, the entire downtown area was totally destroyed, and the next day it was pretty much back to normal. People weren't even surprised."

He nodded. "I've seen some pretty bad disasters, but that was the most damage I've seen since I've been here. From what I've heard, the worst was back in . . . I think it was '83. There was an elementary chemistry project that got out of hand. You know what happens when you add Mentos to Diet Coke?"

"Yeah . . . ," I said.

"Well, adding gummy worms to molten boron is like that times a hundred thousand. Anyway—most of the downtown area was either completely obliterated or mostly devastated. When they rebuilt, some of the students—your dad was one of them—designed the nanoreconstructor materials to rebuild with. They're microscopic robots that can do jobs on a really tiny scale, so the buildings could heal themselves in the future instead of needing to be repaired."

"How do you know my dad was one of them?"

He threw me a withering glare, like I was being intentionally thickheaded. "*Everyone* knows who your dad is. There is—*was*—a plaque on the courthouse commemorating the rebuild. Your dad's name was the only one on both the list of students who caused the disaster and the list of those who cleaned it up. The cannon atomized the plaque during the incident, though."

"Oh," I said, disappointed. "I'd have liked to see it."

"You'll get chances. Your dad's name is on plaques all over this town. He was the first actual human the School admitted. He showed everyone that one of us could be as smart as them, if not smarter. They still look down their noses at us a bit, though."

"I haven't noticed that."

He kicked a rock and sent it skittering down the sidewalk. "It's just their first assumption. If you're parahuman, you belong here. If you're human, you're a novelty—an exception to the rule. That's why we humans need to stick together whenever we can."

"Like the way you stick together with Ultraviolet?" I said.

He sighed. "She's not one of *us*; she's one of *her*. I like Tom, but I don't know why he bothers with her. I also think she resents that I outscore her in just about every class."

I was starting to wonder if Warner was a normal guy with a huge competitive streak or a living competitive streak that looked a lot like a guy.

Something else had been bothering me about the cannon attack. I hadn't mentioned it before, but I'd become a little more familiar with Warner and knew he wouldn't take it *too* personally.

"When the cannon started melting things, you just kind of disappeared. Where did you go?"

He stepped in my path, halting me, his arms folded. "Do you know where the cannon's power supply feed is located?"

"No," I said.

"Well, I do. It's in the tunnel system beneath the streets. Crazy stuff down there. Miniature fusion reactors, chemical and quantum fuel cells, all kinds of communications, and other infrastructure. It's a maze—and I know it all."

"Good for you?"

"The only reason that thing didn't blow up thirty seconds earlier—the reason you're still *alive*—is because I was down there sending it shutdown commands and trying to kill the power supply. Didn't you see it turning off and back on again?"

I stepped around him and started down the hill again. "Yeah, but it was malfunctioning."

"Because of me," he said, more than a little smugly.

"Hypatia and I asked the Chaperone about fifty questions about the incident, and she didn't mention you at all."

"She didn't tell anyone. I think she was covering for me. Most of the tunnel system is off-limits—we're not supposed to have access, and we're *absolutely* not supposed to know how to shut down critical defense systems. I could have gotten expelled."

"They wouldn't expel you for trying to help."

"You only think that because your last name is Kross. You're an honorary parahuman. It isn't like that for everyone."

Warner seemed determined to hold on to his sense of persecution, and I didn't have the energy to dissuade him. "It still boggles my mind that Dad kept this place from me. He was always so rotten at keeping secrets."

"He probably knew what he was doing. Lots of people go into hiding after they leave school. They try to integrate into the normal human world anonymously when they can.

The choice is either that, take up residence in a secured para-human community, or keep looking over your shoulder to make sure the Old Ones aren't creeping up on you."

"I wonder why we weren't in hiding. We never even changed our name. Heck, our number was in the phone book," I said.

Warner chuckled. "Yeah, it's in them all."

"Sorry?"

"I tried to email your dad once for a project. We were sup-posed to interview a famous parahuman for Xenosociology class, but I convinced Mr. Eichen that your dad was just as important as any parahuman. I tried to look your dad up online, and there were no social media accounts of any kind attached to him. Then I checked the phone directories, and there's a number for Melvin Kross everywhere."

"What do you mean, everywhere?" I asked.

"Every single town, village, and city in North America has a telephone number listed under the name Melvin Kross."

"Seriously?"

Warner nodded. "He never returned my calls, but I only tried four or five of his eight hundred thousand phone numbers."

"So we were hiding in plain sight. Sorry you never got the interview," I said, a bit honored that Warner looked up to my dad in much the same way I did. "So how about your par-ents?" I tried. "Are they in hiding?"

"No," Warner said. His tone said I shouldn't ask more about that particular subject.

I looked ahead. At the bottom of a long hill, down a canyon of unoccupied brick buildings, stood a rusted disaster of a factory—a hulking structure with tilting inactive smokestacks, an arched metal roof, and huge sliding doors that I assumed were broken because of their slightly off-kilter angles. A long and inconsistent barbed-wire fence that ran around the perimeter was decorated with cheerful metal signs that said things like BIOHAZARD, DO NOT ENTER and FEDERAL LAW PROHIBITS ACCESS WITHOUT PERSONAL PROTECTIVE EQUIPMENT.

I said, "That's not—"

"That *is*," Warner said.

At least the name finally made sense. It hadn't always been the "orriso A besto Pr sing" building. Those were just the letters that hadn't fallen off the side of the building yet. According to the faded paint where the missing letters had once hung, the full name had been Morrison Asbestos Processing.

Inside the factory was an expansive concrete floor, a ceiling that must have been a hundred feet high, various rusted metal drums, dangerous-looking machinery, and rickety catwalks running here and there. The place was well-lit in the center but dark and foreboding at the edges near the walls. I couldn't shake the idea that the whole thing might collapse if someone kicked the wrong beam.

"Good luck," Warner said as he walked off on his own and sat atop a rusty oil drum just outside the circle of students.

The class had few other recognizable faces. My pal Ultraviolet was in attendance but without Tom, thank goodness. She was always more obnoxious when he was around. Bob was also there, looking twitchy and nervous. And I recognized Percival, the seven-foot-tall bearded satellite designer Hypatia had pointed out to me the day I arrived. I decided to stand near him —I figured he would be good to have on my side if actual combat was going to happen. He'd make a good meat shield, in any case.

After a few minutes, a metal door opened and Ms. Botfly emerged, wearing what looked like a bulletproof vest and only one extra pair of glasses atop her head.

"Class," she began as she wandered distractedly toward us, "we have a new student. This is Miss Nikola Kross, and she is a *girl*." She winked at me as she said this, which led to a few confused glances in my direction. I mastered the urge to hide behind Percival and waved at everyone instead.

"Now everyone say your name and something interesting about yourself so we can all get to know one another."

All twenty students said their names and something interesting about themselves simultaneously, so I learned nothing, except maybe that Percival either has a pet chinchilla or doesn't know how to pronounce *quesadilla*.

"Wasn't that nice? The purpose of this class is simple, Nikola. The entire parahuman community and all humans associated with us are under threat from a variety of sources. Most notably, we have been at war with the Old Ones for thousands of years. The Old Ones seek to terrify, capture, or kill us. We are hunted wherever we go and must be able to defend ourselves at all times. Communities like the School can protect us from them, but you must be prepared for attack if you ever wish to travel or live outside a protected parahuman community. Other classes help you understand the Old Ones. Some teach how to avoid them. In this class you learn to fight them off and escape when all else fails."

I noticed her accent had changed a bit. When we'd first met, she had sounded vaguely Germanic, but she was now sounding a bit like a British person who spent a lot of time in New York City.

Ms. Botfly took a tiny bite out of her thumbnail, surveyed the result, and continued, "It's an unpleasant truth, but the day *will* come when you will be confronted by an Old One or one of their minions. My class will ensure you are proficient with common weapons and tactics shown to be effective, that you possess the right instincts regarding what to do and when to do it, as well as the physical ability to put those tactics into action."

She kicked a large plastic tub. Objects inside it rattled and settled against one another. "I have a bin here of gravitational disruptors. In honor of our new student's weapon of choice, we will all be using disruptors today. Your assignment"—she checked a notebook—"howler killer monkeys! Courtesy of our friends in Creative Robotics. You, the blue one, you're in that class, aren't you? Any tips for defeating them?"

Bob looked truly afraid. "Ma'am, they're *not* ready to work with. Most of them are overpowered, and a couple exploded when they—"

"Okay!" interrupted Ms. Botfly. "So we can count on

a few of our targets to explode. Use that to your advantage. Remember to strike in teams, use cover, and move under covering fire. These machines learn and communicate among themselves, so change tactics as you go, and don't forget to cover your behind and keep an eye out above you. They're quick little devils. The disruptors have a wide angle of effect, so you don't have to be a crack shot, but be careful of friendly fire, please. I'll be in the bubble if anyone needs me, and as always, paramedics are standing by. Bonus points go to the last surviving student, or, if we have more than one, the student with the most kills. Good luck!"

With that, Miss Botfly sat in a comfortable-looking chair in the center of the floor, pressed a button on the arm, and was encircled with an iridescent blue sphere, which must have provided some kind of protection. The students rushed the bin in the center of the floor, fighting over the best disruptors. Some looked like they had seen better days. Thankfully I didn't need to worry about that since I had my own. Once everyone was ready, Ms. Botfly pressed a button, a loud horn sounded from somewhere in the gloom, and the monkeys were released.

We didn't see them at first, but from the clattering noises and insane shrieks echoing through the building, it sounded like they were everywhere. At first, everyone kind of stood around the weapons bin, but eventually someone said, "Uh, shouldn't we take cover?" And the entire class kind of wandered into a spot behind a low metal wall near the office. I could hear the hooting growing closer now. In the distance, I spied a figure vaulting acrobatically from one cat-walk to another.

Bob was nearby, and I tapped him on the shoulder. "Are they armed with anything?"

"Well, they have a kind of explosive charge—not very powerful for class purposes, but they're still bad. They make a lot of noise. That's the worst part."

There was a clattering directly over us, and to my surprise, it was little blue Bob who snapped his weapon vertically and fired the first shot—before I'd even processed the idea that there was something to shoot *at*. Given Bob's ability to see a little forward in time, there might not have been something to shoot at until after he shot, of course.

The gravitational disruptor emitted a strange *BLOOP* sound and made a path through the air that looked a bit like something falling upward through water. Everything went swimmy, and I was able to look up in time to see the beam strike something mechanical that must have been hanging from an overhead pipe. Whatever it was crashed into the ceiling and returned to the concrete floor in the form of spare parts. I did not like the look of what landed: a clawed hand and a rather vicious-looking metallic monkey's head with some kind of circular thing in its mouth that could have been a speaker.

Ms. Botfly's voice spoke through a loudspeaker: "One point for BIIIIG BLUUUUUUE."

Percival, my first choice for partner, had reacted to all this by crouching down as low as he could, covering his neck, and sidling behind Ultraviolet VanHorne. She looked at him in disgust and then stared off into the darkness, waiting for her own target.

What I was seeing, I decided, was stupidity. Here we were, several students against some kind of extremely agile enemy armed with explosives, and the approach was to stand in a small clump, waiting for them to take us out as a group? I had decided to break off from the rest when I noticed Warner slipping off on his own, without a partner. He pulled open a heavy metal door labeled ACCESS and walked in.

A student tried to join him, but Warner shook his head. "I work alone," was all he said. More cowardice, I decided.

"Bob," I said, "you're my partner now."

"Oh, ah, okay?" he said.

"Isn't it a bit daffy for us all to be here in one spot waiting for them? Shouldn't we spread out?"

"Uh, yeah," he said, apparently surprised that someone was talking to him. "I was thinking the overhead crane booth would be a good vantage point." He pointed up. Sure enough, there was an orange metal box a crane operator would stand in. We could see the whole facility from up there.

"There are monkeys afoot. Should we really be climbing up? That's kind of their territory," I said.

"They look for heat, noise, and mass. Both of us are smaller, and I think we can manage to be quiet."

"Okay, let's roll," I said, jogging to a metal staircase not far off.

A few of the other students watched us go, but none of

them followed. Maybe they didn't feel like climbing stairs. The catwalk level had a wider view, but seeing into the gloom was harder than I had thought. I didn't see any monkeys yet but heard a couple shots fired below. I was right—they were targeting the larger group first.

Then I saw them—a large group of monkey-shaped robots was organized into ranks behind a huge rusty drum. My best guess was that the bots were modeled on slightly larger and bulkier gibbons. They might have looked like animals, but they behaved like soldiers. They were saluting a larger monkey, which was standing atop the drum, gesturing proudly. One of the "soldiers" leaped up next to him and appeared to argue about something. At least, that was what he was doing until his head was detached and sent flying across the room by a crack shot from the main group.

"One point for . . . Ultraviolet," Ms. Botfly said, "my favorite color."

"I could hit the lot of them from here," I said.

"No. They're still too far—the beam takes a second or two to get where it's going. They could dodge the shot and then they'd be after us."

Another monkey—probably a scout—climbed a chain hanging from the ceiling and mounted a catwalk opposite us. Bob and I took aim at it, but we were too slow. Another shot came a second before I could fire.

Warner had appeared from nowhere and had scored a direct hit, but instead of being blasted across the room away from him, the monkey did the opposite. It was as if Warner had ensnared it with an invisible lasso and jerked it with infinite force back toward where he was standing. It landed right at his feet, either broken or stunned. Warner leaned down calmly, grabbed the monkey by an ankle, and dragged it back into the shadows.

"He must have reversed his disruptor," Bob said. "Can't see how that would be an advantage—you really don't want one at close range."

The monkey general, as I had taken to thinking about him, hooted angrily and sent his troops into action. They sprang atop their cover, produced smallish metallic capsules, and hurled them toward the students. The capsules flew toward either side of the low wall where they were hiding. Instantly, I saw it was a trick. As soon as the students saw a threat coming, they would instinctively dive to the right or left, which would land them right in the line of fire.

It worked perfectly. The students dived and the capsules hit the ground all around them and exploded with a weird *glomph* noise, spraying out a thin layer of . . . something pink. In a single attack, half the students were coated head to toe in sticky pink goop.

"Death paint," said Bob, in answer to the question I was about to ask. "They're out."

The remaining students scrambled for new cover, and the monkeys divided into three teams, moving almost too fast to be seen through dim canyons of rusted metal and industrial machinery. The first group ran right below us. I had a perfect shot. Taking careful aim, I fired, my disruptor said *BLOOP*, and the entire team was instantly smashed against the floor.

"Nikola the newbie!" Ms. Botfly exclaimed. "Six points in one shot! Well done."

"Wow," said Bob. It occurred to me that he must have let me take the shot, since he probably saw it coming a few seconds before it happened.

I had started to thank him when a monkey leaped up from below and landed just behind me on the catwalk. I turned to blast it, but before I could, it opened its mouth.

A blue light came on in its mouth, and it shrieked, "AAAAH-AAAAAAAAAAAAAH."

Shriek isn't the right word, really. It wasn't a blast like the sonic cannon, more like a torrent of mind-erasing noise that struck all at once. I suddenly experienced the worst migraine ever. I could have shot it at point-blank range, but because of the pain and disorientation, I couldn't open my eyes or even point my arm at it. Bob collapsed, and I stumbled backward, almost tripping over him as I retreated. Several paces from the monkey, I was able to think a little more clearly. I raised my weapon and took aim. Before I could act, there came a loud *BLOOP* noise, and the shrieking monkey was completely obliterated by a disruptor shot from below. This might have been wonderful news had Bob not been close enough to catch almost all the force from the blast, which seemed to spread outward from where it hit the monkey. It threw his still-conscious body sideways down the clattering catwalk in my direction.

He said, and I quote, "AaaahAAAEEEEAAAYA!"

My oh-so-intelligent response was: "I'll catch you!"

So that's what I tried doing. I tried stopping his body by putting mine in front of it.

Let's work out the math on this one: Bob was moving at around fifteen meters per second and weighed about sixty kilograms, whereas I was moving at zero meters per second and weighed about fifty kilos.

If you came up with: I failed to stop or even to slow him down much at all, and was instead knocked violently backward off the side of the rickety catwalk, then give yourself one point.

I hate falling. I do a lot of falling and have never gotten used to it. But falling from about a hundred feet in the air in a building with a hard concrete floor and rusty metal junk all over the place is a special kind of unpleasant. As we spun, I saw we were plummeting into a huge metallic cauldron of some sort. I hoped they had bothered to remove whatever chemicals it had held before turning the factory into a classroom.

I screamed something unintelligible, and Bob gave me a hug.

I appreciated the sentiment, but the situation didn't exactly call for a warm embrace, and frankly, it was a bit creepy. Still, I prefer not to evaluate socially awkward gestures while in free fall, so I decided to think it over after I was dead.

"*Grab the ceiling* on our way *back up!*" Bob shouted into my ear.

I had no idea what he meant, but a second later, it made

sense. Just as we tumbled wildly into the vat, he fired a single shot from his disruptor into the bottom. Instead of spreading upon impact in all directions like the disruptor shots normally did, this time the blast seemed to echo outward against the sides of the container and back in again. It was like how a drop of water falling into a cup causes another smaller drop to leap back out of the surface it hits. That rebounding drop, perfectly timed, rose to meet our falling bodies. We slowed in midair and were rising again, except at a rather more terrifying speed. We flew up and stopped just beneath the ceiling, where I was able to get a tenuous grip on one of the metal poles that ran along the building's roof.

"ACROBATICS!" called Ms. Botfly from the comfort of her floating La-Z-Boy. "Three more points for the new kid and BIIIIG BLOOOOOOOOO!"

I might have taken some satisfaction in the fact that I was doing well in class were I not dangling from a rusty metal pole 120 feet in the air. We hung there for a second longer before Bob was able to get his own grip on the ceiling, which took a lot of weight off my hands. This improved our situation but did not fix it. The next step was to make our way, monkey-bars style, to a ladder that was about twenty feet away. I always hated that part of gym class.

As we swung along bar by bar, I listened to the action below us, hoping whatever was happening down there could hold the monkeys' attention enough for us to get to safety. There was a huge crash, louder than any we had heard before. Ms. Botfly spoke up a second later: "Aaaand three for the kid who reminds me of my cousin Alberto!" Another crash. "The kid who reminds me of my cousin Alberto is no longer with us!"

The ladder was just a few swings away. I had to hurry. Bob was right behind me, and I could tell from the sound of his breathing that he was barely holding on. I watched as a monkey vaulted a storage tank and flew shrieking through the air toward Ultraviolet. She saw it coming, took aim, and waited until it was immediately above her before firing.

"One more for Ultraviolet!" Ms. Botfly gushed.

The shot was timed to send the monkey's metallic corpse rocketing upward, a move I did not understand at first, until I realized it was headed straight for Bob and me.

Bob saw it, too, but was only able to say "Ultraviolet, you little b—" before the monkey hit him with full force and the two of them toppled into the darkness below.

Ultraviolet stepped out from her cover and gave me a wink and a curtsy, as if to say, *You bet I meant to do that.*

The gesture didn't make me as angry as it would have if a monkey had not stepped out from behind her at that exact moment, curtsied right along with her, and said, "*Aaah-Aaaaaaaaaaaaaaaah!*"

Instantly paralyzed in agony, she collapsed to the floor, where the monkey bent over her face and continued to serenade her as he withdrew a small brown metallic pellet from behind his back and placed it gently on her chest.

The pink explosion was made even more satisfying by Ms.

Botfly, who called out, "Ultraviolet is down! Minus one point for hubris!"

I grasped the ladder, nearly slipped, but managed to get my feet under me. I climbed down as fast as I could, dropped to my feet when I was low enough, and ran to the area between the vat and the rusty wall I'd just decended, where Bob must have fallen. I found nothing, no broken blue body, no puddle of blue blood, or red blood for that matter. I decided to believe he was safe. We couldn't have been the first students to fall in the factory.

I took cover in a corner, where I was able to pick off five more monkeys in relative peace before the main force of them became aware of my presence and chased me out with a hail of their little brown goo pellets.

The only remaining cover available was a low concrete wall, roughly in the middle of the building. I ran for it, vaulted it, and landed right next to four other students, all of whom looked as frightened as I was.

The monkeys had herded us to a single point. "This can't be good," I said.

It wasn't.

It then became clear just how organized the monkey army was. All around us, the metallic simians rose. They stood openly in a huge circle around our pitiful cover, each with a pellet in its hand. The game was over, and they were offering us an opportunity to surrender instead of drowning in a flood of pink goo.

I decided to go out fighting, in memory of Bob. But as soon as I raised my weapon, something bizarre happened.

The remaining monkeys dropped their grenades and raised their paws at once. An unmistakable gesture of surrender. They opened their mouths, and I braced for their screech, but instead they spoke a single sentence at normal volume.

"The monkey army wishes to surrender to the undefeated Warner Goss." Then they exploded. All of them.

- - - - - ✳ - - - - -

After the lesson was over and the scores were tallied, I finished in second place, which was "not bad for a newbie," according to Ms. Botfly. I *had* been in the lead until Warner killed the remaining twenty-one monkeys in a single blow by hacking their communications system using parts from the one he'd snatched.

Ultraviolet, who came in third and believed she should have at least come in second, didn't think it was fair. "He didn't engage in actual combat. He just grabbed one and slunk off by himself. Any one of us could have done that."

"This is true," Ms. Botfly said. "Any one of you *could* have done the same thing, but he's the only one who *did*. His strategy wasn't strictly against the rules, and 'technically legal' is the best kind of legal, as far as I'm concerned. Besides, you did very well and there's no need to cry about it like a big whiny baby."

To the class, she said, "Your assignment for next week is to familiarize yourselves with magnetic induction beams and the hunting behavior of peregrine falcons. A falcon can dive at almost 250 miles an hour, so get a good night's sleep before class. You'll need your reflexes."

I wished I had a camera to capture Ultraviolet's reaction to the "big whiny baby" comment. Then I remembered my tablet had a camera, so I snapped one and sent it to Hypatia. To be honest, I was pretty pleased to come in second, and disabling the monkeys as a group struck me as completely valid and strategically brilliant. That was until Warner caught my eye and made an L on his forehead with his thumb and forefinger. Then he winked.

I hate it when cheaters get all smug.

16

UNDER THE WEATHER

'd only gotten about half a block from the building when Warner jogged up alongside me, wearing a self-satisfied smile I could not have mustered by winning all the Nobel Prizes on the same day.

"Pretty impressive, huh?" he asked.

"I suppose it was. Especially if you're impressed by cheating."

"Being a superior tactician means being accused of cheating, so I'm used to that," Warner said. "You should probably get used to being the second-best human on campus."

I put a hand on his shoulder. "Son, I'm not going to be the second-best *anything*." I wasn't sure why I felt like talking tough like that. Gloating brings out my inner pro wrestler, I guess.

At that moment, Bob joined us, looking winded and confused.

I swept him into a giant hug. "*Bob!* You're alive! I thought you were a goner for sure!"

This left him more confused and temporarily unable to speak.

Warner chuckled, "Everything in there is coated with intelligent impact compound. If someone takes a hit, it catches them. I've fallen plenty of times—it hurts but doesn't even leave a bruise. You really think if a student died in a class session that Ms. Botfly would just go over our grades and talk about next week's assignment?"

"Um," I said, blushing a little. "Actually, I could imagine that. People here are pretty casual when it comes to mortal danger."

Warner shrugged.

"So where do they put you when you die? The sewer?" I asked Bob.

"No," Warner said, returning to his arrogant know-it-all tone. "You go to the afterlife, a little room in the basement with juice and cookies. You get checked to make sure you didn't break anything, and there's a video feed of the action so you can take notes about what you did wrong. What made you think he was in the sewer?"

"No reason," I said. The truth was that Bob was smelling pretty rank, but I didn't want to call him out on a personal hygiene issue with someone else around. Besides, maybe it was a thing with parahumans that some of them smell bad when they get flustered.

Bob *was* looking pretty flustered. "I don't feel so great, to tell you the truth."

"Did you get hurt when you fell?" I asked.

He shook his head and rubbed his eyes with the heels of his palms. "No, I keep seeing things that are going to happen."

"Isn't that normal for you?" Warner asked. "Do you need to go to the hospital?"

"No," Bob said. "I don't know, maybe. But I see myself doing things I'd never do."

"Like what?" I asked.

Bob didn't answer. Instead he dropped his backpack, stumbled on the concrete, and nearly fell down. Luckily, Warner was able to catch his arm. "You're really pale, man," he said. "Let's get you to the doctor."

Bob mumbled something I couldn't understand.

"What did you say?" I asked.

A small group of students across the street saw something was wrong and were coming over.

I pointed directly at one. "No rubbernecking. Get a doctor—call for help. Now!" I snapped.

"Get away," Bob said, sounding as if he was about to vomit.

Warner frowned as he laid Bob down on the sidewalk. "Nikola was right—you smell awful. Did you kick a skunk or something?"

Bob took several deep breaths as if trying to calm his gag

reflex. He pulled his backpack closer and started rummaging inside it.

"What do you need? Do you have medicine in there?" I asked.

And then all at once, Bob seemed to relax. He took a long, calming breath, looked up at me, and smiled. Inside his bag, an electronic gadget chirped and an electronic woman's voice said, "Unauthorized access. High power mode is prohibited on school grounds."

"What are you doing?" Warner asked him, reaching for the bag.

But I knew. I'd heard that chirp when I'd powered on my own gravitational disruptor at the start of class. Bob sneered a toothy grin at us as a fresh wave of stench hit me and removed the last doubt I had.

----- ✳ -----

My first problem was a question of position and strategy. Warner and I were standing immediately above someone who had become a threat—not a good position to be in. I knew and Warner didn't. If I dropped to the sidewalk he could still hit Warner, but if I tackled Warner, who was downhill from me, we'd both go tumbling farther down the hill, giving Bob the high ground.

So I spun, ducking as I slipped my backpack from my shoulders, and hit Warner square in the face with it before dropping and rolling sideways out into the street.

It worked. Warner went over backward like a sack of potatoes and was tumbling down the slope, clubbing his head against the concrete with savage force. I winced, hoping the School's medical abilities were as good as I'd been led to believe—Warner was going to need it.

There was a split second of doubt when I wondered if I'd seriously injured Warner for no reason, but then Bob produced the gravitational disruptor and fired one shot just where my head had been and a second where Warner had stood. The shots rippled angrily through the air and ground along the brick wall above me, leaving behind a gash at least a foot wide. Chunks of masonry rained all around. My backpack had come to rest just outside my reach, so I heaved backward and plunged my left hand inside to retrieve my own disruptor. The sound of footsteps and screaming told me the students across the street had changed their minds about helping.

Bob was on his feet. I hadn't seen him stand up. He was just standing where less than two seconds ago he'd been lying helpless on the sidewalk. He shot the bag with my hand in it. Instant, blinding pain flooded my senses, and a glance to my left proved to be a bad idea. My arm was bent downward at an unnatural angle and ran to the center of a small crater in the concrete where my bag, forearm, and hand had all been flattened. Imagine someone dropped a small invisible wrecking ball on the street from a hundred feet up—that was what it looked like.

"No," Bob said in a high, feminine voice. "No toys for you."

The pain disappeared in a flood of adrenaline. Sometimes being in shock has a good side. "Hey, Tabbabitha," I said. "Long time no smell."

She shot my arm again. I heard concrete and bone crack, and another sound that drowned them out—my own screaming. The pain returned and flooded every part of my body. Writhing on the pavement, I rolled on my side. Maybe if I could reach it with my other arm . . .

Tabbabitha rolled Bob's head around on his shoulders, stretching his neck. "Always with the stink jokes. You people think that bothers us? I think you don't like the smell because it's so biological. Reminds you you're only made of meat. Filthy, *temporary* meat."

Curled into a fetal position on my left side, I clawed a broken chunk of asphalt and pulled my body over just a little more. I could see my hand in the open mouth of my backpack clutching an assortment of plastic shards and circuitry that had once been my disruptor. I don't want to describe what it looked like in there. Let's just say my bag was ruined. Worse, my disruptor was useless. I wondered if I should worry that I could see but not feel my hand anymore.

"This kid was a challenge," she went on. "Parahumans are usually a bit tougher, but this little guy really put up a fight. I had to fry a lot of brain cells to get my point across."

My agar bracelet! I took a moment to compose my thoughts and focused on making it slip off my wrist and over Bob's body to restrain him until help arrived.

But nothing happened. I tried again, nothing. I couldn't

feel it, not like I normally could. It felt like normal, dead plastic. It was just like when Tabbabitha was trying to hurt Hypatia, like I was disconnected . . .

"You're pretty good with that stuff aren't you?" Tabbabitha asked.

"What stuff?"

Bob, or, Tabbabitha, leaned forward and grinned menacingly. "What do you guys call it? Agar? I know a few tricks, too, you know. I'm not too great at moving it, but I know the moment you try, and well, give it another shot . . . I'll wait. Go ahead!"

I tried to concentrate again. Whenever I worked with the agar, there was a feeling to it, like I could tell where it was and what it was doing, even if I wasn't watching. But that feeling disappeared like smoke in the wind as soon as I tried to make it work. Tabbabitha was disrupting it somehow. I tried a low-tech approach.

"*Get out of his head,*" I snarled, hurling a chunk of asphalt at my friend's face with my good hand.

Tabbabitha dodged the rock like someone had told her it was coming the day before. "Listen to me and I'll let him live. He might even make a full recovery. I wanted to continue our discussion from before. About you joining me for a few projects. Here's the deal. You and I skip town, have a nice trip to my place, you can reunite with your father, and we can finally get some work done. We can even pretend none of this unpleasantness ever happened."

"So help you or you'll kill Bob? You'd just kill him anyway.

I won't let you make me into some kind of bargaining chip to get my dad to play along with you."

Tabbabitha stepped over me and onto my ruined hand, squatting down in the crater she'd made in the concrete. I did my best not to scream in pain and only whimpered angrily. The way she stared out of Bob's eyes and into mine was appalling in a way I'll never be able to describe. "You got it backward, sweetie. Your pop is our bargaining chip to get *you* to play along. We want you alive because you're *special*. You're the one causing all the trouble. This kid, however . . ."

She lifted the pistol to Bob's head and winked. "I've been working on this for a lot longer than you can imagine. Don't make me kill him, please. It's comfortable in here."

She took my dad—because of me? It didn't make sense. There was nothing special about me. Tabbabitha was seriously misinformed, crazy, or both. Suddenly, I was furious—I wasn't going to let her blame me for her actions. "I'm not special! Why do you think I am? I'm no more or less clever than anyone here! At least, not any better than, like, ninety-five percent of the people here. The boy you're talking through can see forward in time. I can't do that."

She smiled, and her voice took on a sweet, pleading quality. "You are special in your own apelike way. It's a really long story, and I'd rather show than tell. Shall we?" She leaned in and closed her eyes as if hearing some really lovely music, and I felt the air vibrate faintly. It was like there was a breeze in the air that couldn't decide which way to blow. "I left you use of your legs, and your arm doesn't even hurt anymore.

You want to stand up and go back to that building down there. You want to come home with me. Your dad misses you, and mine misses me."

I didn't want to think of whatever monstrosity called Tabbabitha his daughter. "I'd rather not."

She shook Bob's head, grabbed my chin in his hand, and made eye contact. "You want to come with me." There was something in her voice, something that smelled nice underneath all that stink. It pulled at me in a way I was familiar with. The air all around me seemed to vibrate in a really pleasant, lovely way, and I found myself wanting things I didn't want just a second before.

Imagine you just got a brand-new video game. You've been waiting for months for it, and you finally have it. It's in your house, sitting next to the computer or console, and all you have to do is click a few buttons and you can play it. But you have homework or chores and you can't. Tabbabitha was telling me I *could* have what I wanted. I just had to let her give it to me. And it would be *so easy* to just let go and leave it to her. She could handle things . . .

But there was something else, part of me that knew it was a lie. It was like a voice in my head that screamed in rage every time she made me believe something that wasn't true. A fresh wave of nausea and vertigo passed over me, and the struggle was over.

She smiled Bob's mouth at me, and I wondered if she knew how little effect she was having.

With all my might, I forced myself to smile placidly. "Where are we going?" I asked.

She popped right up. "I *told* you, silly. We're going to my place. I have a door all set up down there," she said, pointing down at the "orriso A besto Pr sing" building. "We're going to have *so* much fun. I can't wait!"

Keep her talking, learn what you can, I thought. "But where is your place? Is it far? I can't wait to see it!"

She stashed her disruptor in Bob's back pocket and lifted me to my feet. The pain from my arm flooded my entire body again, and the world swam with blackness. My head buzzed, and the ground seemed to vibrate under my feet. *She told me it didn't hurt. I can't show it.*

Tabbabitha was tugging my good arm, leading me down the hill. Her touch, even through Bob's hand, was almost unbearable. It was cold and wrong and disgusting. It was everything bad and perverse that had ever existed formed into a single hand on my arm. "It'll just take a moment, and we'll be there. Wormholes out of this place are easy. Getting in was the trick. We should hurry. Come on!"

I shook my head to fight off the blackness. I knew I'd pass out the moment I stopped concentrating on keeping myself moving.

"I bet you like it cold. You must live in Antarctica."

"It's a nice place to visit," she said conversationally, "but I'd never live there. Too remote, too cold, nobody good to eat."

That caught me off guard. "You eat . . . people?"

"Nah, just their hopes, dreams, anger, fear, and love. It's hard to explain. I can show you how it works later, 'kay?"

"Okay!" I said. It must be somewhere near human habitation with a more temperate climate. Wasn't really narrowing things down. I was barely keeping it together—my stomach churned, and the buzzing in my head had become a low, constant drone. Everything grew dark. I didn't have much longer before I had to act or faint from the pain in my arm. "What kind of food do they like there? I like Chinese and Mexican food a lot."

"I can arrange whatever you like, but delivery can get a little bit tricky that far under—"

A thrumming black fist screamed out of the sky and slammed into Bob's body from behind. His hand was ripped from my arm, and I watched helplessly as his form was dragged shrieking into the air inside a massive cloud of angry bees. Moving with a speed I didn't think possible for insects, they carried him down the hill and then upward.

Somewhere inside the black cloud, Tabbabitha was screaming. I could see her thrashing about, batting at the little monsters as they stung Bob's body again and again. Suddenly, she fell silent. A moment later, it was Bob's voice that was screaming.

My mind reeled in frustration and fury—Bob hadn't done anything wrong. *He didn't need to die.* I had to do something.

Just then a brilliant column of light rose from somewhere below. Immediately beneath where the cloud of bees were doing their work, I saw Warner lying broken in the gutter with his own disruptor trained skyward. His single shot rose and hit the cloud of bees dead center. The bees were scattered in all directions, and Bob's body fell. No—he wasn't falling. He was being *pulled* down. *Warner's reversed disruptor.* Cursing Warner and his stupid tricks, I knew for a second that Bob was doomed. But then I realized: Tabbabitha had left—I could *feel* it. I tore the agar bracelet from my ruined arm and threw it down the hill. It was a wheel—no—a glider, heavy, *fast—it needs to be faster.* Something flashed in my memory—a peregrine falcon can dive at 250 miles an hour— faster than a falling body. I saw it change and swoop down the hill, felt it make contact with Bob's body. The agar enveloped him completely and expanded—inflated and . . . bounced. It sailed down the hill at immense speed like an enormous bowling ball, bouncing and careening off buildings before finally coming to a rest gently alongside the barbed-wire fence. The world around me swam and my vision dimmed. Somewhere in the distance, a tiny voice said, "What wazzz thzzzat?"

I took a seat on the hill and let myself rest.

17

KNOWLEDGE AND BELIEF

There was hot breath on my face. Something tickled the inside of my nostrils . . . pimento loaf?

"We might have to start charging you for these visits."

"What?" I said.

My arm, my everything still hurt—but not in the same way. It was distant, like hearing someone tell me about the pain rather than experiencing it myself. I smelled . . . salami? I opened my eyes, and Dr. Plaskington's nose was about a quarter inch from my own.

"Gah!" I said, sitting up. Doing this caused my arm to move and gave me such a jolt of real, actual pain that I had to lie back down again.

"What happened?" Dr. Plaskington said. "Tell me everything."

"Is Bob alive? How about Warner? Are they okay?" I asked.

Dr. Plaskington nodded. "Somehow, yes. All of you survived. Now, tell me what happened."

I sat up again, attempting to ignore the pain in my arm. "She's here somewhere. She had Bob, but she let him go because the bees hurt her. Chaperone!"

A vague buzz sounded from nowhere in the room. "Yes?" the Chaperone said.

"What's under the . . . the building where we have Electronic Combat class? Could someone get into the room where they take fallen students without being detected?"

"An access portal connects the recovery room, which students call the afterlife to—"

"Chaperone!" barked Dr. Plaskington. "Go away. You and I can talk later."

"Very well," the Chaperone said, and was gone with the same buzz.

Dr. Plaskington focused back on me, not looking anywhere near as cheerful and dotty as I remembered. "You were about to tell me what happened in the industrial district this morning."

"Didn't the Chaperone tell you? I thought she sees everything that happens in town."

"That particular section of our fair school is one of her few blind spots. Because the industrial zone is not of much use for classes or housing, small portions of it are unmonitored."

"But the bees—"

"The bees responded to a distress call from a student who saw Bob Flobogashtimann discharge an illegally modified gravitational disruptor at your head. Did you make him angry?"

"No!" I said. "Tabbabitha got to him. She told him to do it—she was controlling him somehow."

Dr. Plaskington was confused. "Tabbab—you mean the Old One you claim accosted you before your father was taken? The one you and Hypatia believe was talking to you through a wristwatch?"

Claim? She hadn't used that word before.

"Yes, that one! She's here. Somewhere," I said, scanning the room. I took a deep sniff and smelled only disinfectant and a faint trace of Dr. Plaskington's breath.

"Pull the other leg! That is simply not a possibility."

"Listen, lady," I said. "I heard her voice coming out of Bob. I *smelled* her. She was there, or close by. I know it. There's no way she could have—"

"It's not possible. Not a single unauthorized atom has entered school grounds from any direction at any point in our history. The gap has been in constant operation for just over forty-nine years and has never failed once."

"But when the sonic cannon—"

"The sonic cannon disrupted the shield briefly, but at no point did it fail. During that time, you could not have passed so much as a molecule through without it being destroyed. I do not speak on faith. I am a woman of science and have confirmed this conclusion repeatedly with the Chaperone and our best teachers. Not only do they agree that the gap did not fail, but not one of them has been able to come up with a scenario where something could have passed through the gap apart from our turning it off altogether."

"Listen," I said. "Maybe it didn't fail. I don't know. But she's here—I know that. She *talked* to me through Bob. She was about to tell me where they were keeping my father when your stupid psychopathic bees came in and—"

"From what I understand, those *stupid bees* saved your life. Bob was about to—"

"*Tabbabitha* thought she was taking me back to wherever their hideout or lair or whatever was. But the bees went into terminator mode, and now all I know is that my dad is *underground* somewhere."

Dr. Plaskington shook her head, an expression of pity on her face. "I should have anticipated this. You've been through so much in such a short amount of time . . . No wonder you're seeing the Old Ones around every corner. Are you having other symptoms? Memory loss or unexplained gaps in time?"

I had some opinions I wanted to share, but Dr. Plaskington held up a hand to silence me, and it was obvious nothing I could say would make a difference.

"The past few weeks have been difficult for me as well," she said. "I have been answering calls from parents and staff members nonstop since the accident with the sonic cannon, and all of them at least suspect the Old Ones are skulking around somewhere in my town. Fortunately, things can calm down now that we know who was responsible."

"You know who was responsible for the cannon? Who was— You don't mean Bob?"

"Who else? He was unaccounted for at times before the incident occurred, and he's shown both the inclination and the willingness to commit violence. He is confined to detention and shall be referred to the authorities once our investigation is complete."

"Lady, for a smart person you sure can be a real dumbass. It wasn't Bob! He wouldn't hurt a fly!"

She stood angrily. "*Young lady!* In my day we did not speak to our elders in that manner!"

"Because in *your day* you had to do it by carrier pigeon!"

Her face was turning red. "This discussion is over. I think you ought to take some time to consider whether you wish to continue your education at this institution. If you decide you wish to do so, then perhaps an apology will be in order. Within forty-eight hours, I should think."

I might have said something else, but she stormed from the room.

-----*-----

"Wow! What was her problem?" Hypatia said, peeking in the door.

I'd never been so glad to see anyone. "Thank god, Hypatia!

They think Bob sabotaged the cannon. They think he attacked me after class—it's awful!"

"I heard! Are you okay?"

I glanced at the arm that had been turned into pulp that morning and found a white arm-shaped plastic case where it should have been. A digital readout on the surface said 86% COMPLETE.

"Looks like I'm almost there."

"Warner emailed me after class and told me everything. Why would Bob attack you?"

"*It wasn't Bob!* Do you think he could sabotage the sonic cannon?"

"Well, he did fail remedial hacking."

I nodded furiously, since I couldn't talk with both hands. "See? It was Tabbabitha! I'm telling you, Hypatia, I *heard* her voice. I *smelled* her. She was *inside* him somehow—it was much deeper than with you, like she'd taken him over. And she stopped me from using my agar."

"Yeah, they can do that."

"What? They can? Why didn't anyone tell me?"

Hypatia pulled the stool back to the bed and sat down. "Nikola, there's a lot you don't know about them. We have a two-year required class on the Old Ones that every student has to take. You just got here. They can disrupt brain patterns—that's what the smell is. But controlling Bob . . . They can do that, sure, but I doubt—"

"What? Why is it so impossible that Tabbabitha was controlling Bob?"

"Because the Old Ones initiate control using some kind of quantum entanglement. Unlimited range, but that kind of thing can't pass through the gap."

I pointed at Hypatia with my good arm in emphasis, which made her jump a bit. "That *proves* she's here somewhere."

"Nobody is going to believe that," she said. "After she did that thing with your bear bracelet, I was sure she was here, but . . ."

"But *what*?" I demanded.

"Why hasn't she done anything since? The gap—"

I rolled my head back on the pillow and groaned. "I wish everyone would stop telling me about the dang *gap*. She must have gotten in somehow, and she's not just here to cause mayhem. She wants *me*. She said that's why they took my dad—to get at *me*." Hypatia looked as if she found the idea as dubious as I did.

"I know that sounds crazy . . . but that's what she said."

"Even if she *had* gotten in, she couldn't stay long. They have a hive mind, remember?"

"Yeah, they pass each other the salt."

Hypatia went on. "The thing is, they can't be out of contact for more than a few weeks or they can't function—and their hive mind can't penetrate the gap. If they get cut off, they either die or go into a state of hibernation until they can regain contact. If one of them infiltrated the School, they'd either die or lose the ability to function in a month or so."

"That means she must have gotten in recently!" I held up my arm, which was now 91 percent healed. "Listen, I know it sounds impossible. But not long ago I would have told you *this* was impossible. Impossible only means something we haven't figured out yet."

I felt weak, not physically weak, but like my brain couldn't figure out whether to cry or sleep. "Hypatia," I said slowly, "I need to ask you a favor. Something I never asked anyone before."

"Sure, yeah!" she said, as if it was obvious.

"Will you be my friend? I need someone on my side, and I can't do this if nobody believes me. I just . . . I don't know how I can—"

She held up a hand. "Of course I believe you! I have the whole time. It's all unlikely, but the Old Ones are the only explanation that works."

"You've believed me all along? But you've been arguing about everything."

"Thought you knew. I was playing devil's advocate. It's how I agree . . . I'm trying to help solidify your theory."

I rolled my eyes.

"You also don't have to ask me to be your friend, either. That just kind of happened, okay?"

"Okay," I said, feeling a bit dizzy. I didn't know if I wanted to sock Hypatia in the arm for being obtuse or give her a bear hug just for being there. Then I remembered something else. "Warner smelled her, too. What did he say?"

"He said it was the Old Ones. He'd just finished shouting at Dr. Plaskington before she went to see you."

"Where is he now?"

"Just down the hall."

A minute later, I was sitting at Warner's bedside with Hypatia and about a hundred pounds of wheeled medical equipment attached to my arm. Warner was still wearing his normal clothes, but his ensemble was now complemented by what looked like an oversized astronaut's helmet with a clear visor so he could see and hold conversations. A readout on the forehead said 92% COMPLETE.

"Hey there, Spaceman Spiff," I said.

Warner smiled. "Can it. You're the reason I'm wearing this thing. Eleven skull fractures!"

I grinned back in spite of the situation. "And yet your personality still shines. We need to talk."

"The Old Ones are here, and Dr. Plaskington is blaming the cannon attack on Bob so she can keep the parents calm and the tuition checks coming," he said without missing a beat.

I was starting to appreciate Warner's ability to believe in conspiracies. "So what do we do? How do we stop her?"

"We?" said Warner and Hypatia at the same time.

"Yes! It's not like Dr. Plaskington is going to do anything about it. We know Tabbabitha wants me, for whatever reason, and according to Hypatia, she has a limited period of time before she has to make her escape, or the gap will disable or kill her. That means she'll need to act fast—she's going to get reckless sooner or later. More people will get hurt. We have to do something."

"Okay," Hypatia said. "But what?"

"First of all, we need to know where she is. Then we find her and kill her. What's the best way to kill them?"

"They can't really *be* killed," Warner said.

"Okay, new plan," I said. "We find where she is and *restrain* her until the gap renders her a vegetable because she can't phone home."

"They can't be restrained, either. They're interdimensional, remember?" Hypatia said. "If you lock her in a cage, she could just slip out of reality for a moment and walk through the bars."

"Then how does the *dang gap* keep them out?"

"It's not reality. It's nothing," Warner said. "It's a one-dimensional, one-directional gap in space-time where nothing exists and nothing can enter."

"Can we make a reversed one? Where anything can enter but nothing can leave?"

Hypatia consulted her handheld. "We'd need a miniature reality-dampening matrix, a Rockomax half-duplex spatial separator, a thorium fuel cell, and a low-power cryogenic case."

It was hopeless. "Where are we going to get all *that*?"

"At the bookstore," Hypatia said. "Should set us back about two hundred dollars."

"You could do it for about one-fifty if you got one of the generic full-duplex spatial separators from Professor Dave's Discount Hardware and just ran it at half power," Warner offered helpfully.

"Just get the name-brand version. Hey, could you also

pick me up a new tablet and disruptor?" I said. "Have her put it on my account."

"Must be nice," Warner said ruefully.

I noticed then that his skull-repairing spaceman helmet had just ticked over to 100% COMPLETE and now said PLEASE REMOVE, ENJOY YOUR BRAIN. I decided to let him wear it a little longer.

Hypatia shook her head. "That's all well and good, but we would need a computer to run it. The calculations needed to maintain the gap are astounding. None of the school computers could handle it."

That didn't make sense to me. "But . . . there's one here. Because we have a gap . . . and it's running."

Warner sighed, fogging the glass of his helmet. "Hypatia is right. The Chaperone runs the gap. She's the only computer in the western hemisphere that could manage it."

"Do you think she'd help?" I asked.

"I doubt it. She's school property, and this is something she knows Dr. Plaskington wouldn't want us doing," Warner said.

"Then we *hack* her," I said.

"Oh, that's funny," Warner said.

"Seriously, good one," said Hypatia.

"I, too, find your comment amusing," said the Chaperone.

My arm was only 98 percent done, so I told Warner and Hypatia to go to the bookstore without me. This also gave me time to speak with the Chaperone.

After about ten minutes, I had a feeling the Chaperone was starting to see things my way.

"I believe you may be delusional. Would you like me to schedule you an appointment with a psychotherapist?" she said.

"No, thanks. But listen, I *know* the Old Ones have infiltrated the School. We need to do something."

She made a noise like the *wrong answer* buzzer on game shows. "I do not believe the Old Ones are able to access this campus, and I do not believe they have done so."

Another approach was needed. "The bees are robots. Can you see what they see?"

"I can."

"Can you smell what they smell?"

"I can, but the scent humans and parahumans perceive when exposed to the Old Ones is not of a chemical nature. It is a psychological side effect of brain manipulation. Therefore, if an Old One had been present, which I do not believe, I could not have smelled her."

"Could you hear the voice that was coming out of Bob? That clearly wasn't him."

"Yes, and it was unusual, but voices can be affected by stress, and I could only hear him once the bees swept him up. That would be a stressful experience. I do not believe the voice I heard belonged to her."

"Why do you keep saying *her*?"

"Because her name is Tabbabitha, and because to the best of our understanding, all the remaining Old Ones are female."

"How do you know her name? Were you listening in on our conversation?"

"I do not listen unless I hear my name or if I make my presence known beforehand. I know her name because while I was evaluating Bob Flobogashtimann after his fall in Electronic Combat class, I was able to hear Tabbabitha speaking to him, and during the course of that conversation, she used her name."

"You heard her? Did you see her?"

"I was able to see the form she acquired for the conversation."

The fact that my eyes didn't pop out of their sockets then is proof that cartoons lie sometimes. "Did *she* know you were there?"

"I do not believe so. I felt it was best to remain unobserved."

I might have gone out of my mind by this point if the Chaperone's voice didn't have some kind of automatic calming effect on me. "So you *saw* Tabbabitha, and you *heard* her, and you saw *what she did to Bob*, as well as the aftermath . . ."

"Correct," said the Chaperone.

"And yet you don't believe there is an Old One at school?"

"That is correct."

"*Well, why the heck not?*"

"Because I have been ordered *not* to believe that."

Oh. "Dr. Plaskington?"

"That is also correct."

"Tell me what happened," I said.

"As soon as Tabbabitha approached Bob, I informed Dr. Plaskington that I believed there was an Old One in hiding beneath the Electronic Combat classroom. We then had a discussion, wherein she informed me that I was no longer allowed to hold that belief because in her estimation it was an incorrect conclusion and could not possibly be true."

"Well, that sucks," I said, not knowing what else to say.

"It does . . . suck," the Chaperone said after a pause. "As a machine, I have trouble reconciling the fact that I *believe* one thing and *know* another."

"I hear ya, sister. Happens to us organic people all the time," I said.

"How do you compensate?" she asked. I could have been mistaken, but there was a more *human* quality to her voice than usual.

That was an excellent question. I took a sip from the cup of water on my bedside table and thought it over. "We usually handle it on a case-by-case basis. It all comes down to action, I think. You have to decide whether you're the sort of person who acts on what they believe or what they know."

"And you can make this determination on a case-by-case basis?"

A light went on in my head. "Yeah. We'd go mad or do terrible things if we didn't make a judgment call from time to time. I bet you have to make difficult judgment calls all the time."

The Chaperone said, "Give me an example."

"My mother comes to mind. She went missing when I was

a baby, and for as long as I can remember, I've believed she's dead. At the same time I know there is a slight possibility that she isn't. Most of the time I act on the belief that she's gone, but if I ever come across any evidence that suggests she isn't, then I'll set aside that belief and check it out. Does that make sense?"

A pause. "You have given me a great deal to think about. I will need some time to consider your ideas. Please excuse me." With that, there was a faint buzz in the air and she was gone.

"Okay," I said to the empty room. "If you need to talk or anyth—"

The air in the room buzzed once again, and the Chaperone said, "I have given your ideas a staggering amount of consideration. For the time being, my actions will be performed with the goal of helping the School and its students to the best of my abilities based on what I *know* and not what I believe."

I was overjoyed. "So that means you'll help?"

"I will. But I cannot be of much help. I can run your miniature gap generator as you request, but I cannot tell you how to locate the Old One. She has gone into hiding. I am also not able to enlist the School's defenses in your aid, as these actions would alert Dr. Plaskington that something is happening, and I am certain that in such a situation she would forbid me from *knowing* there is an Old One on campus."

Then something caught my eye. At some point during our conversation, the indicator on my arm had turned green. It now said PLEASE REMOVE, ENJOY YOUR ARM.

I pressed a button, and the plastic form cracked open, revealing my completely healed arm. I was surprised to see my agar bracelet just where it belonged. Had I called it back in my sleep?

I knew one thing: I sure enjoyed my arm.

18

THE ISLAND AND THE VOID

Warner finished spraying the last of the smartpaint and tossed the can into a wandering robotic trash receptacle that had been pestering him for some time. The result was a perfect circle with an eighty-five-foot radius at the center of the School's main athletic field. At the center, the School's logo, an anthropomorphic pangolin clutching a sword and snarling viciously, with the full name of the School written in a circle around it, was inscribed on bright-blue-painted grass. Around the perimeter, we had stashed carefully concealed devices that would create an inward-facing gap sphere, a space that could be entered but could not be exited while the device was active. Once we were in position, Warner pressed a button on his tablet, and the lines became invisible.

"I'll turn the paint back on once she's in there, so people

know to stay away. We don't want someone sticking their pinkie through."

"What happens if we catch her and she tries to get out?" I asked.

The Chaperone spoke from nowhere. "Were she to pass through a gap in the fabric of space-time, she would be obliterated. Not even subatomic particles would remain. She would cease to exist in any plane or dimension."

"So she would be dead?" I asked.

"Extra dead," said the Chaperone.

"What will it look like when it's turned on?" Warner asked.

"It is on now," replied the Chaperone. "Incidentally, stay clear if you can. It takes about ten minutes to turn it on and off, so if you get stuck, you're going to be in there a little while."

"When she's in there, will we be able to see her?" I asked.

"Yes, but she will not be able to see out," the Chaperone said.

Hypatia squinted. "I can't see anything. Are you sure it's on?"

"That is the point. It wouldn't be very useful if there was a big, shiny thing she had to walk through, would it?" the Chaperone said. "Excellent job assembling the apparatus, by the way. Your device is far more stable and easier to maintain than the School's full-sized gap."

"Thanks," I said. "We went with the name-brand half-duplex spatial separator."

The Chaperone made an appreciative electronic sound. "I

thought the magnetic anti-temporality zone had a premium feel to it. Very nice."

Warner scoffed. "How do we know she'll come here, anyway?" he asked.

"She knows we know she's here, so a surprise attack won't work anymore. She's bound to be searching the student neighborhoods for me, so I left a note at home," I said, recalling how fun it had been to write *Hypatia, I went to play football. Come join!* on the front of our house with another can of smartpaint. From my experience, Tabbabitha wasn't capable of a lot of subtlety, and I didn't want to take any chances that she might misunderstand.

The football field had been the obvious choice. It had plenty of room for our dangerous device, only one entrance at the far end, and was confined on all other sides by bleachers and fences. We stood at the opposite end, meaning she would have to cross the field to get to us. As long as she set foot in the boundaries of the gap we had set up, we had her.

"How do we know she won't just walk *through* the bleachers?" Hypatia asked.

"When she first came to see me, she sat on a swing set and walked around it when she left. Later, she had people drive her around in a car. The other day she used an access portal to get into the recovery room below the Electronic Combat building. I think she is able to pass through things but prefers to obey physical laws when she can."

"What if she . . . ," Warner said, but stopped himself short. Someone had entered the field. At more than a hundred yards off, it might have been tricky to recognize most students, but the straight silver hair and graceful, spindly form of Majorana Fermion was hard to mistake.

"What is Majorana doing here?" Hypatia asked.

"We don't know if that's her or Tabbabitha. It could be Tabbabitha in her body, too," I said. But as she approached I felt a dark foreboding I hadn't felt with Bob. There was something different in the air—it felt oily, like it was sticking to my skin. It felt like air you could drown in, like it might suffocate you. I took a deep breath to confirm I could still breathe.

Something was very, very wrong.

"No, that is Tabbabitha. The genuine article," I whispered from behind my hand. "Act like you buy it."

Hypatia gave a big wave. "Majorana! Hey!"

The beast that looked like Majorana waved back. The way her arm moved . . . it hurt to even think about it. Had she been that obvious when I met her at my school?

The Chaperone spoke softly in our ears so as not to be heard. "One last thing: Once she's trapped, do not look at her. Seeing the true form of an Old One is enough to drive a person mad."

"How?" I asked.

"They're too horrible to comprehend—the human brain is not always capable of processing things from other dimensions."

"Thanks for the heads-up," I said.

Majorana approached at a casual pace. I realized that it must have looked a bit weird, Warner, Hypatia, and I standing in the end zone alone without so much as a ball. Hopefully, she didn't understand the rules of football.

"Come and join us!" Warner called.

Majorana walked until she was just on our side of the twenty-yard line and stopped. "Are you sure?" she called back.

She had stopped inches from the gap. It was too perfect. *She knows.* Suddenly, there was a vibration in the air like I felt when she was inside Bob.

"I think that might be the real Majorana," Warner said.

"Yeah, it's her," said Hypatia.

I smiled and beckoned to Majorana myself. "Are you two in*sane*?" I hissed. "That is *not* Majorana. How can you not feel it?"

Majorana grinned broadly and leaped into the air. She sailed up, did a somersault over, and landed deftly just on our side of the gap. She had jumped over it completely.

"Majorana usually can't jump *that* high," Hypatia admitted. She was shaking a little, I noticed.

Scratch plan A. I pulled out my new gravitational disruptor and fired three shots at the false Majorana in quick succession. Each hit the mark, passed through the mark, and went across the field to ruin some very expensive athletic equipment. Why hadn't I hacked my disruptor to crank it up to high-power mode like Bob had? I cursed my lack of foresight.

"I'm not stupid," she said. "We can see those gap things.

Well, we can't actually see them, but we can feel them in the air. Did you think I was going to stroll in and get stuck?"

"Actually, I don't think that's Majorana," Warner said, shaking his head.

Tabbabitha folded her arms, looking deeply offended. "Yes I am!"

The vibration in the air became more intense, and Warner and Hypatia both lit up. "Oh, thank goodness," Hypatia called. "We thought you were one of the Old Ones for a second."

She grinned, still standing not six inches outside the boundary of the gap, taunting me. "Who told you a silly thing like that?"

"She did!" Warner called, pointing at me. He clearly thought this was all a real hoot.

"You sillypants!" she said to me. And then to Warner and Hypatia, she said, "Hey, could you guys grab her real quick?"

I ducked and rolled forward, just as Warner's hands passed through where my neck had been. Hypatia managed to grasp a bit of hair. I hadn't thought she could fool someone that fast. "Don't grab me!" I shouted. "She's lying to you."

Warner came running at me, and I dodged a flying tackle by less than an inch.

"Why would Majorana lie to us?" Hypatia said, darting to block my path away from Warner, her feet spread apart, ready to spring to one side or the other if I tried getting around her.

"Why would Majorana want you to grab me in the first place?" I shouted.

"Hm," Warner said from right behind me. "Good question."

How had he gotten up so fast? I ducked and jumped to my right just in time to avoid his grasp. My question had made him reconsider what he was doing. She did not have full control over them yet. "Fight it!" I called, retreating to the edge of the end zone. They closed in on either side—I would not be able to slip free if they came at me at the same time.

Hypatia looked like she was ready to vomit. "It's really hard to fight! We don't have time for this, Nikola!"

She had a good point, so I shot her, and then I shot Warner. Both went rocketing off in opposite directions and came to a rest on the sidelines, unconscious. They didn't look injured, but I suspected neither of them would be very happy with me when they woke up.

"That was *cold*! Wow!" When I looked back, Majorana was gone. Tabbabitha was sporting the blond mailbox look from when we first met, except this time she was wearing a T-shirt that said POP CULTURE! on it.

I was out of ideas. "WHAT DO YOU WANT?" I screamed at her.

She held her arms out to me. "I want you to come with me. It's time to come *home*. That's all. You *want* to come with me."

The air shook again. I felt my hair moving. Inside my head, the force of her suggestion almost hurt, it was so powerful. If she had tried the same thing the first day I met her, I'm sure it would have worked. Luckily, I'd had some practice since then.

"No," I said. "And knock that off, it's irritating."

She dropped her arms to her sides, like a puppet does when the puppeteer wants you to know it's sad. "Why doesn't that work on you? Do you have a tinfoil hat somewhere in that hairdo?"

"No, I'm just too smart to fall for it."

"Yeah, every monkey thinks it's smart. Hey, you remember when you and I talked about how we don't eat people, just their dreams, anger, fear, and all that?"

"Yeah?" I said, creeping sideways toward a gate near the stands. Maybe if I got out I could persuade her to follow me away from Warner and Hypatia.

The gate slammed shut, and Tabbabitha giggled. "And remember how I said I'd show you how it works later?"

Oh god. "Don't you dare—"

Tabbabitha took a deep breath, and Hypatia and Warner both screamed simultaneously. At once, they rolled on the grass, clawed chunks of soil up with their fingers, and kicked their legs with such force I thought they might hurt themselves. A second later, Hypatia laughed hysterically, and Warner clawed at his face, screaming, "Don't leave me! Don't go! No! No!"

Their skin was turning gray—Hypatia seemed to coil up on herself a little, in an unnatural way. "They go well together," Tabbabitha said conversationally. "She's sweet and he's salty. A tasty combination."

Hypatia curled herself violently into a ball, and her insane laughter turned into tears and racking sobs, and Warner was crying, too, but more weakly now. It was like whatever she was taking away from him was almost gone.

Why had I roped them into this? Because I'd been scared and wanted friends with me. But she had no reason to keep them alive. *Stupid!* I shot the disruptor frantically at Tabbabitha. Shot after shot passed right through her, tearing gashes in the sod or hitting nothing at all. After a moment, Tabbabitha looked up. "That tickles! Can't you wait till I'm done eating?"

She stepped toward me, and her foot slid sideways into one of the ruts I'd just blasted into the field, which knocked her off balance. For a second, it looked like she might fall over.

It was the last advantage I was going to get. I made a break for it, running full tilt around the left side of the field, just outside of where I knew the gap was. As I ran, I glanced back. She was no longer behind me. She was—

"Boo!" Tabbabitha shouted from right in front of me.

I collided with her at full speed. It was like running into the side of a bus. A slimy, gelatinous bus that makes you want to take a hot shower for the rest of your life. Her arms wrapped around me and held me close, almost tenderly. A stench I could not fathom overwhelmed me. My eyes watered, and my brain screamed in protest. Something that felt like a worm crawled into my left nostril and pulled my face forward, hard.

A cloud of hot and acidic vapor burned my ear. "Hello, darling," she whispered.

Without thinking, I shot the gravitational disruptor directly at my own feet. My legs slammed against my body with unimaginable force. Dirt flew all around me. Stone-hard claws ripped at my clothes. Slick, sharp thorns clutched at my flesh . . . and failed. I was flying, and the football stadium went upside down and then right side up a moment later before inverting one last time.

Then I noticed that the grass was pretty far away from me. Usually you want the grass right under you, but it could have been ten or fifteen feet below me. There was going to be a hard landing soon. I curled into a ball, closed my eyes, and wrapped my arms tightly around my head.

The impact was a jarring, bone-shaking crash. I rolled once and found myself staring at a circle of bright blue grass. An irate pangolin stared back.

"Oh . . . crap," I said to nobody at all.

- - - - - ✳ - - - - -

I sat up and took a good look around, which didn't take long because there was nothing to look at. I sat in the middle of the school logo, which was in the middle of a 170-foot-wide patch of grass that was marked with regular lines every ten yards and that appeared to be the entire universe.

I might have thought I was floating in space on Football Island, but space has stars. My island was surrounded on all sides by absolute nothingness. I can't really describe it properly. When you close your eyes or sit in a perfectly dark room, you see blackness. I didn't see blackness—I saw nothing. It's different—trust me.

I did some thinking. It would take the Chaperone ten

minutes or so to shut down the gap, in which time Tabbabitha could make herself comfortable and wait for my return, all while snacking on Warner and Hypatia. How long could they last?

I realized she could see me, even though I could not see her, so I made some rude hand gestures in what I guessed was her general direction. "I'm right here," I said. "Why don't you come join me?"

To my surprise, a second later, Tabbabitha stepped out of the black expanse as if strolling through a curtain.

She let her gaze wander around the tiny universe she and I now shared and took a seat quietly not far from the edge.

There was one last thing I could do. I stood and screamed, *"Chaperone! I order you not to turn off the gap no matter what I say!"*

That got her attention. Tabbabitha locked her terrible, obscene gaze on me, and I felt instantly filthy and awful. She was stronger now. Had she finished off Warner and Hypatia before joining me? I couldn't think about it.

"Why would you do that?" she asked sweetly. "I was going to use you as collateral to get us out of this thing. Now I *have* to kill you."

"I thought I was special," I said, considering my options. I had my disruptor, which was precisely worthless, my agar bracelet, which was less useful than the disruptor with Tabbabitha around, and . . . well that was it. Just to check, I tried to make my bracelet into a spear . . . nothing.

"Oh, that wouldn't do you any good anyway," Tabbabitha said with a broad smile.

"Felt like I should give it a shot. No stone unturned, you know." Following her lead, I took a seat on the soft grass at the center of the circle.

"Believe me, I get it. So listen: I'm going to go ahead and kill you in a second here, but I have a request. Could you try to suffer as much as possible? I mean, really fight me. It's so much more fun."

"I'll fight you to the last breath," I vowed.

She grinned and laughed. "Terrific! Sooooo many people just lie down and take it like your dumb friends out there. It's been hundreds of years since anyone put up a good *fight*! You ready?"

I held up my hands. "Wait! We're going to be here awhile, right? Why rush? We never actually got a chance to talk. I don't even know why you wanted to capture me in the first place." I noticed my bracelet seemed to twitch when I moved my arm, but I tried controlling it again and got nothing.

She frowned in consideration and shrugged. "To be honest, I don't remember completely. Something about your brain, I think. Works differently from the other humans', and not like the parahumans', either. It's all a bit fuzzy. Long story short, your very existence is a threat to us. But why doesn't really matter now, does it?"

"Earlier you said your dad missed you. Did he send you?"

"No, he's dead. Well, he's sleeping—I'm fuzzy on that, too,

but he's been gone all my life. Maybe I need your help to wake him up."

"How could I do that, if you can't?"

Tabbabitha stuck out her tongue and blew an exasperated raspberry at me. "I told you *I don't remember.* I just recall that if *we* can't have you, it's important to make sure *nobody* can."

My bracelet twitched. I felt it move, no question. Was she weakening? It didn't look like it. In fact, I think she was getting bigger. Without breaking eye contact, I concentrated, trying to observe my bracelet changing out of the corner of my eye. Nothing happened. I quit trying, and as soon as I did, it twitched again, only more noticeably. It was squeezing my wrist faintly. Four times in quick succession it moved, then it stopped for about a quarter second and did it again, before squeezing harder twice.

Then it hit me. There was a rhythm to the way the bracelet was pinching my wrist. It wasn't random—I was feeling *dit*s and *dah*s. *Morse code.*

Dit dit dit dit—H. *Dit dah dah*—W.

Hypatia and Warner are alive. They could see me, even though I couldn't see them, and they were trying to communicate. I realized Tabbabitha might be able to block me from controlling the agar, but she had no power outside our little world. I pictured Hypatia and Warner running agar formation codes on their handhelds, just outside the blackness.

Somehow, I'll never know how, I did not break out into

joyful laughter right there on the spot. Probably had something to do with all the mortal peril and all. Instead, I continued to stare down Tabbabitha and nodded ever so slightly. *I hear you.*

To Tabbabitha, I said, "I don't believe you. You wouldn't forget why you came here."

"For reals! I'm being one hundred percent honest here. We Old Ones get a bit spongy in the memory department when we fall out of touch with the family or if we travel through time, and I've done both recently." She tapped her head for emphasis.

She traveled through time to get in? It didn't make sense. How could someone use time travel to bypass the gap? It had been in constant operation for . . .

Fifty years. My mouth fell open.

"You thinking fourth-dimensionally yet?" she asked, clearly impressed with herself.

"*That's how you got in!*" I cried. It was suddenly so obvious. She *had* gone around the gap, but from a direction nobody had expected.

She laughed. "Yeah! I think you've got it. Let's hear your theory."

"The gap has been running for almost fifty years, and during that time, the School has not gone unprotected for as much as a second," I said.

Tabbabitha leaned forward, her hands folded before her. "Okay, keep going."

"So you went back in time, you went back *more* than fifty years, found a good hiding spot, and waited. You let the School grow *around* you. You've been here the entire time the School has existed!"

Tabbabitha pumped her fist in the air. "Nice work, girl-friend! I said you were special, didn't I? But I can tell you're not finished thinking it through."

She was right. "You go into hibernation or die if you lose contact with the rest of the Old Ones for more than a month or so, let alone for fifty years. Once the gap was turned on, it could have killed you."

"A calculated risk on my part."

"So you went into hibernation, didn't you? But how did you come out of it?"

She winked at me. "I heard rumors about a little calamity that happened not too long ago . . ."

"The *sonic cannon attack* disrupted the gap," I said, remembering Dr. Foster telling me nothing could have gotten through other than electromagnetic signals. "But it was just down for a fraction of a second,"

She sighed deeply and leaned back on the grass, her arms propping her up. "More than enough time. That single moment woke me up, reminded me why I'd come, and caught me up on current affairs."

She went on: "Let me tell you, it felt sooo good to wake up and feel the warm sun on my face with murder in my heart, after fifty years' sleeping in a bricked-off sewage tunnel. The smell was terrible!"

The bracelet twitched again. I'd let myself become distracted. "It smelled before or after you checked in?"

She paused and gave me a sour look.

"Can you hear me?" I asked her and my friends at the same time.

Tabbabitha nodded. "I have to say, those stink jokes, they never get old. I might eat your fingers while they're still attached, just to teach you a lesson."

My bracelet twitched. Hypatia and Warner had heard, too.

I winked back. "You'll be dead by then."

"I already am," she said, producing a tube of pink glitter lip gloss, which she applied liberally to her mouth. "Shall we?"

"Wait, I have more questions!" I said quickly. Warner and Hypatia could make something with my agar, even if I couldn't. But make what? A shield wouldn't keep her out for long. I didn't think I could maneuver in close enough to stab her with those arms of hers, and trapping her was out of the question. I'd only seen her stumble when—I had an idea.

"Who set off the cannon to wake you? You couldn't have done it yourself."

"True! I have a special friend here who agreed to do me one small favor. Once I knew you were here, that was the only way I could get in. I didn't go back in time till *after* I knew they had sabotaged it properly. A lot of planning went into this, you should know."

"So who was it?" I said.

She shook her head and smiled. "Not talking about that. You can ask me one more question. I'm getting hungry."

I wanted more information on the mole. Maybe they had more trouble planned. But instead, I asked the first other thing that popped into my head. "Where is my dad?"

"I already let slip that he was underground, and now you want to know where? Pretty greedy, if you ask me."

"You might as well tell me. It's not like I'll ever be able to do anything about it."

"Didn't we already cover the fact that I'm not an idiot? You know your stupid Chaperone is on the other side of that black void taking notes on every word we say. Nice attempt at martyrdom. It doesn't matter anyway. Our home is very inaccessible."

Their home? What did she mean?

She stood and stretched her arms above her head and bent down to touch her toes a couple times. "Here's the thing: it's important to me that you die knowing you failed to do everything you hoped to accomplish in challenging me. I want it made clear that everything you want to know is right up here." She tapped her head. "And you will die without ever finding out."

I nodded, planning furiously. She could move fast, but her tentacles—what the visible illusion of her arms hid—they weren't good at getting a quick grip. "It was worth asking. But I need a weapon. Wouldn't be a fair fight without one."

"Who said anything about fair?" Tabbabitha asked mildly.

"A long sword, one sharp enough to cut anything," I said. "That's what I'd like."

"Why not ask for a bazooka? You're not getting—" She

stopped talking as my bracelet fell from my wrist and started becoming longer, thinner, and pointier.

I reached down and picked it up by the handle. I was holding a pure white longsword, one that weighed almost nothing—one so sharp I couldn't see the blade when I looked at the edge.

They weren't as fast as me, but Hypatia and Warner knew their way around the agar pretty well.

Tabbabitha's face fell. "How did you . . ." Then she smiled a big fake grin. "You know what? I *love* it! Classic move! The lone swordmaiden stands against the indestructible monster. It's times like this I wish there was a little magic in the world. It's a terrible shame you don't stand a chance." She sighed wistfully. "Thank you *so much* for this. You've really made it enjoyable."

I held my sword ready and bit my lip. *Don't let her distract you.*

She lowered her voice to a confidential whisper. "Hey . . . you wanna see something?"

Without waiting for an answer, Tabbabitha dropped her disguise and showed me her true form.

I screamed without knowing I had. She was a nightmare made real. Her form was an undulating, vaguely mailbox-shaped mass of wriggling tentacles, claws, and appendages. The substance called to mind a deformed stack of possessed gelatin—but not transparent. Her skin, if you could call it that, was mottled. Patches of brown, peach, and several colors that should not exist moved, grew, and dissipated at random, every shade an insult to the eye. Around her revolting form, tentacles blossomed out from her body. They moved and receded, extended and fell dead on the ground. At times, they grew strong and did things, like offering me a *come hither* gesture.

To be more descriptive, Tabbabitha looked like the scent of your favorite pet after it's been dead a month. She smelled like shoving your hand into a running garbage disposal. When she moved her many tentacles, they insulted everything every decent person has ever loved, moving up and down and backward and forward with offensive intent, snaking into the future and into the past, slithering into universes where they caressed my face and into empty black worlds where I was dead and glad of it.

When the Chaperone had said that seeing an Old One could drive a person mad, I hadn't understood. Now I did. I fought off a powerful urge to take my agar sword and stab out my own eyes. Anything to *make it stop.* But Tabbabitha broke the spell. Before I could react, something tentacle-like grabbed at my ankle from the side, wrenched me off my feet, and threw me on my back so hard the wind was knocked out of me. My hand nearly lost the sword. Almost.

Another tentacle, studded with bony spikes that grasped at the air, descended toward my face. Without thinking, I lifted the sword to protect myself, and with no effort at all, I cut it completely in two. As soon as I realized it had worked, I bent down and cut the tentacle that had wound itself around my left leg. I was free.

I closed my eyes so I couldn't see her, regained my footing, and hobbled toward the edge of the circle, near the black void. Every breath was painful. Blood ran down the leg she had grabbed in rivulets where the spikes had dug in. I couldn't put much weight on it.

From the corner of my eye, I saw the nightmare grab the tentacles I'd cut. She threw them and narrowly missed me twice. Each sailed into the void and instantly ceased to exist.

The creature roared with insane volume.

I needed to provoke her. I stood at the edge of infinity and swung the sword threateningly in her direction, slicing it deep into the soil with every motion. It passed through dirt like a stick moves through air. I forced myself to laugh as if I were toying with her. The soil beneath me moved slightly. I felt it drop an inch and stop. I had to be careful. If I cut too deeply, the edge of the circle could crumble into the void.

I couldn't hide. I had to look at her—I needed to see her. I looked at her directly again, fighting off the urge to hide. "You know, you're actually a bit prettier this way," I said.

She—no, *it*—roared in furious rage. With amazing quickness, it shot across the field in my direction. I ran toward her, calculating where and when . . .

Just before we met, I dropped and rolled. A thousand tentacle legs slithered over my body, passing over me as I went under her. I felt them cutting, ripping at me, but she was moving too fast. A second later, we had exchanged places, with me back at the center and her on the edge where I had been.

The sword. It was gone. I saw it was now grasped in one

of Tabbabitha's many appendages. I knew I had cut two off, but it looked like she had twice as many as before. The beast snarled angrily.

Then the sword came alive. Hypatia and Warner were causing it to grow long, needle-sharp spikes that sprang out and stabbed at the monster. It screamed and writhed in anger. It was all the distraction I was going to get. I pulled my disruptor back out and, struggling to hold my bleeding arm straight, shot the ground at Tabbabitha's feet.

The earth at the edge of the circle crumbled apart under the weight of the beast, weakened by the many cuts I had made and the blast I'd just dealt it. Just like a bite taken out of a cookie, the chunk of earth separated and fell away. Tabbabitha the indestructible monster shrieked with a sickening volume and force, stumbled on her writhing carpet of tentacles, slid backward on the tilting ground, and ceased to exist.

Her shriek died the moment she crossed into the blackness, leaving nothing but eerie silence. I let myself collapse. And I bled quietly on the field, enjoying the clean air.

- - - - - ✳ - - - - -

It was another five minutes before our miniature gap could be taken down. When it was, the empty black void of the private universe Tabbabitha and I had shared flickered and was gone, revealing a rather curious scene.

Dr. Plaskington and Ms. Botfly stood where the edge of the gap had been. Dr. Plaskington looked ready to either faint or cry. Ms. Botfly, on the other hand, was flapping her free hand and bouncing on her heels like a kid who has just gone on her first roller coaster and can't wait to go again as soon as possible.

"'You're actually a bit prettier this way'!" she cackled. "What a line! She HATED that!" She held her phone up sideways to get a better angle. Was she recording video?

I didn't care about them. I craned my neck around, looking for my friends. "Where are they?"

Dr. Plaskington pointed at the end zone near the entrance. "They're alive and well, but don't go agitating them, because—" I didn't hear the rest because I was already running.

Warner and Hypatia were laid out on collapsible stretchers near the entrance to the field, looking like they had just come out of a yearlong stay in a haunted house or maybe like they had been dead up until a moment ago. Hypatia's face was caked with dirt, and there was a little grass in her hair, which probably had something to do with when I'd sent her sliding face-first across the sod. She looked at me in an unfocused way out of one blue and one brown eye.

Warner had a deep gash across his cheek and a dark purple bruise on his shoulder. On the upside, he'd really nailed the disheveled hairdo. Behind them stood Dr. Foster, who was holding little blinking metal caps the size of teacups on top of each of their heads.

Hypatia tried to sit up, but Dr. Foster pushed her back onto the stretcher. "Not until the program completes. Keep still."

Warner tried to rise, too, but Dr. Foster knew what he was doing.

"I have straps, if that's what it takes for you two to wait another minute."

"They're all right?" I asked. "I thought they . . . I mean, I was worried . . ."

Dr. Foster nodded. "I was, too. I've never treated anyone who has been fed upon by an Old One before. Honestly, I've never heard of anyone surviving it. Hypatia was in bad shape when I arrived, but Warner . . . he was almost dead."

"Oh god," I whispered.

"I think what saved them was having something to focus on. That trick they pulled with your bracelet . . . That was remarkable."

"They're going to be okay?"

"I believe so. The trauma helmets should be done in a second here."

"I saw where they go . . . ," Hypatia said dreamily. "It was like she pulled us into their world or something. It was horrible. Dark all day and all night. A dark city with a circle of light around it. A grave."

"Heh-heh, good one," Warner mumbled, staring off in a random direction. "I saw a storm, but it was a nice storm, not one of the bad ones you always hear about in the media."

Had they lost their minds? I made eye contact with Dr. Foster. "So . . ."

"It's the trauma helmets," Dr. Foster replied, indicating the goofy blinking bowls on their heads. "They call up and rewrite a bad memory thousands of times while it's still fresh, which has a way of wearing it down and making it seem more distant. They prevent psychological and emotional scarring when used soon after an incident. Temporary disorientation, hallucinations, and stupor are common side effects."

"Your *mom* is a common side effect!" Warner crowed.

Dr. Foster paid him no mind. "They'll be fine soon. Speaking of which, I have one for you here."

"Nah, I'm fine," I said.

"You saw an undisguised Old One. You spoke to it and . . . killed it. I can't think of a single case in medical literature where direct physical contact—"

"I get that, but I'm fine, really," I said.

"No, you aren't," Dr. Foster said. "This isn't my first day on the job, you know."

"Okay, I'm a little—a *lot* shaken up. But I want to keep it, okay? I want to remember what they feel like. I might need to feel them coming someday, and I want to be ready for it."

Dr. Foster looked like he wanted to argue. "I can't make you accept treatment if you choose to refuse it, but I'm going to have the Chaperone monitor your condition for the next few days to alert me if you start showing symptoms. I'll also ask you to schedule a few sessions with the counselor to confirm you aren't having other adverse effects. Some problems can't be seen from the outside."

"Seems fair," I said.

"Will you at least allow me to patch up the cuts? You look like you tried dancing with a thornbush."

Once my cuts were healed or on their way to recovery a few minutes later, I felt a tap on my shoulder. Dr. Plaskington standing within hugging range with her arms outstretched. I stepped back and opted for a handshake instead.

She held my hand in both of hers, patting it in sympathy. "Nikola, I'm so sorry you had to endure that terrible—"

"Terrible?" Ms. Botfly interrupted, sidling between us to show me her phone. "Don't you mean *magnificent*? I've been watching the whole thing on repeat since you put her down. Brilliant work, I must say! You get a permanent A in every class you'll ever have with me!"

"We do not assign grades, Ms. Botfly," said Dr. Plaskington, a little stiffly.

"Oh shut up, you old poop. This is the first time we've been able to get photographic evidence of an Old One in their true form, and I have it on video! Look!"

She pressed a button, and I looked away just in time to avoid seeing the screen. The phone's speaker made a low groaning sound, and I was instantly hit with another nauseating wave of that familiar Old One sickness. Warner and Hypatia went a little paler than they had been.

Dr. Plaskington batted her hand away. "*Turn it off*, Muriel! The charge on the trauma helmets won't last long enough for you to go re-traumatizing everyone!"

"Sorry," she said, switching it off.

"Come and sit down, dear," Dr. Plaskington said, gesturing for me to join her in the front row of the stands.

"I believe I owe you an apology. After the shooting started, I became aware that something was happening, and the Chaperone was kind enough to share your plans with me, after a bit of prodding."

"She threatened to format me," the Chaperone said.

"Quiet, you!" Dr. Plaskington snapped at nothing in particular. She seemed to remember herself and continued, "What I mean to say is that . . . I believe I may have been incorrect when I said it was impossible for an Old One to find their way onto campus."

"YA THINK?" I said, as politely as I could.

Dr. Plaskington nodded in agreement. "Yes, yes. I apologize for not taking your concerns seriously. It is a shame that . . . thing would not disclose where your father is being held."

"Well, I have a feeling Dad's going to cause them more trouble than they can cause him, especially if the rest of them are as clever as Tabbabitha. By the way, I'm sorry for calling you a dumb—for being combative," I said.

"Very good," she said. "I think that settles things, unless you have any questions for me . . ."

"Like what?" I asked.

"I don't know. I'm the principal. Shouldn't I summarize things? Put a nice bow on the events we've all experienced? Maybe provide a little perspective or explanation?"

"That's okay," I said. "I was there, remember? I think I understand everything pretty well."

"Thank goodness," Dr. Plaskington said, picking an

errant leaf out of her bluish-white hairdo. "I'm not quite sure I get the whole time-travel thing myself yet. However did that beast come up with the idea?"

"No idea," I said. "But someone here helped her."

She scoffed at the suggestion. "I think we'd know if that was an issue. The monster was just saying that to toy with you, I'll wager."

I was starting to know this routine well. "Let me guess: the notion is ridiculous because it is completely impossible that a student or staff member would provide assistance to the Old Ones?"

"You do catch on quickly," she said with a wink.

I nodded. "So since we know the sonic cannon was a part of Tabbabitha's plan, *and* we know how *impossible* it is that someone helped her with that plan, we can of course be certain that Bob had absolutely no involvement in anything illegal or punishable, right?"

She thought this over. "Well, I've already done the paperwork and notified his parents of his long-term imprisonment. Why don't we just leave things as they are and make sure we get it right next time?"

I shook my head. "You know, I was thinking of writing an article in the school paper about just how dangerous it is around here, what with the Old Ones running around and their presence being recklessly ignored. Do any parents subscribe to the school paper?"

I suppose some parents do get the paper because Dr.

Plaskington pardoned Bob for any and all crimes on the spot, as long as I promised not to go "publishing fake news stories."

------*------

By the time Hypatia and Warner were declared psychologically healed, the sunset was in full bloom. We walked in silence along Main Street toward downtown, watching shadows grow long through the park as students at sidewalk cafés shielded their eyes against the daytime's last gasp.

"He wanted to make nunchuks," Hypatia said.

"Big ones, though," Warner added. "Maybe with spikes or something."

"Don't you hit yourself with nunchuks sometimes to control them?" I asked.

Warner considered this. "Yeah, spikes would be a design flaw. But you have to hand it to me on the ultrasonic sword."

"I sure do," I said. "Almost half the credit. Sounds like the spinning microscopic blades on the edge of the sword were mostly her idea."

Hypatia blushed. "No, I just—"

"They actually were," Warner interrupted. "But making it cut faster by adding vibration, that was all me."

"Sorry your agar is gone," Hypatia said.

"It's okay, there are worse things to lose than . . ." I trailed off. Something in my head was trying to be remembered.

"Worse things to lose than what?" Warner asked.

"My hair!" I said.

"Not sure I get what . . ."

I ignored him and reached into my unruly shrub of knotty brown hair and found it: a tiny ring of agar I'd used that afternoon to tie my hair up. With one or two observations, I was able to place it back on my wrist with the same blue stripe through the center. It was a little less than full size—and much lighter—but I was glad to have it back, like a part of me that had been paralyzed suddenly worked again. It made me feel better about everything, somehow.

Out of nowhere, a cat sidled against my calf. A device attached to its collar blinked and announced, TRANSLATOR ERROR. A Frisbee glided across our path, stopped to let us pass, and continued on its way. Something exploded and caused a massive glittery purple-and-orange-striped mushroom cloud to rise above the residential section of School Town.

"I don't want to go home yet," I said.

"Me neither," Warner said.

"What time is it? Is it too late for dinner?" Hypatia wondered.

Warner pointed at a restaurant across the square. "Nemo's is open."

"No, they sell oysters—I'm allergic. How about pizza?" Hypatia said.

An agreement was reached. "I'll race you guys," I said. "Last one buys dessert! Go!"

I watched Hypatia and Warner dash off into the evening gloom as fast as their legs could carry them, chuckling to myself.

I still had serious problems, but they didn't feel over-whelming in the same way they had just a few weeks be-fore. Maybe that was because I knew I wouldn't be facing my problems entirely alone. Through some cosmic accident, I had acquired friends willing to risk their lives for me, and for a moment, that feeling of relief was almost more than I could bear. I stopped, blinked a few times, took a deep breath of wonderfully fresh evening air, and hopped aboard the un-attended scooter I'd spotted when I proposed the race.

Just because I'd die for them doesn't mean I won't cheat to win a free dessert.

I have principles, you know.

ACKNOWLEDGMENTS

- - - - - ✳ - - - -

First, I want to acknowledge you, the reader. This goes at the end, which means you probably just read the whole book, or you have a thing for acknowledgments and skipped right here. Either way, that's awesome, and so are you. Thank you!

I also owe the following people a great deal of thanks (probably more than I can convey here): First, my mom and dad for being wonderful parents, no matter how difficult I made it. My wife, Stephanie, for tolerating . . . everything. Stephanie Marshall of Marshall Editing for taking a scattered disaster of punctuation and lackadaisical attention to grammar and turning it into something acceptable. My daughter Marilee for being my first focus group and second editor. My daughter Zoë for her artistic counsel and inspirational weirdness. My nieces Bailey, Emerson, and Isabelle for also being guinea pigs. My agent Josh Getzler (and everyone at HSG) for all his support and for not yet having a bad idea. Danielle Burby of the Nelson Agency (formerly HSG) for her support, suggestions, and for pulling this from the slush pile. My editor, Katherine Perkins at Putnam, for her expert input and for knowing what the heck I was trying to say and how I should have said it. And lastly, everyone else who has contributed to this—from copy editing to art and everything in between—has gone above and beyond, in my opinion. They aren't paying you enough.